Dog Horse Rat

ALSO BY CHRISTOPHER DAVIS

NOVELS

Suicide Note
The Sun in Mid-Career
A Peep into the 20th Century
Ishmael
The Shamir of Dachau
Belmarch
A Kind of Darkness
First Family
Lost Summer

NONFICTION

Waiting For It
The Producer

PLAYS

A Peep into the 20th Century

FOR CHILDREN

Sad Adam-Glad Adam

Dog Horse Rat

CHRISTOPHER
DAVIS

VIKING

VIKING
Published by Penguin Group
Viking Penguin, a division of Penguin Books USA Inc.,
40 West 23rd Street, New York, New York 10010, U.S.A.
Penguin Books Ltd, 27 Wrights Lane, London W8 5TZ, England
Penguin Books Australia Ltd, Ringwood, Victoria, Australia
Penguin Books Canada Ltd, 2801 John Street,
Markham, Ontario, Canada L3R 1B4
Penguin Books (N.Z.) Ltd, 182–190 Wairau Road,
Auckland 10, New Zealand

Penguin Books Ltd, Registered Offices: Harmondsworth, Middlesex, England

First published in 1990 by Viking Penguin,
a division of Penguin Books USA Inc.

1 3 5 7 9 10 8 6 4 2

LIBRARY OF CONGRESS CATALOGING IN PUBLICATION DATA
Davis, Christopher, 1928–
Dog horse rat / Christopher Davis.
p. cm.
ISBN 0–670–82580–8
I. Title.
PS3554.A933D64 1990
813′.54—dc20 89–40339
CIP

Printed in the United States of America
Set in Bodoni Book

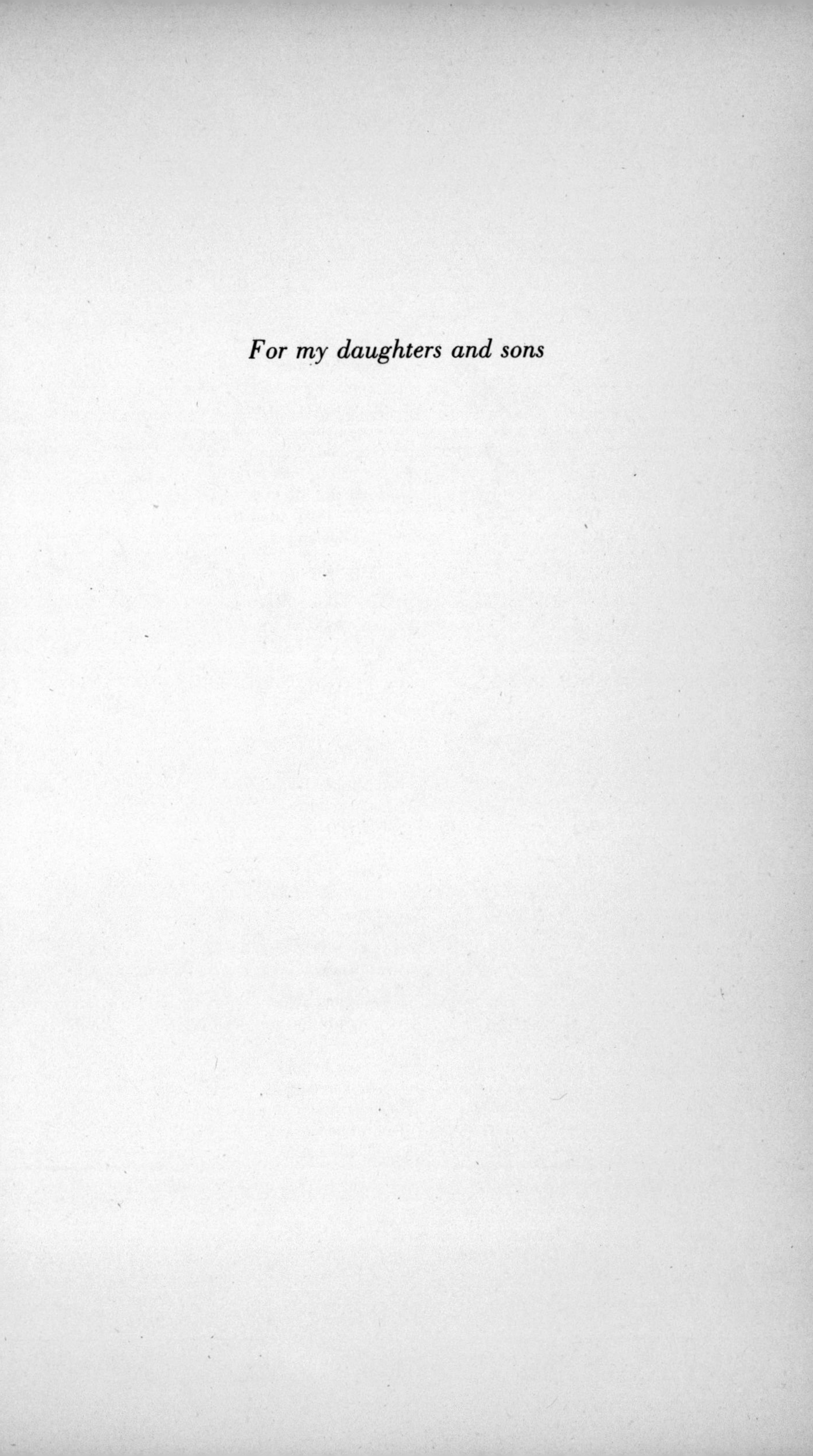

For my daughters and sons

Why should a dog, a horse, a rat, have life,
And thou no breath at all?

—William Shakespeare, *King Lear*, V, iii

One

1

They found the guitar he remembered. There was the TV too, about ten years old, a nineteen-inch-screen black-and-white. He'd seen its light flickering when he drove by at night in the summer with his brother, getting the shape of the land and house and outbuildings clear again. There was a typewriter that looked pretty good and was probably worth something. They walked through the house, lighting matches as they went, dropping them anywhere when they burned down, on the carpet, into easy chairs. Maybe the place would burn. Let it burn.

He remembered how two years before, going by with his daddy in the pickup, he had seen the dark-haired boy sitting on the edge of the porch, the guitar in his lap, his sister in the shadows, just her hands visible. She looked as if she was listening. And the father, tall, thin, glasses, half bald, standing on the other side of the road in the flower garden, a hose in his hand, facing the house, listening too, he guessed. Royal and his daddy, partway drunk both of them, going fast past the rich white house in the dusk, Royal looking quickly right and left to fix again this picture of money: the dark boy bowed over the shining box, stroking its strings, the sister, the father with his sad face turning to look up at the old house. He decided right then, if Van agreed, that he would return sometime when the people were back in the city and take away as much as he could carry.

He didn't care where the big blue-topped kitchen matches fell, just dropped them. They flared and showed edges of brass and what looked like silver, but Van said it was most of it shit: where were the guns Royal had seen? Van had explained that all they could really use were cash, guns, TVs. The typewriter maybe. They couldn't use anything that would give Freddie trouble on resale.

Van was working on the floor above, slowly covering each room. Royal could hear him.

He had the guitar in his hand. On his head was the cocky hat the man used to wear when he was in his garden. The few days Royal had been employed before he quit, the man used to look at him from under the porkpie with its camouflage pattern, his brown eyes sleepy with his power over him, tell Royal what was what: do this or that. Royal didn't have to decide himself, the man said or seemed to say, where to dump the leaves he raked. Just listen. And he took him by the elbow to where he wanted the leaves dumped. "Get your fucking hand off me," he wanted to tell him. The man—he was a teacher of some kind; his name was Corbin—looked right into his eyes with his sad brown ones, talked soft, smiled as if whatever he said to this dumb country boy didn't matter much anyway, was not worth his time. He kept his hand on his elbow as if Royal was a fool and couldn't follow instructions without being shown.

Now he had the man's hat on his head, its brim down all around, pushed forward over his eyes the way the man wore it, and the boy's guitar in his hand.

"Roy, are you looking?" Van called from above.

He held the guitar, with its inlaid decoration, by the neck.

Van came down in his heavy boots, confident in the dark, using his night vision and what he called combat instinct. He had on pieces of his uniform. They both wore the thin transparent plastic gloves Van had lifted from the regional emergency room when he was in for stitches for a cut the summer before.

"You told me you saw guns."

The older brother spoke from the landing, his voice quiet. He had sewn his corporal stripes back on, restored his own rank. You could just see him, the shine on his boots. His deer-skinning knife in a soft scabbard was pushed down into one of the boots. He was combat ready.

"I saw them with Brownings going into those woods in back of the house."

"In the summer?"

"They were going up to try them. I heard them firing. We have to look, Van. They prob'ly hid them somewhere."

They stood apart in the darkness. Royal thought his older brother could see him plainly. Of Van, in the darkness of the house, in the November cold, he saw his shape, the gleam on his boots and on the frames of his glasses. He waited, trusting his brother.

"We don't have suffish at this point to justify the thing," Van said. He came down the stairs. "Nothing on the second floor. There should be. The TV's not much. He said he won't take anything but practically new. Shouldn't there be silverware?" Seeing in the dark: "What's that?"

"A guitar."

"It's not worth much."

"I don't want to sell it."

Royal saw Van's face lean into a match. He was lighting a joint. They stood in the blackness of the rich man's house, passing it back and forth. It got to him quickly, so that suddenly he smelled his own and his brother's sweat. He heard some night bird calling and then the traffic on the state road a mile away.

"You said you saw fishing gear, Roy. You said you saw him go with his wife to play golf. There should be power tools and equipment."

The marijuana had sharpened Royal's vision, also it had grown fractionally lighter. He saw his brother's face, the breath from his mouth in the cold.

"They kept horses too," he said. "The girl rode. There should be all that gear somewhere."

They finished the cigarette. Van put the remains into the snuff can he'd brought it in, and they looked again, this time starting in the basement and missing nothing. At last Royal heard his brother's voice penetrating all the rooms of the house. "Here it is. I found it." It took him a while to locate him, bumping into corners of furniture, and when he did Van said again, "This here," in a satisfied tone. Not wild and triumphant, but as if this was only one more night's work and here was its reasonable result. Van had done this kind of job a few times with friends Royal didn't know, never before with his brother. This action had been Royal's idea and his plan.

Van said, "There's a few good things here."

They were in a windowless storeroom under the stairs at one end of the rambling old farmhouse. Van used his flash, putting its light here and there for Royal. Objects leaped up sharp-edged. Fishing rods and reels of various kinds hung on pegs. There were wading boots, boxes of tackle and whatnot, a pair of Browning shotguns in canvas cases, a .22 with a telescope sight, set across nails in a beam, two bags of good golf clubs, one black leather, the other, the woman's, white. There was a good electric typewriter; a Sony color TV, almost new; hand tools, power tools—a drill press, a rotary saw, a chain saw, and so on. A lot of valuable things. There were saddles on racks with bridles and other gear hung above them, also riding boots and the hard hats. There was a collection of liquor in two grocery cartons, a wooden box of wine. Van twisted the cap off a bottle of Scotch, and, kidding, turned the light on himself and drank, his long throat working. The up-from-under light put black holes in his face.

He handed the bottle to Royal.

"Make sure you want that guitar. You can't play it, and you're too impatient to learn."

The job was all but done. They could relax, take their time. Van was coming down from the strain, making conversation. Royal had forgotten the guitar was still in his hand.

"You mean I'm too dumb."

"You know I don't mean that, Roy. Don't put yourself down. The value you put on yourself is how people take you. You run around saying you're dumb, people believe it and act accordingly. It's in your control. That's our daddy's doing, the way you put yourself down. He's not too bright himself, so that's how he sees other people."

Van was respectful in his dealings with the younger brother. He didn't talk down to him. He tried to teach him but did it in a way that was inoffensive. "You don't want to bad-mouth that person," he had once said of one of Royal's teachers. "Just let it go for now. She's against you temporarily, so you have to show her. Be polite and do the work, enough to show you don't give a fuck. Then, when you can, you'll even up the balance, tell her who you are. I learned that long ago. Never be something just because a man or woman says you are."

You judged yourself. You didn't let anyone do that for you. If someone did you a wrong, you evened it up and got the balance back. But there was the other balance, and if someone did well by you, you acknowledged that too.

Van had come back from the service, his papers clouded,

though he had not been tried. They'd exercised their prerogative, took his stripes and what benefits they could and fired him, Van told Royal, because he refused to let anyone sit in judgment on him. Then they'd dropped their charges to save the expense of prosecuting. It cost the government more than twenty thousand dollars to try a man, someone had told Van, and they were not about to waste the money on him. Then there was the accident the month before his discharge, which had hospitalized him—the artillery truck turning over. No benefits on that, not even a line in his official jacket, though the dismissed charges remained for any future employer to read. Never mind: you forgot it. Van did whatever needed doing, he said to his brother, and what he couldn't handle he just let go, let it ride for the time being. When he could, by whatever means necessary or possible, he did his best to restore the balance.

It was all a question of control and balance.

The Scotch and the pot had made Royal clearheaded, as if he was watching himself. In the picture in his mind the young boy was bent over the guitar in the summer evening. He wore jeans cut off at the knees and a clean white sweatshirt with printing on the chest. A college. His head was bent so you could only see its top. It seemed to Royal that in this house it was always summer, always evening. The boy, about his own age, his sister sitting in shadow, the board-sided house clean and white, its windows bright with the sunset. The boy was about to speak or maybe even sing, his bare feet crossed under him. On the other side of the road Corbin, who had treated Royal like dirt, his green snake of garden hose in his hand, was turning to listen. They were like people in a movie about a happy family. After he'd quit he used to drive through with Van or friends, see the house and woods on the one side, pastures and pond on the other, and throw out his empty Coke or beer onto their lawn. Flip the beer can out onto their neat lawn. When he came by again it would be gone, so he knew someone had to go out and pick it up. They were snobs. A professor in a college and his family.

He'd seen the man's wife once or twice. She had hair so blond it was almost white. Smiled at him with white teeth. Someone in town he'd talked to, he didn't remember who, said she was an artist. Once after the incident over where the leaves went and his quitting, driving through, he gave his cowboy yodel of derision, let it carry back on the wind. He figured they knew who it was and got the point.

He lifted the guitar, hesitated, and drove it against one of the support timbers, smashing it.

"Hey!" said Van.

Then he said immediately, "Hold it." And then again, low: "Hold on, sonny. I'm serious."

Van turned off the flash. Royal did not move.

There hadn't been any cars at all on the road outside, but a car was coming now, going down its gears as it moved up the rise. Pencils of light pierced the storeroom through spaces between the wall boards and circled the room as the car's headlights ran across the house.

The car went past.

"It's okay," Royal said.

The older brother remained stubbornly still. "Cars don't come up here this time of night." And then: "Why the fuck did you make a noise like that?"

They'd planned this burglary on principles laid down by Van West working on the basis of what he called worst case or critical point contingencies: if they found nothing of value; if they were seen coming in, the stolen car noted at any stage; if they couldn't handle what they found—antiques, rugs, which their contact wouldn't fence, or something too heavy or strong for them, such as a safe; or if they got surprised in the act. What they would say and do. Van had it all laid out. If it was worked out up front, you were freed of responsibility in it and could just go ahead like some kind of machine. Whatever you anticipated made you that much more efficient. Royal's action had not fit in with the plan.

After a time, the car long past, Van put the light on, turned it on his brother, then on the remains of the musical instrument. Royal expected more, but Van only said mildly, "All right. We'll let that go."

A minute or two later Royal found the real hiding place.

It was at the back of one of the holes made by the beams running behind a frame wall. He had been using a box to stand on, pushing his hand into one hole after the other. Now he held out a bundle of silverware—knives, spoons, odd pieces—all wrapped in a soft cloth. Van looked it over, nodded in his serious way without comment, set it aside, and waited.

Royal brought out two silver cups and several platters with inscriptions on them. There were other pieces of silver and china. Van said the china was no use, leave it.

He found a piece of machinery wrapped in a rag.

"It's the distributor rotor for that pickup in the barn," Van said. "That means we can take it."

Royal heard the excitement in his brother's voice.

Now he had found a metal box. He held it open under Van's light. "Shit! Look!"

It was filled with jewelry—pins and rings, bracelets, a gold pocket watch. Under it all was a neat packet of cash with a thick red rubber band around it. Royal took the light and held it on the box while his brother counted.

Two hundred in twenties, four fifties.

"Good," Van said. "Good boy."

Directly into their pockets. Untraceable.

"You can take something for Pauline," Royal said, referring to the jewelry.

Van nodded.

It was Royal's find. It was as if he was giving something to his brother: "Pick it out, Van."

"You take something too."

Van chose a brooch with a cluster of dusty red stones. The gold had an old look and showed dully in the light. He slid it into the pocket of his tunic where he'd put the cash.

"This justifies the risk, don't it?"

"Yes."

Royal smiled.

He took a bracelet and put it in his jacket pocket. Van set the box aside with the other things they would carry out. Royal, standing on the crate, tried the remaining spaces at the top of the wall. He said, "I don't think there's anything else." Then he found a flat metal object folded in a piece of taped plastic. He passed it to Van and, reaching deeper, breathing the old dust, first touched, then lifted out what he already knew was a gun.

"This here's the clip to an automatic pistol," Van was saying under him. "Loaded. You can tell by the weight."

Royal had the gun in his hand now, feeling its heavy balance against his palm. It was not big, but its coldness, the authority of its weight, made his heart pound. He wanted to put it in his pocket, pretend he had not found it. He suddenly felt he had to use a bathroom, then a sexual stir and tightening.

"You find it?" Van asked.

He handed him the gun.

"An old Mauser automatic," Van said, his light on it, looking closely. "World War Two prob'ly, a souvenir some dogface brought back. It's a good little weapon. There's some nicks in the blue, but they kept it clean and oiled. Equivalent's our .32 caliber."

Van would say later that his concentration on the gun was so intent that what there was to hear from outside the house could not reach him, could not get through. In any case he did not register the sounds in time to back them off the mission and get away. There were soft steps, a scrape. Royal would say he'd heard nothing up to that point.

It was while Van was putting the gun in his pocket, saying in his normal voice—too loud, he would blame himself: "I believe maybe we'll take a chance on that truck, Roy. Leave the car." He turned out the flash and said suddenly, low, strictly, "Now, this here is it, Royal. Whatever goes down from here on, you do everything exactly like I say."

There was someone on the porch.

Royal would recall that in these seconds his mind was clear and his body in his charge, that he was sweetly in charge as he would be with Lou, any woman, sliding down the hill to climax. It's going to happen now, he thought.

He heard the loud shaking voice from the porch outside the storeroom and suddenly recalled the boy's name, which he thought he'd forgotten. It was Michael. The girl, the sister, whose own name he never heard, had called him Michael.

"Is anyone in there?"

Royal heard nothing from his brother, not even the sound of his breathing. It was as if Van had left him alone.

The shaking voice said, "It's Mike. Is there somebody here?"

And then, unbelievably: "Is that you in there, Roy?"

It was when he heard that that Royal's control of himself left him to the extent that he couldn't be sure for a long time how it all went down, the sequence of the events, who did what and when and why.

2

Van also said later it was a matter of whose point of view it was. If it came to a court case, you wanted the best of it presented through counsel. That's what counsel was for. But you yourself had to prepare first, because in this case you were the witness, the only one who knew. Van went over it with him afterward: what was the aggravating circumstance, the burglary felony, putting that in perspective against what was mitigating. It was the boy who brought the gun to the scene. Soon that would become enough of the fact for Royal that he could slide one picture over the other, see the one or the other or, changing viewpoint, both together as something else, and each would be correct. It wasn't that he would forget or not know but that, with Van's coaching, he could to an extent, where it might become needful in this total fuckup, choose which reality: the right way, the mitigating way.

The first way, Royal heard the sound of the clip, going into the grip of the pistol, then the barrel being pulled back to put the round up. His brother hesitated for maybe two seconds. He lifted his boot high, pushed the door straight out, and shot the boy.

That was it.

Period.

"Come on, sonny," Van said to Royal then. "Take what you can carry of that stuff I stacked there and haul it down to the car. Stay there. Don't look at him." Van's voice sounded natural. The same as always. Nothing had happened. "You don't need to look at him."

He saw the boy anyhow. He was lying on his side, kicking one leg out. He was pulling it up tight to his waist and kicking out straight over and over. One arm was hidden under him, the other curled on his chest, the long hand dangling loose. His head was down on the porch boards as if he was tired but couldn't sleep. His mouth was open and he was making a high "Uh-uh" that didn't stop. His eyes were wide open and looked concentrated like he was working at what he was doing, as if that could save him. There was no blood to see. He looked too big, too old to be the boy Michael. It might have been the father or anyone, a stranger coming in. You had to step around him the way he filled the porch, hug the wall.

Royal went down the road fast to where the car was. There was another car parked right behind it, a rusted-out VW with a soft top. No one was in it. He got into their own car with the goods he had been able to carry and sat there. He did not move again. He thought probably he couldn't even if he wanted to, but he did not try. It had gone suddenly cold and damp, the way it does before light. After a period of time he heard another shot.

Van came down with goods, piled them into the back, went up the hill again. When he returned he had most of the rest of the stuff they had selected.

"There's nothing to tie us to it," he said, "but here's the story in case."

3

Van said, "All right. Where were you?"

"You told me to get out to the road before he came up on the porch, which I did. I saw him, but he didn't see me. He had the gun in his hand at that time. Then I came down, saw his car behind ours."

"You had the starlight to see his gun, just make it out."

"That's all I know about it."

"All you know and all you need to know."

Van kept going over it. His voice was steady, but he breathed in short flat gasps, and though he drove carefully the car kept drifting from side to side of the dark road. He held the bottle of Scotch between his knees and took sips from it. Royal didn't want any.

"Two shots. The first goes wild into the porch wall. We fight over the weapon. I'm trying to disarm him, prevent the disaster. The second round took him, this accident, and he went down." The second shot Royal had heard was the one that went into the wall. All he needed to do was turn around their order in time, make it first. "Where we went wrong," Van said, "we panicked and left the scene. We should have called the police and stayed by him."

"I should be in it, say I was there and be the witness for you."

"They'd only figure you'd lie for your brother, so it's wasted. I want you out of it."

They stopped for Van to piss in the water runoff beside the road, and even there, ankle deep in cold mist, he kept at his brother, rehearsing him, made him tell it to him over again. He stood with his head back, taking breaths as if he could drink the air.

"Shouldn't we tell somebody?" Royal asked. "Just call it in without names? Maybe they can help him still."

"He died right while I was there. It's done with."

Royal said nothing.

"Too bad," his brother said. "I'm sorry for it." When he got into the car again he sat and chewed angrily on the skin around his thumbnail, staring out into the night. "I put you in danger there."

And later:

"Well, you saw me in a different light tonight, sonny. The other man."

After that, as they drove, he kept asking, "Are you okay?" And he said, "Well, I shouldn't have let that round off at him. He had friends he was going to meet there prob'ly, and one of them happened to have the same name as you, that's all. It was a coincidence. I thought he knew it was you in there, and that triggered this whole thing. I just plain and simple fucked up. Well, it's over."

He drove with care now, no more drifting, sitting straight, his chin up as if he couldn't see out without sitting up tall, though he was normal height, slowing almost to a stop even for the black-and-yellow signs that showed the road's curves.

"We can't sell any of the stuff to Freddie either, because we have a manslaughter on it now. I don't even know why I brought it. I'm not reacting right. That's the shock to an extent. You get more or less shock out of an event like this. You're going to feel it too, Roy, if you don't already."

His voice and manner were calm. He kept figuring angles, rehearsing everything, making changes in the story. He would say, "Let's go over it once more, Roy."

Royal would tell him the story of the events of the night.

"All right," his brother said at last, satisfied. "Now that's the truth."

They had come down onto the river road. Van turned abruptly into the yard of what had once been a farm. The house and barn had burned the year before. He stamped hard on the brake, stalled the car, put his head onto the steering wheel, and passed out. Royal leaned across and punched the car's lights off. Then he took the bottle, which had tilted and was beginning to spill, from between his brother's knees, sat back, and waited. On his left under a thin fringe of trees the river reflected the last of the starlight. Hills rose on the other side. Night sounds, which had stopped with their arrival, started again. After a time he got out of the car, a new-model Pontiac, took a mouthful of liquor, and spit it out. His erection would not subside. He stepped behind one of the two big sugar maples that had marked the front yard of the house and, thinking not of Lou but of other girls he knew, picturing them naked in the act with himself, tried to bring himself off. He could not. He could neither urinate nor come.

His hands were dark with the dry dirt from the Corbins' storeroom. He stood against the tree, his quilted vest open, jeans open, the big cowboy belt buckle hanging heavily. He stared down at the curled tips of his heel boots. When the erection eased at last he was able to urinate, grunting and sighing.

He looked around then. A shed was leaning against its

collapsing frame, inside it an old horse-drawn hay rake. Boards weighted with cinder blocks covered what appeared to be a well. Looking things over this way, pissing, he felt better, in command. He did up his clothes, went and lifted off the blocks, kicked the boards aside, and dropped the bottle in. The well must have been good still, because there was a deep splash when the bottle hit.

After a time, knowing almost to the minute when his brother would come out of it, Royal crossed the yard and stood at the driver's door of the Pontiac. When Van looked up he opened the door for him, caught him under the arm as he stumbled getting out, and led him a few steps away. The older brother vomited, Royal holding on to the back of his belt so he would not fall.

Van said presently, "Shit."

He looked around.

"Where is this?"

"The Daley place. They say they burnt it for the money."

"I heard that too. I knew the grandson, Frank, on football. He could've burnt it. He was capable of about anything."

Van sat on the engine hood, legs folded under him, looking everywhere but at Royal. For a minute everything was ordinary, as if it was an ordinary conversation, except for the fact he wouldn't look at him. Then he said, "Well, I messed up somehow. I can't remember how just yet."

Royal was silent.

"I fucked up. I did, not you, Roy." He paused. "That boy. Was that it? Well, I know it was."

"He came up with his daddy's gun in his hand, and you fought him."

"That's right. That's right. Where's the bottle?" And when Royal said what he had done with it: "Okay. That's just what you should have done, the way I am."

The older brother had a little mustache, and he sat chewing it thoughtfully. The metal-rimmed glasses he wore caught the light that was beginning to come from the hill above them. Royal realized he was shaking, the aftereffect and the cold.

Van said, "I feel bad. You don't get used to that ever. It just gets worse. I never thought I'd run into it again after all I've been through and seen."

He said, "It's coming back now. It was when we were into that box. Seeing the cash made me lose my concentration. If we'd heard him, we'd have gone out the side door, carried out one or two things, the cash, the TV, and gone out. I wasn't concentrating, and we lost the opportunity. Now we have this casualty to deal with. We shouldn't have taken the goods at all. That was dumb. It was poor performance and no excuse. Right at this point my concern is for safety, yours and mine. This is a major felony with the manslaughter, and I'm anxious about it. We have to go about everything in the right way. That's my position."

He sat thinking.

After a time, Van directing it, they put the thin gloves on again, dropped everything but the cash into the well, covered it the way it had been, drove back into the town of Bradford, and returned the car to where they had found it, in the lot behind a wholesale hardware store. There was no reason why anyone would know it had been taken. Then they walked two blocks to the pickup they'd come in, divided the cash, and drove to Whitehouse, which was their town.

Royal was still shaking.

"That's the shock. Take your time to feel better, but don't take too long about it, Roy. It's almost light."

Van had stopped on the main street. After a few minutes he said quietly, "All right. I want you to calm yourself now." He said, "I believe we can get away with this. If they suspect us for some reason, I think they'll give us the benefit of the doubt. We have our story clear, the facts in the case, in the event we need it, but I'm known, there's respect for me, and I don't think it will come to it. At the worst, what they'll have on us is a manslaughter charge. If it comes down, that's what they'll try us on, not first degree. We'll have the two felonies on us. They'll dismiss lesser charges. The weapon was his, belonged in the family. The burglary and the manslaughter. Worst case. And they'll drop your manslaughter because you'll turn evidence on me. But I think we can beat both."

He let Royal off at his place and said, "I'll get an empty bottle and put it in the truck. What we did tonight, all night"—he looked at his watch—"until five this morning, we parked there on that road by the sandpit where we go, talked, played the radio, finished the bottle."

They had played the radio off and on in the Pontiac as well as in the truck. Country music.

"You remember some songs we heard?"

"Sure."

"Listen. I don't downgrade the seriousness of it. You're on your own now for a while. What are you going to say to Lou?"

"Just what you said now."

"And you're all right?"

"Sure."

Van said, "Listen. These things happen. You know it, I know it." He asked again, looking at him carefully, "Okay?"

Royal nodded.

Van gazed through the metal-rimmed glasses at the younger man, calming him by his look and voice. He said, "You're all right. I can see that."

4

Royal was married to Louetta, three years older, Van to Pauline, who had been Lou's classmate and best friend in school. Van and his wife had a baby and shared a mobile home in Whitehouse with the West boys' father and stepmother. Royal and Lou rented a bedroom and bath with kitchen privileges on a widow's farm outside town.

Lou came down in her nightgown. Royal stood at the half-size refrigerator, the door open, pushing aside the few things in it. He said, "Shit. Why isn't there ever anything in here?"

"You want me to make you a sandwich?" she asked.

She couldn't find much either, and finally she went into the widow's end of the kitchen to her refrigerator and got some ham.

"I'll explain to her."

She made a sandwich and sat with him. "You don't seem like you've been drinking," she said when he told her where he had been all night.

"Van did most of it. He was more or less off the deep end. He wanted to talk."

The brothers had plans. They were going to borrow to rent local pasturage, fence it, raise beef cattle, then when they had sufficient profit buy western land in Montana or the Dakotas, where acreage was still cheap, maybe get in under the Homestead Act, which still had more advantages to it than drawbacks. They would start up again out there. Van had a little saved. Pauline had an inheritance from her grandmother, which she just kept in the bank, wouldn't invest. Van thought he could talk her around. They would pick up the rest by whatever means.

"Was he bad?"

"You know the way he gets every once in a while. He had to let some of it out."

He had opened a beer, but it stood untouched on the table. He did not eat the sandwich. Every time he looked at her she would pick up on it, glance into his face to see what was wrong. There was a rush of water in the waste pipe behind the wall, which meant the widow, Mrs. Marquette, was up.

Lou asked, "What's the matter?"

"Not a thing."

He was not really thinking about anything.

Lou took the sandwich for herself. She wore her cotton nightgown. As she ate, unconscious of what she was doing, she smoothed her breasts. She was thin and blond, her long, fine hair parted in the middle. Now it was loose, but during the day she tied it back. She used little makeup, drank wine sparingly on the occasions when they went out, but did not mind Royal's drinking. She did not criticize him for the time he spent away from her.

He watched her. At last, to see what it would feel like, looking at her, seeing her image blur, he thought: Well, this is doom, bringing it to the surface.

He used the word in his mind. He kept looking at his wife, letting her blur and come back.

If Lou was eating, she was content. She liked to work. She

planted and maintained Mrs. Marquette's garden, did the canning, and cleaned the house. She took the bus in to shop, cooked for both families, and so on, so that the woman didn't charge them for rent, only their share of the utilities. The two were friends. Louetta liked to eat but did not gain weight the way most women in Whitehouse did in winter, Pauline for example. She liked TV. Royal would come in late at night and find her and Mrs. Marquette, the old woman with her Bible, a plate of cookies in front of them or a cake, Lou looking at the big book over the old woman's shoulder with curiosity, the way she would at a magazine, then both of them glancing at the TV, as if one was as interesting as the other. He wondered at the way she could be friends like that with old people.

The word stood in his mind now but did not bother him. Doom. He was all right. Seen in one light, in this place, this point in time, it was the way it had been just afterward—as if nothing had happened. Or it was as if it was still waiting to happen and did not need to. It seemed to him that this was the real part of the night and that everything would go on from this time forward.

In bed he fell asleep right away, but soon she was shaking him. "You're having dreams, Roy, carrying on and talking."

"What did I say?"

"Nothing I could understand."

He said after a time, "I'm sorry for Van is all."

"What's he into now?"

"The same thing it always was. How they did him over there. He can't keep fighting them all his life. It wears him out."

"I'm sorry for him too."

A wind had come up. He didn't know the names of the trees it shook outside their window. He thought then that he didn't know anything worth knowing, only a handful of things to get by with, and that was it. "If you're going to solve your problems, you need to know something," Van had said to him, advising him not to quit school when he was old enough to do it.

"They do that to a man," Royal said. "Take the best he has and don't give him anything back. He don't say much, but I know he's hurt."

"You said he talks about it to you."

"He tells stories, but it's like he jokes."

He had begun to caress her, running his hand nervously up under her nightgown. She took hold of him.

"Don't that hurt?" He was so hard.

He held her by the wrist, put her hand away from him.

"Well, what *are* you upset about?"

"When you did it with Bobby Argyle before me, what was it like?"

She looked down at him in the early light. She did not know what he meant, she said.

"Did you take hold of him?"

Surprise made her laugh.

He had begun to shake as he had earlier and could not stop. He pushed her away, but she kept moving back to him in the bed until, stiffly, shivering, he let her hold him, one hand behind his back smoothing, the other between his legs caressing him. She soothed with her voice. Her voice now was just like his old family court mother's, dark, easy. He had told her once how she sounded when she was like this with him in bed, and it made her laugh in the same way she just had.

Now he said, "I can't help thinking about Bobby. It makes me feel so bad."

After a time he asked, "Who else did you do it to?"

"Now, you know nobody but Bobby. What are you asking for? I told you everything I did before you."

"What about your friends you told me about?"

"I told you."

His hand, as if it was free of him, smoothed her under the flannel nightgown. She did not let go of him. She told him again about how she and her friends, three or four girls together, would sit around on winter weekends, January, February, if they were alone in one or another's house, and they would bring each other off in turn or bring themselves off, the TV going, maybe some skin magazine one had stolen from her brother or father open on the table, not that they cared so much for that. It helped make the mood was all. There was coffee cake out, Cokes, whatnot. Like a tea party. Once or twice there would be a boy with them, a younger brother. That didn't trouble Royal much, because he himself could become the boy, the witness, in the picture in his mind. They'd all be so quiet and sweet, lambs with each other, just children. They knew no better, never thought it was wrong. Lou still did not, she said. It made her laugh, looking back. They would curl up together talking, caressing each other, sometimes naked under their dresses, watching the Saturday cartoons or some game show, the snow piled up outside the windows, stuffing themselves with cake. She'd said they brought themselves off, but really, she admitted, that was a rare accomplishment. They were more or less like innocent barnyard creatures with each other, heifers butting or playing, or lambs. What were they—eleven, twelve? Twelve at most. She thought maybe one of them once was thirteen. Maybe one of them, no more, had breasts worth looking at at that age. Though Royal was free to guess and thought he might know, she never mentioned the girls' names because that wouldn't be fair on them. It was just a childish event, to be replaced in time by whatever more grown-up way came next. It wasn't anything, she said, but she told him all about it in detail, the intimate details of her friends' bodies, and he came into her hand and over the front of her nightgown, so that she yelled, "Roy!"

She had to get up to take it off. "Oh, my Lord! What a deluge!"

He watched her naked in the light that leaked around the window shade, the particular nameless tree outside rushing and scraping in the wind. The space between this and the earlier part of the night had widened and deepened.

She dried herself. "It's cold! Why that woman won't put some heat in this house!" She held her breasts, heavy for someone so thin, supporting them as she used the towel.

"Bobby Argyle," she said scornfully, laughing. "That poor nothing."

"Why is he nothing?"

"You don't need to be jealous of him, Roy. He was nothing to me."

"Why wasn't he?"

He was pleased. She made everything easy, something you could work with if you took it slow. The other shore of the night was just that. You ignored it if you could or dealt with it in its time if you could. If not, Van would work on it, sit with his stitched suede heel boots up on the coffee table in their stepmother's mobile home, notes in a clipboard on his lap, cigarette going, work it all out, make the lists, analyze existing facts. He gave himself to Van and to Lou. He felt the shivering excitement of being at the start of everything. You're on top of the biggest hill, and they're going to shove the sled off hard right out into the sky. He felt the easy, floating, doom-filled excitement of being about to fall into the sky. Van waiting. Lou watching, saying, "It'll be all right." Van saying, "Leave it to me." They were all doomed in the same way, all together. It was out of their hands.

She stared at him in the half darkness. He was getting up as she got back into bed wearing his pajama top.

"I have this thing for you."

He turned on the bureau light under her posters. John Lennon. Mick Jagger in a big frilly shirt like a woman's eating the lollipop microphone. She stared squinting in the brightness, her thin hair scattered across her shoulders.

"Your side of the bed's getting cold!"

He was searching his clothes.

"What is it?" She laughed.

She looked at the gold bracelet in his hand, then took it from him. Now he was counting bills, cash, smiling self-consciously. He stood in the pajama pants, light on his narrow naked body, his red-gold head bent to hide his self-conscious pleasure, counting the money, and Louetta, still with pleasure in the tone of her voice, saying, "Oh, Lord, what kind of trouble are you in now?"

5

They were in the roadhouse they always went to. The day bartender was a woman named Alice Daley. They knew her. She was the aunt of a high school classmate of Van's. They knew all the regular customers and were related to a few. Van always asked Alice about her nephew, who was in the Marines. He was courtly to her. "I understand you were sick for a while. We missed you." That kind of thing. He was serious. He did not kid her. "You stay away too long, this place would fall apart."

He would nod, take in her responses, listening carefully. Then when he was through, that was that. It was as if he had found out what he had to know on her behalf to protect her interests if a need arose. Then he would turn to something new, someone else, take that up.

Van sat with a beer and the Bradford paper on the table in front of him. He used a glass, poured a little at a time, making it last. He was not really drinking. Royal had a Pepsi.

Cold late-morning light came in through the front and side windows. The place was called the Antlers, and they had the various racks mounted on the walls, the antlers with prize spreads. It was famous for them. There were the usual notices and licenses and beer ads, games. There was a shed on one side to tie horses or park snowmobiles and tourist cabins in back, everything of peeled varnished hemlock logs. On the other side was a miniature golf course the owner had built. It had not caught on and was fallen into disrepair. You could see through the front windows an arm of Whitehouse Lake across the state road, tall pines in a thick screen around it.

Alice Daley, every time her eye fell on Van with his paper, said, "I can't get over it," or something like it.

Two morning drinkers were in, John May, who kept a camp on the lake and was known as an ice fisherman, and Tommy Solent, a hunter and guide, whose business card was taped under two of the prize deer racks to identify him as the one who had taken them. Van knew them. They all knew each other, cutting across generations. If you knew a man's son, then the father was a friend. You took their daughters out, went to their funerals and so on. They came to your wedding, the football games.

John May said, "Well, it's too bad."

"I never knew one of those people. They kept to themselves," Alice Daley said. "I wouldn't have known one of them by sight, but still it's a terrible thing."

It had been forty-eight hours.

Royal could see the headline upside down. Van had a ballpoint pen and was drawing over it, filling in the letters. CORBIN DEATH. TRAGEDY SHOCKS RESORT AREA. Royal would not read the story, but Van had read every word. The father was an important man. He held posts and wrote books, Van told him. He was a professor. There was a story on it in *The New York Times*, on an inside page, and in the other papers Van had looked through in front of the Whitehouse Pharmacy. He'd bought the *Bradford Star*.

"They're robbing camps more and more. People come in

from the outside and do it, professional burglars come up from New York City," May said. He and Solent were tough old outdoor drunks who did not show their drinking except, after a number of hours of it, in their reddened blue eyes. Both had been friends of the brothers' father since grade school.

Van West asked, "How do you know it isn't someone local?"

Royal knew his older brother was talking for his benefit, telling him something. He was not kidding around, yet he was. He would look up from his work with the pen at Royal, eyes heavy and humorous behind the round metal-rimmed glasses. He'd smooth his little mustache. His expression was cool as marble. He wore his jeans and boots and old pile-lined denim jacket, a dusty brown flat-crowned rodeo hat pushed back on his head. He smoked his little brown cigars out of a tin box he kept on the table in front of him, using the lid as ashtray. He was serious.

"Royal worked for the man once. He knew the boy who got killed. What was his name?"

Van pretended he could not hear the answer. Royal said, "I didn't know the boy's name at the time. I was only there a couple of days. It says in the paper it was Michael."

Van asked, for the others to hear, "I suppose you can't make any kind of guess about what happened there, can you, Roy?"

"No, I'm just sorry about it."

"Where was the camp?" May asked.

"Roy here's the expert."

"On Coldspring Road, out of town about eight miles. They're not so far from the river. A big property. They kept horses. The people next door farmed it for them."

Tommy Solent, who was sharp drunk or not, said, "If I was you, I wouldn't talk about knowing them, young fellow." His morning drink was whiskey and coffee in a big mug. He wore farmer-looking clothes—work pants, quilted jacket, a John Deere cap.

"They'll know he worked for them," Van said.

"He don't need to advertise it."

John May was rolling dice against the bar for drinks, not paying attention now that he had expressed his sympathy.

"Just where were you, Roy," Van asked like a detective in a movie, "between twelve and three A.M. on that particular night?"

Royal could not help glancing at Solent. "You know I was with you."

"Can you prove it?"

Royal laughed.

"I mean, I'd lie for you, wouldn't I? My own brother?"

He supposed he understood what Van was doing, keeping things natural, open, but also teaching him. Van would ask the kidding question, then point his chin at him and give him that hard look. If you worked with fire, the look said, you had to understand what it would do, that it could burn.

The older brother had turned to the comic pages and was starting to work on the puzzles. "I shouldn't joke about it," he said. "I'm sorry for that boy anyway but especially since if those criminals were professionals, they prob'ly didn't mean for it to happen. I saw a lot of that where a life is thrown away out of carelessness or some freak coincidence. Or it just happens. Your own shell does it. It's the boy's first day on the line and he's ignorant, inexperienced. Then the medics have too many to deal with or they're somewhere covering their ass, and the boy just lays out there quietly bleeding to death because he's too shy or scared to yell or thinks he better keep still, it's safer. I've seen that. It's all a lottery how it turns out. Am I right, Alice? I pity that boy and his family just like you do."

He meant what he said, Royal saw. He felt sorry for the dead Corbin boy.

People came in. A township highway maintenance crew in work boots and mackinaws.

"This is the worst thing to happen around here since those campers were killed in the woods," Alice said, beginning again with each new person. She was pitying. Tears stood in her eyes. She was a big woman, unmarried, always dressed in men's jeans and down vests or college sweatshirts. She usually had a cigarette going on the edge of the bar so that there were black scars up and down its length on her side of it. "My heart goes out to those poor dear people."

One of the workmen said, "They'll never find out who it was. You can tell from the story this was professional, people passing through from out of state. They come in on purpose this time of year to rob the summer places. They got surprised at what they were doing and killed the boy. They're a thousand miles from here by now. In Canada or Florida."

Alice said, "There are people around here capable of it, some of the ones from Four Corners, places like that."

Most of them did not see it that way. Outsiders were responsible.

"It's part of the Mafia's business," a man said. "They sell lists of houses, location, contents, when they're empty. They keep files. Professionals go out in a van and burglarize. They're in New York State Monday, North Carolina Wednesday, fence the goods, go to the next place on the list in some midwest state."

"Well, I just pity the family," Alice would say each time.

Royal watched her, saw the beginning of tears.

"That's it." Van would nod. "That's who suffers in the long run."

* * *

"You did well. You had the right answers," Van said in the pickup.

"I didn't say much."

"That's even better." He said, "Let's go up there. Drive by."

"What for?"

"To look it over. It's a natural thing to do. You worked there, we wait a decent amount of time, let them get themselves together, then we go and take a look." He said, "As far as we're concerned it's an interesting news story, Roy."

He said on the way, "When I asked you where you were on the particular night—"

"I told you."

"You watched Solent to be sure he was going to believe you when you did. That's the only thing I have to criticize on the way you acted."

They had talked briefly on the phone, but this was the first time they'd met since the event. Van asked questions. "What did you do with your cash?"

"I have fifty on me. Lou's keeping the rest."

"What did you tell her about it?"

"I gave her the bracelet, and she saw the paper. I didn't say anything. I guess she thinks you were in on something and I'm holding for you."

"If she don't ask, don't tell her, not that it matters. I told Pauline and Daddy to try it out. I said how it went down. How the boy had the gun and we struggled for it."

"What did Daddy say?"

"He said I was a fool."

"I think the more people who know, the more we talk about it, like in the Antlers now, Van, the more they'll connect us down the line when they begin to remember this day. How interested we were. I mean even if they see you're joking the way you were. I don't think you should do it."

"Okay. That's all right. Is that what you think?"

Royal saw his brother was angry.

"Only I believe that right now this is just the correct approach, Roy, and I advise you to go along with it, but you know I want you to speak up. What is your best judgment here?"

"Well, I said. We shouldn't talk about it even in the family. The way I just let it go with Lou, let her have her own ideas, but I don't say anything."

"All right. I see what you mean."

Royal looked at his brother's profile. His nostrils were pinched white with anger.

"Never mind my advice, what I advised," Van said. The road had begun to rise and serpentine as they came into the foothills of the mountains. They were silent. "Well, maybe I better go with your judgment," Van declared at last. "Maybe I can't tell anymore."

"What I'd say, we shouldn't go up there to the place right now."

"That's your judgment? All right."

Van drove on slowly, climbing, for half a mile, then pulled over.

"Do you feel sick?"

"Some. It's always there. This incident, this tragedy, has brought it to the front of the cage, and I'm going to have to deal with it in a serious way sooner or later, see someone. I just don't want anything else right now. It's enough handling this incident and the complications of it, it seems to me." He said, "Listen to that idle. I'll have to work on this car, tune it up for Mona."

After a time, not looking at Royal, he said, "Here's this. I'm asking now. Are you going to trust me?"

"Yes."

"Because I say to you right now in all seriousness, Roy, you have to have trust to survive in a thing like this."

The younger man was silent.

"It's your future at stake, depending on how you do right now. This is life or death. It's no time for dreaming. All right? I remind you who has both the experience and the instinct. Survival with honor. I use that word. That's what we're talking about here. But I don't know how many times I've said to you and meant it it's your estimate of the situation too, your decision as an individual, so don't just say yes to me without thinking it through because we're brothers or because I have experience or, like this, I lose my temper a little because I'm hotheaded. You have to put it all in the balance and decide."

Royal said, "Well, I say go on and do it, that I trust you."

"I'm no leader of men, Roy. That's the worst kind of shit as far as I'm concerned. I have a trained instinct and that's all, and I know a little bit about how to react under the gun and maybe not get hurt. I think it's right to talk about this in a certain way to certain people, for example in the Antlers or in town. I try it out with Daddy and Pauline, who I trust, to see how it goes down. I want to drive up to the site here and look at a few things, let you see a few things, show it to you. Because that's my instinct."

"Well, I decided, Van."

"Say I'm off the wall in a certain sense, those particular episodes, and then I have to trust you, put myself in your hands. You see? I trust you. Do you believe that?"

He got out, came around to the passenger side of the pickup. "I don't feel like it. You drive."

"That's all right."

"Go on. Put you in control."

They drove by the house. Curiosity-seekers. They'd read the story, had nothing to do. They were dumb country boys.

There was a black van in the driveway with state police tags on it. There was a blue-and-yellow state cruiser. The VW Royal had seen with a college sticker across its back window had been pulled onto the lawn, one of its wheels right in a flower bed. A brand-new '76 Olds with a Connecticut plate was parked behind it. There were two men up on the porch talking quietly to each other, official-looking in dark overcoats and city hats. A couple of state troopers in the cowboy-style hats and bright black leggings were in the drive. The house, long and low, one section built onto the next in the New England style, was of white-painted clapboard with a cedar shingle roof and two chimneys, one at either end. It was set above the road at the back of a big lawn on their right in the direction they were driving. The porch where the men stood and where the brothers had been two nights before ran along most of the front. Behind it a wooded hill rose steeply. Everything was neat and buttoned up, the lawn clear of leaves.

"Is that the girl?" Van asked.

"I guess so."

She was seventeen, eighteen, just coming out of the front door between a pair of dark evergreen shrubs. The sun was bright, though it was cool, and it made the white house glare behind her. She was carrying a leather handbag and what looked like a notebook and glanced up into the sun as she came.

"That's the sister."

She was taller than he remembered and looked older than the two years would account for. Her hair seemed darker. He thought she looked right at them in the truck, and he saw that her eyes were clear. She was not crying or anything. She looked like she was busy, on her way somewhere. Then he remembered the time he had worked here and seen her cry. She was maybe fifteen and had been, he guessed, at some kind of horse show.

He saw her father drive up in the truck towing the horse trailer, the girl in the cab beside him. It was late evening. Royal was in the barn, and he looked out through the open door, hearing the truck and then the father's voice. The father, Corbin, got out of the pickup wearing that hat and a shirt that looked like an army shirt, old work boots. He let down the gate of the trailer, then went around, came in through its front door, and backed the horse out, a little red-colored one with white legs, and then stood with it as if he didn't know what to do next. The girl would not get out of the truck. He said something to her, and she didn't answer. Royal could see she was crying, probably over something that happened at the horse show, some prize she didn't get, Corbin standing with the little horse, looking mad as hell.

"I guess we messed up their Thanksgiving a little," Van said. "Interrupted their dinners. I'm sorry for that."

A trooper stood at the foot of the drive. He looked into their vehicle as they moved slowly past staring like tourists, gave them a hard look but no harder than you would expect in the situation, as Van would say later, and waved them on. The driveway was blocked with red traffic cones marked NYS. Across the road three troopers were working their way down the slope through the brown fall pasture toward the pond, heads bent, searching. One swung a metal detector. Another carried a canvas sack.

"Look at them," Van said wonderingly. "What do they think they'll find? They have the gun. We gave them that right there on the porch."

Then they were past and going down the winding secondary road to the river. Van did not speak for a time, then he said, "Shit, they're so stupid. They have the gun. What do they want? They just go by the book like robots. Do whatever's next on the list."

Royal said nothing.

They passed cars parked on the shoulders and saw hunters walking up into the hills.

"Do you want to go out one day?"

"Sure."

"We'll do it," Van said as they descended to the river. "Get our licenses and go. We'll get you that prize buck."

They drove by the Daley property with its scorched foundations and scraps of rusted farm equipment buried in the grass. Van said, "Don't slow."

"This is where we were."

"Is that right? I don't think so. I don't remember this place." He said, "Now you see, you slow down there, and that's poor judgment. That place don't have a thing in the world to do with us. You know I don't mean I really forgot, but before we ever got near to it I studied how I was going to react. Even though it's just us two and we're both involved."

They drove the rest of the way in silence. Royal stopped in the dirt drive of the Marquette place and sat looking down at his hands. He did not want to leave Van. The older brother said, "All right? Do you see where I'm going with this? You can't act like you dreamed it, Roy. If you do that, you're not in control. You wind up blaming yourself for something you never did. Certain things happened. Certain other things did not. Get it straight. The reason we went up to the site. What did you notice? What struck you?"

"I don't know. The girl. Seeing the place."

"That's it. You saw the place. It's there. Do you know what I'm saying? It happened."

Royal shook his head.

"It happened is what I mean! It wasn't some bad dream. You go and look at it, you see the girl, feel bad, see the cops out doing their stuff, everyone out there in the light, and then you're in control, you're not pretending or dreaming, because in a dream anything goes. This way only certain definite things happened, took place. This went down in one way and one way only, but it really went down. That's what I'm after with Tommy Solent and Alice and so on. It's why I made you go up to the place. Because you're in a little state of shock here, a little dream. That's your tendency. I have to snap you out of it so you can deal with this, and that was my approach."

Royal was silent.

"Do you hear what I'm saying?"

"I guess I do. You say it loud enough."

"I don't think you hear me." Van stared at his brother. "Listen. Wake up." He said, "Jesus, you piss me just a little, Roy. Do you know that? You're really like you're asleep. Please wake the fuck up."

Royal said nothing.

"Go on. Let me have the wheel of this car. I got to get home."

Royal was afraid Van was sore at him, but after supper the older brother was back in the drive, fresh-shaved, wearing a pair of clean, pressed Levi's, his jacket over a new western shirt with pearl snaps. It was a nice night, not too cold.

"Come on, sonny. We're going to do some man's drinking."

He kidded Lou in his serious way, an arm around her waist. "When are you going to give my little brother a son and heir and all? Get in touch with me if he won't do it. That's the West tradition. If the younger brother can't, the older must. Jesus, you're thin! Pauline's a cow, does nothing but eat."

"I eat."

"Well, she sits and watches TV all day with Van Buren West Three in her lap, and you work it off somehow. That must be the difference. Nervous energy."

He went to spend a minute with Mrs. Marquette, leaned

over her, one hand on the lounger, the other on her thin shoulder. She liked him, though she wouldn't show it.

"You don't have no fat either. I worry about you women."

She had her TV on and the police emergency scanner sitting on the table beside her, its red light searching up and down its range. Now and then a voice crackled out of it. She was knitting something.

"How's my sweater?"

She shook her head. You could see she tried not to smile.

"You're not going to give it to Roy, are you?"

"It's for my godson in Bradford," she said in her flat French-Canadian voice. "For Christmas."

Van had come up and worked with Royal a few times, helped the neighboring farmer take what little hay there was off the fields, cut wood, and whatnot, and never accepted anything for it but his sandwich and beer. He would call her by her first name and use a certain tone because he saw she liked it, shy as she was. He said now, raising his voice since she was more or less deaf, "Well, we better have the medical report over with. Give us the short version, Annie, because we need to start on our drinking."

He got her going on her symptoms, listened, asked the right questions.

In the truck he said to Royal, "She talks like she's going to die in a week, that old woman. Does she ever say anything about her will?"

"She wouldn't leave the place to us, and she don't have any cash."

"You don't know. That family in Bradford, they're no blood. You and Lou are all she's got."

"She won't do it, that's all. I know."

"You think she don't like you enough, but that's your lack of self-confidence talking, Roy. Play your cards right, wait, and see." He said in a conversational way, "I was thinking. The girl today looked like a nice person. She looked good too."

He meant the Corbin girl. He had mentioned her before casually. He would keep touching on it. It was like a test, but not about the girl.

"I guess so."

"Did you get to know her, Roy?"

"Not much."

"I can't believe you'd miss a chance like that, wouldn't take your shot."

He went on about it, kept it out in the common light of day. It was as if the brothers had had some minor trouble, a little adventure, nothing they couldn't talk about.

"I didn't like how that trooper looked into the car at us," Royal said to show he could refer to it.

Van had the country station on and was beating time with the heels of his hands on the steering wheel. "Well, he's supposed to do that. They don't want people rubbernecking, getting in their way. Maybe he even noted our license. That's all right. It's just his routine work."

After a silence, Royal said about the girl, "We talked once. I took a break, and she saw me and brought me water where I was cutting brush for him. Maybe someone told her to. She wouldn't sit down. I wasn't there long enough was the trouble, never even knew her name. Or I forgot it. She seemed all right today." This was important. "She looked just sort of normal. There she was coming out of the house, and you couldn't see anything special about her. It was just, except for the cops, like she wasn't part of it."

"Well, she liked you all right. Brought you water. Maybe she didn't care for her brother. That happens."

Royal searched for the recollection of her sitting on the porch listening to the boy play his music. The image was changed.

The brother was not in it now. Just the girl sitting back in the shadows. It amazed him that the boy would disappear from the mental picture like that.

"It could have been someone else we saw today," Van said. "There was a girl from the college come over with his friend, the one named Roy who found him. The paper gave her name."

"No, it was her all right."

The Antlers was two deep at the bar, all the tables taken, the dance floor crowded. The brothers were acquainted with most of the people in the place. Van got beers, leaving the change from a twenty on the wet bar top knowing it was safe, and moved around the smoky, noisy room, joining in one group or another for a while, then moving on. He bent politely over the women, listened to everyone, even to young boys, in his sober old-fashioned way, respectfully, nodding quietly, giving his own opinion on whatever it was in due course. A lot of the talk was about the killing.

Royal stood under the blackboard with its list of hunters entered in the sweepstakes. Two men already had bucks with racks of six and seven points, one with eight. There were prizes for the heaviest, the lightest, the most points. Next to the board was a joke set, a pair of one-inch plastic antlers mounted on a tiny varnished shield, the name of the bar owner on a card under it: "Taken at night by Jay Cooney." There were old photos tacked up everywhere, ski resort patches, postcards from local people on the road, on vacation in Florida, so forth. Royal studied it all, though it was as familiar as the things in his own room. Now and then he looked out over the crowd. He held his beer bottle by the neck, tipped it up, capped it with a thumb to keep it alive, looked through its bright glass at some group or individual.

He had felt better with the first few sips. A beer in your own kitchen was one thing, this was another. The beating country music from the jukebox soothed and filled him. There would be a good loud fast one, then one of the dark old ones, its sad bass tones working in his throat. He really felt better, eased. The beer was good to him. The place had the strong yeasty smell he liked. He liked the high noise. The tide of the crowd around him was like his own pulse. He heard the remarks, comments about the crime, coolly. It was all right. "They should bring back the death penalty," a woman he didn't know said. "You won't stop it unless you kill them. That's how you stop them." She stood with her back to him about three feet away, a brown sweet-looking drink in her hand, the men she addressed, cowboy types, staring down at their boots as if they were embarrassed.

Looking around at these people, no matter what they said, he felt safe in their midst. He saw John May and Tommy Solent, one at either end of the bar, as far as they could get from each other, propping it up. It was as if they'd never left the place since that morning, which was a possibility. It was good to see them. There was a cousin of some kind on the brothers' mother's side, a Porter, standing at the short pool table in back, a stick in his hands, chewing on his mustache, looking the situation over. He had some kind of record, had served a state sentence before he was twenty-one. There were rough men here, a few with county or state prison files, some on the other side, but good people, Royal thought, all honest in their way. Van was talking to Paul Beam, a prison guard at Locust Grove Correctional. He was telling the man a story, raising his green bottle of Canadian beer to drink now and then, the big guard quiet, nodding at whatever it was.

If someone addressed him, Royal would talk for a while, then back off. He wanted to stand aside and watch, feel good, at the same time keep an eye on Van. He had three or four beers, using the money Van left on the bar. He watched Alice

Daley matching her check stubs with the cash, getting ready to turn over to the night man. She was a good woman and tough too. Royal had seen her put men out of the place, big men, for drunkenness and bad-mouthing people. She was still hard at work, not tired at all, it seemed, laughing at the jokes, wisecracks. He thought it was too bad she had not married, though you saw she could never have been much on looks. Then he realized, focusing on it, that she must be related to the ones who owned the burned-out house on the river road. All right. He watched the night bartender start to set up for his shift, an old-timer named Cole on his social security, working for next to nothing plus tips. He'd make a hundred, a hundred and fifty dollars on a night like this one, a holiday night, never bother to report it to the IRS. The brothers knew him, had known him for years, fished with him once or twice. Good man.

There wasn't a person in the place who would not be on their side if it came to it, help them out, say a good word for them. Fifty, sixty percent of them anyhow.

Royal felt eased and distant. Later the brothers would smoke some of the local pot a friend of Van's grew in the river cornfields, mild stuff, come off the evening of drinking, unwind, get the little extra help they needed to sleep. There was that to look forward to. And Lou at home in their bed. It half turned him on just to think of her name. It was like the final thing in its place.

In a silence he heard Van say clearly, "Shit, it could have been anybody. It could have been me."

Beam, the guard, wore his dark-green uniform pants with the black stripe down the leg, an old leather jacket on top, a baseball cap. He was almost six and a half feet, had a down-curving mustache and long black hair almost to his shoulders, unusual in the position he was in. He'd played tackle for the two years he was at the state university in Poland, New York, and looked like all the other Beams Royal knew, all living in the mountains to the north and west, all big, beards, long hair, trappers, bear hunters, whatnot, always at the county fairs for pony pulls and logging competitions. Mountain men. Half of them, the respectable ones, became prison guards, the other half collected public assistance, hired out in logging operations, and scratched the earth to farm.

Van's military citation was taped to a piece of cardboard and mounted behind the bar along with an antiwar cartoon, presented by him as a joke after his discharge. Royal was staring at it. Van's words had brought him down, brought him back. He looked over again. He could see his brother was probably drunk, though he hadn't noticed him drinking that much. Van stood close in to the tall guard, red-eyed, a grease of sweat on his forehead, looked up at him squinting as if the light was too bright. When he wasn't talking or drinking he chewed angrily on his thumbnail as if he was thinking hard about what to say next.

The woman who had spoken about the death penalty earlier said, "The boy wasn't dead when they found him. I believe he died in the outpatient."

A lie.

He would not listen to her or the men with her. Van's recklessness took him down. The safe feeling went. He kept his gaze on his brother. He knew he was still talking about it. You could tell. It scared him to death. He tried to get Van to look his way, warn him. The older brother's face was pinched and pale with sweat. Under the little mustache his mouth had grown small, the way it did when he'd gotten drunk and was being serious. And as he talked and talked Royal could see the gap where the lower teeth in front were missing. He had been in a street fight, a civilian riot in Saigon, he told his family. The plate they'd made for him with the two teeth on it was uncomfortable, and he kept it in his pocket except to eat, sometimes didn't use it then.

Royal spoke his brother's name. It sounded loud enough in his ears to be heard on the moon, but Van did not look up.

With all his talk, the careful planning, the advice, this was what Van wanted, Royal saw.

It was Paul Beam who looked over at him at last. He gave Royal a slow hunter's look, the gaze clear. He wasn't drunk. It hit Royal then. He didn't know why it was, but he didn't think he was wrong. He understood what he should have known the three years Van had been home from the war, that his brother was sick, that he wanted to die.

6

He half avoided Van, waiting for what had to happen next. It had begun to rain in the counties, a cold steady drizzle that turned the paintless Marquette farmhouse black and stained its ceilings in old patterns of damp. The woman would not use her heating system. Lou fired up the little wood stove in their room, which made it smoky and too hot. Neither one of them was employed at the moment. She had had a job at a Bradford motel cleaning rooms but been let go after the season. Royal's last job was in the Sunrise steel locker factory, but he'd cut himself, taken a leave, then learned he was laid off. He couldn't get his job back from the man who replaced him. There was no union. Van had worked for the locker manufacturing company too for a period.

After his discharge, if things went bad or wrong, Van would feel a nausea that unfit him for anything. He would force himself to get sick, go into the rest room wherever he was and get it done, then sit on the toilet, lean his head back as he had in the car at the Daley place, and black out. He would not talk to doctors. He said it wasn't physical. People and the situations people created did it to him, and he included doctors in that. At first after his discharge he would sit with Royal in the

Antlers, all but ignoring old friends, even relations, sit in the back by the table shuffleboard and other games no one used in the day. Royal would wait until he saw the nausea and fear come into his brother's face as he stared out at his old world, then would try to make him leave before he got into a fight or got sick. After a time the episodes eased off, almost stopped, then returned depending on circumstances.

Van had held jobs since the army, but the recurrent sickness, the people who caused it, as he said, forced him to quit them. He could not deal with people on that basis. He would not be pushed or ruled. It made him sick to be. He said he looked around at the world as it was now and felt its sickness as the cause of the sickness in himself and despised it. He'd held two different positions in the paper mill. He worked for a month in the locker factory and quit because of the racket. The longest he'd maintained a job was on a cutting machine in the paper carton factory in South Bradford, work he liked, but because they seemed to feel they had to rule him, require him to submit one way or another, the episodes began again, came with greater frequency, and he had to leave. It was pride, Van admitted. He did not admire it but could not help it. He said he saw some of the same thing in Royal, anger and pride, only less pronounced. It was why Royal had left the job at the Corbin place, quit on the spot when the man tried to push him too hard. The difference was that where Royal could cool off and be more or less all right, Van would feel the steep slide of the episode, feel the darkness come on so fast and strong he would have no choice but to ride with it to the bottom, if necessary take the people who caused it with him. Take them along by fighting them. It was wrong. He didn't like it. It only hurt him in the end. But it was how he was now.

Royal tried to tell Lou about it.

"I guess he's drinking too much," she said.

She didn't seem to care.

She had the money and the bracelet in her possession and had to realize a little of what was going on, but she kept turning away. "Why don't you talk to your daddy about it?"

He wanted to tell her he thought Van was trying to hurt himself, do himself an injury, but couldn't get into it without involving her in the whole story. He guessed it was wrong to give her information she didn't want, that might implicate her in some legal way, even though a wife can't testify. Finally he decided she was thinking the same thing he was, that she was scared and wouldn't talk to him for that reason.

It made Royal look at her differently, guessing at thoughts in her he couldn't refer to, thinking she was afraid, maybe of him.

For the first time since Van's discharge Royal avoided him. He would put on his sweater and nylon school jacket with the hood, walk out to the state road in the rain, hitchhike into town or go the other way into Bradford, which was a lake resort and had shopping centers and movies and entertainment parks. He stayed away from the Antlers. Neighbors gave him rides. He drove around for a day with Mickey Hagy in his Nova, uncomfortable on the broken front seat. Mickey had been in school with him until he dropped out after the first year in junior high to farm with his father. Each fall he started to look for a winter job, then gave up. He said he didn't care. He was typical of Royal's class at school, which was known to have little ambition.

They stopped at the body shop on the mountain road where Mickey's cousin worked, pestered him for a while, shot the breeze. They picked up some beer, went by the high school, and watched the majorettes, baton twirlers, whatever they called themselves, in the parking lot in front of the school, practicing for the Sunday game. The girls had bright-colored flags which they whirled, threw up in the air, and caught, one leg back, a hand on the hip. Half the time they dropped them. The rain had turned into a mist, and the flags looked wet and heavy. It was cold, their hands were red, and they wore thick tights under their little skirts.

Neither Royal nor Mickey said anything. They sat in the car, which smelled of rust and oil, and watched as if it was a show put on for them. The girls were small, young-looking. They didn't interest Royal much, though you always picked one out and thought about it. That was automatic.

He held the six-packs between his feet on a heap of snow chains. Mickey was big and red-faced, mostly silent. He drank steadily. Royal was already warm and felt a buzz beginning. The girls and their flags were bright in the rainy air.

Mickey did not say a word about the Corbin killing, showed no interest in the subject. He let Royal pay for the gas and beer and whenever they stopped to eat but didn't comment on the fact that his friend had more money than usual.

They drove upriver to the power dam, took the car out on the dam itself, which you could do, and stopped. They looked at the lake on one side, the low white tumbling river on the other, and drank their beer. The rain had picked up again, and its needles drove steadily into the metal-colored water. There were black-looking evergreens on either shore, picked out here and there with white. What were they, the naked, thin, white trees? He lived here, ought to know the names. At the far west end of the lake was the place called Four Corners, just visible from the dam. It had been in the trees, but the rise of the artificial lake revealed it to the world. Just about everyone in it was named White or Austin, both families distantly related to Royal's on his father's side, something no one bragged about much. They'd intermarried over the years, and they had various physical and mental problems, more or less mild ones, that were passed from generation to generation. None of them went to school beyond eighth grade. They grew corn and potatoes, did odd jobs to survive, and hitched or walked into Whitehouse Village to the feed and seed or grocery with their food stamps and a little cash to buy the day's supply of food and heating oil or kerosene. They carried their ragged children to save their shoes but also because they didn't like them to mix with the town children.

Royal gazed down the lake's length. The Austins and Whites were family too. He didn't mind the idea so much right now. He imagined he could feel the Austin blood and bone in him. They were thieves along with everything else, helped themselves to anything that didn't require work or money to haul away, got their names into the Arrests Record in the Bradford paper every other day. Some called them gypsies. It was strange, but it comforted him now, the thought of this particular shared blood.

The owner of the body shop where Mickey's cousin worked was also a farrier. He'd done jobs for the Corbins, shoeing their horses. In winter he worked at a harness track in Pennsylvania, but he was back now for the holiday. He had come into the shop from his house. "It's a damned sin," he'd said, because he thought the boys were talking about the local killing and it was on his mind. "They were good people. I was up there any number of times, did their show horses. They always come down and talked—the mother did—come down and talked to me. They didn't put on airs. I didn't know the boy, but I read in the paper where it said he went to college at the age of fifteen. He was smart. I was out there the start of this past summer for their horses. You just can't believe it, a thing like this happening."

He went on about it. No one else said anything, as if it embarrassed them.

Now, sitting in the Nova with Mickey, power lines singing overhead, the crows calling, it came to Royal why the thought of the blood comforted him. It was because of what the blacksmith said about the boy. That he was smart. Here was what it was: You were what you were born and not responsible.

He tried to fix the thought, which kept sliding away because of the beer. He did not use the name in his mind, but he thought: That boy was what he was, a boy genius call him, at age fifteen, whatever it was. Royal was what he was. Exactly. No more and no less. You couldn't change it. It was as natural as the difference between the kinds of trees, as natural as the leaves they put out and dropped. You did what you did because of blood.

It was in the blood and the bone, and you were not responsible.

They came back the long way, on the far side of the lake, and Hagy turned into the sand drag track, which was in Sunrise, ten miles south of Whitehouse. It was closed for the winter, the saloon boarded up. He pushed the Nova's grilleless nose through the wooden gate that was barring the way, broke the light chain, and drove out onto the oil-dark yellow sand without a word. This was how he was going to show his drinking. It didn't bother Royal. Mickey drove the track a few times at normal speed, then accelerated and did some turns at nearly ninety. He did stops at high speed, hitting the brakes suddenly and locking the wheels left or right so that the car skidded and spun into the banks of sand, tilted up a little, then banged hard. It made Royal yell, opened him up so he shouted with laughter, but Hagy was quiet about it, as if it was a job to do. The track was soft with rain, so it wasn't too dangerous. He took a few more turns, then, when he felt right with it, nodded and began to push the car with its rebuilt engine harder, taking the turns with care at the tight ends of the track where the sand was plowed deep, swinging out, cutting close, but not slowing much. They pretended they were in a race, passing other cars, getting a split second's edge, Royal narrating it like a TV announcer.

He felt good in the speeding car beside his friend. He decided Mickey Hagy knew what had happened, all about it, and didn't care, that what the farmboy was saying in his way was that it was all right with him, whatever fell. It was all right because of blood.

The rain would pause, then start again, clouds sitting on the mountains.

In the evening Royal walked past the Methodist parsonage across the river in the old part of town. There were lights in its windows, the broken-down little church next door dark and cold-looking. At the end of the street was the house he'd lived in the two years his father was in prison and his mother doing her worst drinking not long before she died. This was the house of his court mother, the foster mother, Mrs. Gladys Tower, and this was the church she'd taken him to—took him to the services, put him in the boys' Bible study class, made him go with her to polish the woodwork and put the flowers around, help in the charity rummage sales. She was mad for religion, but she was good to him. He'd liked her. Now and then, until she died young of something or other, he used to see her in the village. He'd wave, but she seemed not to know him, and he didn't like to go up and speak to her. There were things he remembered and other things he forgot about his life there with her, but even then, when he was sixteen or so, seeing her in the street, he thought all that was in the past and belonged there. You didn't dwell on the past.

Now he looked at the house.

He'd lived with her and her two sons and daughter, plus her husband, who had been an assistant plant manager at the paper mill, been retired with heart trouble at the time, and never had much to say to Royal. Mr. Tower had been dead eight years, Mrs. Tower three or four. The children were gone, new people had the house. It made you shiver to think of it.

The day he left to go back to his father and new stepmother, Mrs. Tower told him to remember God loved him. He believed she said she did too. She had said so before. What was he then? Ten, eleven years old. The daughter's name was Amanda. She was older and read books. The boys were older too. Amanda read to him a few times out of books she liked. He didn't know what became of any of those kids, where they'd gone, but thinking of them he felt an ache in his shoulder at the collarbone. The thought of those old slick-paper picture books, remembering the smell of the house and the flowers in the church, made him feel the way he did with Lou, with any woman if he was in the mood. Strange but true. He thought of that church, of Mrs. Tower and the books, and that was what he wanted back.

He wandered around the near-empty streets of Whitehouse. It was as dead as the moon. A few kids out or hanging around in front of the pharmacy, a kid in his dad's pickup cruising Prospect, leaning out to yell at the ones on the sidewalk, bang his hand on the outside of the door.

Royal was past that now. It was childish to him. He got a soda at the chain grocery and walked out to the place.

Van dropped by once or twice, stayed in the driveway. His own car was in the garage, getting money spent on it at last. This was still their stepmother's truck, which their daddy could not drive now and she rarely used. Van had cleaned it up. In the rack behind the seat, in addition to their father's old spinning rod, was a Winchester, new to Royal.

"Thirty-aught-six," Van said. "Picked it up used, couldn't resist."

He was as clean as the pickup, hair cut short almost army style, clean-shaven except for the mustache, creases in his jeans, boots polished. At the same time he looked pale and had smears under his eyes, the eyes themselves red as if he was getting stoned too much. He had a few sore spots on the backs of his hands, which he picked at.

He gave his brother a look that said he knew what he was thinking.

"I figured we might have to make a stand for it after all, sonny."

He smiled under the neat mustache, watching Royal.

"I have the new gun, three boxes of cartridges, you have your twenty-gauge. Trouble comes, I'll phone, swing by and pick you up, your gear, and we go up into the lot."

He meant the mountainside woodlot, sixty acres, belonging to their stepmother, Mona.

Royal did not say anything.

"We'd use that old hut there. Sugar shack, whatever it is. Stand them off. People could carry supplies in to us on the deer track." It had been their daddy's idea and Mona's. They were in earnest, he said, though Van smiled telling it. You never knew what he took seriously. "They have it worked out. We go up, secure our perimeter with a few bunkers, put wire out, live on a fifty percent alert, live the life of dog soldiers. You should have heard Mona. It's all those stories I told her." He said, "Don't you smile, sonny," though Van was doing it. "It may come to it."

"Okay."

"It won't be no vacation if it does, but we'll manage. Just bring your firearm and a shovel, because you got to dig your toilet."

He took the gun out and showed it off, its Nikon scope and so on. Royal sighted it on various things, tried its action, not caring much, though he did not want to hurt Van's feelings. Louetta came out, stood in the drive, and looked at it too, admired it.

"We don't see you much."

"Ask this husband of yours. He's avoiding me."

After a time they all went in, took beers out of the little refrigerator, and stood leaning against the counter at one end of the old kitchen, while Mrs. Marquette watched TV at the other and her scanner made its static.

Van kept hinting.

"We might just have to do it, sonny. Take our stand."

Lou ducked her head away as if to say this wasn't for her to hear. Royal looked at him.

"Hell, she's deaf as that door there," pretending Royal was worried about the widow hearing.

When he said goodbye, Lou said stiffly, "Don't be a stranger now."

Royal walked out with him.

"Lou can't help you on this if you don't put her in the picture," Van said. "They surprise her with it, she'll maybe say the wrong thing."

"You said don't tell her anything."

"She ought to know what to say."

"You keep saying they can't tie us to it."

"You have to work on worst contingency, Roy. Clues we don't know exist, clues only a police lab would understand. All that's missing is the connection, though I don't believe they'll ever make it." He got into the cab of the truck and gave his new rifle a thump as if for luck. "You want to come to the Antlers?"

"I don't believe I will."

Royal wanted to say all they had to do was be quiet.

"You almost gave it to Paul Beam the other night," he declared finally. "It seemed to me."

"Naw, I didn't. I knew that was what was on your mind. I was just being Van Buren West, the one Paul knows. I talk the way I always do. I don't hide or minimize or show fear, Roy. I'm myself." His voice was quiet, no resentment in it. "It's just as well you don't come. I have a date tonight. Janet Colby."

"Why make Pauline mad?"

"She don't care. Daddy says you ought to come see him and Mona once in a while." He had carried his bottle out with him to finish it. Now he handed the empty to his brother. "You see the paper?"

Royal shook his head.

"The father's here still. Staying at the Holiday Inn in Bradford. He told the paper we need mental help."

Royal was silent.

"I guess you think it might be halfway true, at least in my case."

"I don't think that."

"Never lie unless you have to." He grinned. "The man said the killer or killers ought to come forward because they may require help. He wants to see it doesn't happen again, the senseless killing, study us to see in what ways we're crazy."

Royal said nothing.

"He doesn't know the instigator was his own son." He started the motor, fixed his dark, worn-out gaze on his brother. "I won't fuck this up, not this time. As I've stated before, the way I have it worked out, the fallbacks, it doesn't involve you. You're clear. I only say you ought to talk to your wife because you want to touch on all the possible combinations. If you treat her like a cop, maybe she'll go and act like one. I just mention it."

Van said, "I know what you think—that I want to throw it all away. Look at me. All right? I know what I'm doing."

He found Lou standing against the table as she had been, her head bent over her nearly untouched bottle of beer. Mrs. Marquette was still watching TV, that end of the room dark except for the blue light from the screen. The woman had arthritis and shifted from place to place with effort. As Van had said, she had few relatives, no close ones, and Louetta, like Van, thought or hoped she might leave them the place or part of it. Lou was too proud to do anything for it except to do right, and she really liked the old woman, but it gave her something to wish for and look out for. Royal was the pessimist concerning it, an attitude, she said, that hurt their chances. It was always to this possibility, the thing she wished for, that Lou would refer when he did something risky—that they might get on the bad side of the widow. Now, as if she had only waited for him to come in so she could show her emotion, she gave him a sad look, glanced at Mrs. Marquette, emptied the rest of her beer into the sink, and went upstairs.

Royal slept poorly these nights. It was a drowning kind of sleep. When he finally fell into it, he did not want to be where it was and, as if he was drowning, struggled hard to escape and breathe or just to quit, not to breathe. He did not dream. The sleep itself wounded him with fear. It was not the ordinary world of sleep. It was like a life all but stopped. It was unconsciousness, floorless, formless. He would slip struggling into whatever it was, the unconsciousness, wanting it and afraid of it, like a drowning man fighting to find the bottom.

That was one thing. The other was he could not get enough of Lou. He would put a towel over the lamp to close the room in, give it color. They took off their clothes. She would get onto the bed, but he would stand and look at her, inspect her, while she had to laugh. But she also groaned in a kind of exasperation of embarrassment and sexual power. She told him to be himself, which this wasn't. Be normal. It scared her, but he saw she didn't turn away from it. To be looked at, all but inspected, and not touched. So that when he did touch her it was like she was hit with electricity, a hot wire.

"Oh, Lord, it's good that old woman can't hear."

She spread towels on the bed, rolled up the cotton rug and pushed it against the rattling door.

"Just be a good baby, Roy. Babe, what is it?"

He was too close. Before, when their lovemaking was wrong, it was absence, but this was presence. Before, she would say, "Where are you?" He would be off in some dream. Now he was too close for comfort. She'd had rheumatic fever at the age of eight and had a heart murmur. She thought about her heart and was secretly afraid for it. He could not do what he did, she said, and she not be killed by her heart.

Royal would be erect soon after his orgasm. Lou would get off as she wanted and was ready again if need be, but she also wanted to go to sleep, to hold him against her breasts like she did, her baby. But he would remain erect. Wood, stone. It was as if she was embarrassed for him, he saw, as well as for herself. But he kept the light on, looked at her, standing with his erection. The light glowed pink or blue from the towel. If he had to, he would hurt her, he thought. He worked to make her complain that her heart would stop. Then, for no reason she could see, he would suddenly turn off the light, get over onto his side of the bed, and start down his road, begin that private struggle with unconsciousness.

He wanted to hurt her. The way she showed him her feelings, the sad looks. He held her arm tight, hurt her breasts, pushed his mouth down on hers until he knew her lip had to be cut. He would feel his teeth in her like that, the slippery saliva, get a little salty taste from her blood. He just about knew he wanted to kill her. Only not really. It was because of the woodenness and that he got no real relief.

He blamed her, but to explain it he blamed the weather.

"This fucking wind!"

The rain.

The big tree at their end of the house would strike at the window as if it wanted to break it. The rain kept on. There were old saucepans here and there for leaks, which made a racket. "How the hell can I ever get to sleep!"

He saw she knew all about it, the burglary and everything else, but wasn't going to speak. She would not get involved. And he couldn't say anything as Van wanted him to, put her in the picture. It was how they were with each other.

"Don't use bad words, babe."

She did not criticize beyond something like that.

Or, half laughing about it: "My poor heart. You'll kill me with love, like the song says."

Later he would fight with his floorless sleep, trying to join it, live in it the way it wanted him to, then fight to climb back out, sucking in air, trying to be awake.

The morning with its sensible light was like being saved, though flashes of practical fear came with it. He lay watching Lou asleep. The light that kept him from going crazy flooded the window and filled up the old floor, which Lou kept scrubbed and waxed, like a pond. In the light he didn't see how he could ever have wanted to hurt her, though he could remember wanting it.

She would wake too, look at him. All she allowed herself was they shouldn't do anything to upset Mrs. Marquette. He thought: Either she meant the noise they made or that he might be charged in a murder. He couldn't tell which.

The rain stopped. It got colder. He had no work, so he hung around the house half the morning until he and Lou started to argue about some little thing, some job he should do. The long Thanksgiving weekend felt like it would not end. He went into town to look at the newspapers in their rack in front of the drugstore, then passed by without bothering. They were nothing. He saw a few people. Mickey Hagy drove by in the Nova, the rear of the car jacked up high, and turned his head away, didn't know him.

Royal had coffee at the Nook, sitting at the counter, and changed a fifty, watching to see if the woman would react. He stood on the sidewalk again, then couldn't remain still and started to walk out along the river. That was it with Mickey. He had given Royal a day to show his old friendship, then didn't know him. One day.

That was it.

The people who lived around here were strange. He was one of them, yet knew it. They gave just so much. They said, "Well, I know you, your daddy. You're one of us." But that was the end of it. You were on your own then, sink or swim. A token, and afterward, cold as the climate, they could watch you go down, drown, and not blink. Strange but true. "Well," he said, "fuck you all," bitterly. He thought: To hell with Mickey Hagy. But he also thought that maybe he was the same, would have done the same.

He wandered the countryside, stood on a bluff above Stag Road and looked down on the landfill and the graded lot full of orange highway trucks and utility pickups with WHITEHOUSE TOWNSHIP on them. He could hot-wire one, head north. He could be in Canada in an hour and a half, two hours. Escape. He'd take the truck out to the farm first, hide it in a shed, get some spray enamel, disguise it. He thought: They tell the possible criminal, I'm your friend, your blood—cousin, brother, friend. I'll help as much as I can so long as I'm in the clear, but it's on your head in the end. Forget innocent until proven guilty. You're guilty. Be it on your head. The man, unconvicted, had to find out how to pay or get out of paying on his own in the long run.

The short run. That's what they gave you. A day.

There was a bulldozer pushing at the mountains of junk, making flames rise. Two kids were stripping an old VW body. They had a fender off it and were looking at what was left of the engine. He heard one say, his voice rising clearly, "It looks like a good head on it." He knew these boys, who were a few years younger than him. Good kids. They could be friends if he knew them better. He knew everyone around here a little, yet no one really. He tried to think of the boys' names.

He felt almost old standing there looking down. The second-growth scrub hid him. He could see himself being Royal West right at this minute. The trees with the chalky bark, the smooth gray-barked tree with a few dry red leaves left on it, another that smelled sweet as spice when you broke off a branch, the low growth that stayed green through winter: he saw himself in this world. There were the two kids in warm mackinaws, the buzzing dozer, crows and vultures lifting off from the garbage heaps, beyond them everywhere you looked the goods of the world: old kitchen appliances, beds, whatnot; the heavy sky like cement. It built pressure, excitement in him. It was as if the best thing in his life was about to happen. Never mind Hagy.

It began to snow, came stinging down, each hard grain distinct. The sky fell lower, sat on the foothills around.

He had brought his dark glasses, the aviator wraparounds. Now he put them on.

A farmer he knew by sight picked him up on the mountain road, drove him five miles, and dropped him. He didn't speak when Royal said thank you. Like a piece of machinery fitting into place, a blue transport van rolled past, pulled up on the graveled shoulder. Royal thought he was getting a lift, then he saw it said LOCUST GROVE CORRECTIONAL FACILITY, MOUNT MASON, NY, on the door. The driver got out, lifted the truck's short hood, and looked inside. The convicts—on their way to prison or being transferred, mostly black—stared out through the heavy mesh that covered the windows. The black pink-nailed fingers poked through and rubbed clear patches on the steamed glass. The men gazed out at him and at the slick empty roadway as if wondering where in the world they were. Royal was looking into the face of a con. It was as staring and smooth as a baby's above the thick curving nails hooked in the mesh. The reddish eyes looked into Royal's without embarrassment. It was the way a kid stared at you: you were made of wood and couldn't look back. The man was doing his time. He wasn't in charge, had no care, like a child with his parents in back of him. He gazed at Royal with innocence, as if he had just been created.

Royal felt the excitement, the pressure. It was a sign. Punishment made you innocent as a child, so he supposed it had its good side, never mind the men who ran the system, bad as they might be. It had its purpose.

Wayne and Mona West lived in a little village of mobile homes south of Whitehouse. There was a long rank of metal mailboxes mounted on a rail out at the paved road. A dirt drive led up a rise between scattered rows of the houses to the back of the property, where stood the homestead and barn of the enterprising farmer who leased the sites, his house prosperous now, freshly painted. He had his own mailbox and beside it a joke box mounted on a fifteen-foot pole, with AIR MAIL stenciled on it. The community was called after the dozen elms, tall and mostly sick, that bordered the drive, but the sign with the name, The Elms Mobile Court, hadn't lasted a year. His daddy's place—Mona's really; she brought it to the marriage—stood by itself in some evergreens, the town cemetery visible beyond it through the trees.

There were two cars parked in front.

"It's about time," his father said in his slurred voice when Royal walked in.

Iris, his oldest sister, was there, a baby on her lap. She nodded. "What's it doing out?"

She hadn't seen him in a month, but it was as if she'd talked to him that morning and he had said something to make her tired. She was thirty-four, thin and worn, the child with her her sixth. Her husband, Tom, worked in the paper mill in Sunrise.

"Snow's starting."

"We'll see enough of that before we're through," she said. "You find anything to do yet?" And when he did not respond: "You ain't trying, Royal. There's jobs there if you'll only look for them."

His daddy was on the divan in the narrow living room, legs wrapped in a quilt. His face was gray and pale, with a waxy shine to it on one side. He was partly paralyzed. He talked with one side of his mouth, looked with one eye, used one hand. But he was getting better, the doctor said, and barring another stroke would keep improving. He was alert, usually mad about something the way Iris was. He kept an aluminum walker by the sofa and used it to get to the kitchen and bathroom. He didn't dress or go out. It was always too hot or too cold for it. Mona lay back in the old recliner, her legs up, a coffee mug in her hands. There was cake on the table where she could reach it. The place had been left to her by her first husband—that, a pickup which she'd traded since, some cash, and the woodlot on the west side of the river.

Van's wife, Pauline, came in from the kitchen and smiled at Royal. Younger by nearly thirty years, she was already as heavy as Mona. She was pretty, usually had a smile. The baby, Van Buren III, was in the bedroom, asleep. Iris's baby was naked on her lap except for a diaper and rubber pants. It was sucking a bottle.

"It's hot in here as usual," Royal said.

His father watched him with the one eye in a way that made Royal nervous.

"Van said you wanted to see me."

"I didn't. Mona did."

"We wondered what you were up to," Mona said comfortably. "We halfway expected you to Thanksgiving dinner."

"I couldn't come."

"Your daddy just wondered where you were at. How's Lou?"

"Good."

"What have you been doing?"

"Nothing much."

His father snorted.

Pauline said without anger, "I hope Louetta sees more of you than I do of Van."

"Well, I don't know. I don't think she does."

It was hot. The windows ran with condensation. Two or three cats were lying around and a fat dashhound dog with a pointed graying muzzle. It sat at Mona's feet, its popping wet eyes following sharply as she took her cake. Royal didn't care for little dogs much. The rooms looked like a bomb was dropped a minute before—clothes, dirty dishes, saucers of dog food, cat food everywhere. It smelled. Royal wanted to be out in the air.

Pauline said, "I believe he thinks that place—what do you call it, the Antlers?—that's his home."

"Well, I guess that's his home away from home," Royal said.

He did not mind Pauline, or Mona either. They could criticize and not make you feel bad.

"He'll be an alcoholic before he's thirty," Iris said. "So will you if you don't ease up on all that beer. The pair of you get through a case before midnight, and that's too much for anybody's system."

He couldn't tell if Iris knew. Probably she knew something but didn't want to talk about it. The only thing different about this place from some public place, Royal thought, was that they did not talk freely about the killing, trying out their ideas and theories.

"Now here's this," his father began in his slurred, rough voice. "You were going to paint that porch out there we built on last summer. It's too late now with snow coming."

Iris had a few more things to say about Royal and Van and their responsibilities. Then when she had packed up her baby and left in one of the cars parked in front, and Pauline went into the bedroom, Wayne West said in a different voice, "You're a fool. You and Van both."

Mona shook her head.

"I can't do anything the way I am," his father said. "Mona's hands are tied. She can't afford to get involved."

His wife bathed and shaved him every noon, and his flat gray cheeks shone. The smell of aftershave cologne mingled with the other smells in the house. His clean thick gray hair stood up in spikes. Mona had come to sit next to him on the arm of the divan for the talk. She held his wasted right hand in her plump pink one. The TV was on without sound, and her eyes moved comfortably from the screen to Royal's face and back. They could have been talking about some easy family problem.

"You ought not to have gone up there in the first instance. You think you're going to do something nobody ever thought of doing, but in fact they turned the idea of that place down long ago because it wasn't practical. It was thought of. You don't do places like that just because they *are* known. There's a watch on them. Look at that. What are they laughing at?" A game show was on the TV. "Turn it up."

Royal moved to do it. The foolish roaring of the studio audience filled the narrow room.

"We can't give much. We don't have it to give. We'll help you out on the basics if you have to hide, but what use is that? You can't live out of doors in this weather without a fire, and the smoke would show where you are. We considered it but decided you can't use the woodlot on account of Mona getting into it, so you'd have to go right up into the wilderness, and that's going to finish you off even if nothing else does. So for right now what do you have? If you act, leave town, that will give you away. So where are you?"

"I guess we just sit tight."

"That's about it. You're in this backwater for the moment. Stay there. Sit tight. Figure your approaches. Don't do anything, say anything, or touch anything. See what happens."

"I guess Iris knows."

"I can't say. Not from me she don't know. No, you're right, Royal. Stay still and don't draw attention to yourself. Then we'll see. Suffish unto the day."

Royal saw how his father kept his easy con's style, weighing things up: what were your chances, what were your best approaches? The voice of experience. He was like Van in that, but he was also like the rest of the town. He would help, give so much, and then that was it. The rest was up to you.

Royal said, "I believe Van is talking a lot in the Antlers and so on. Not about anything direct, I don't mean." His daddy did not hear or understand, and he repeated it: "Van draws attention to it. Drinks and does it."

Pauline had come in from the little bedroom she shared with Van when he was home, their baby on her hip, a redheaded two-year-old boy still half asleep, his fat cheek creased and bright where he had slept on it, both of them with their eyes turned on the roaring game show.

She said, joining the conversation, "Van talks when he gets upset, not when he's drunk so much. But he seems to know what he's doing even then. He has pretty good control over himself."

Royal spoke to Lou about it directly for the first time. She listened, didn't say anything, just shook her head a little now and then. The way he told it, it was like an image that kept getting clearer in his mind. The intent and so on, the burglary, which you admit is a felony, Van's involvement, that the boy brought the weapon to the scene, so on and so forth.

"I was down the road at the time I heard both shots."

She just shook her head.

She wasn't calling him a liar. She was saying don't tell me. He went on anyway because telling it each time made it clearer. There was a hole in the leg of Lou's jeans, and she kept poking a finger into it and then smoothing it over. He looked at her face and saw her eyes had reddened as if she would cry.

"It was more like an accident than anything else."

She said nothing. He thought she might suggest that if he told them, the authorities, they would take that into account, that and the fact he had come to them of his free will, so they would not have to go to the trouble of the investigation, the expense, searching for clues.

She was silent.

She didn't cry, just sat with her mouth tight, looking down. They were in their bedroom. It was late afternoon, with the sun out at last but almost gone. They sat on their bed under the slanted gable-end ceiling. He looked through the window at the nameless tree, now hung with beads of ice. When he turned his head slightly, looking, they flashed into rainbows in the sun's long light. Beyond the tree was rising pasture land that had once been cleaned by grazing cattle but was now grown up with brush, the setting sun on the upper rim of it. What would you plant there if you farmed? He knew little about farming. If they ever got this place, in the unlikely event, he would need to learn, maybe take the course at the community college.

"I think it will all blow over," he said finally, and when she made no comment: "If not, we have our fallback positions. In the first place we say we were together with a bottle somewheres else. Then, if they put him there, he leaves me out of it. If he can't do that, if I'm involved, it's only the stolen vehicle and the burglary on me. Accessory." He went on, outlining the story again, making it clear.

She looked at him with the red eyes, then looked away. "Well, you go on out now for a while," she said. "I want to be alone, do some work around."

"Okay."

He couldn't move, couldn't leave it alone, kept going over it.

She said gently, "Go on, Roy. I don't want you here."

He meant to ask if it was all right, how she felt, but couldn't.

He found Mona's pickup in the Antlers parking lot. Two cars down from it was the Whitehouse-Sunrise township black-and-yellow, empty but its radio going on quietly. Van was at a table in the back of the place with Janet Colby and another couple. He would not look his way, though Royal knew he'd seen him come in. Van had a hand on Janet's shoulder and was talking into her ear, while she smiled down at the drink on the table in front of her. Van's hat was on, pushed back. Janet wore a quilted vest and a lot of silver. She listened, nodding, fiddling with the drink and smiling in the slow sleepy way she had, her chin tucked in. She was older, in her mid-thirties, and twice divorced. She'd been a grade school teacher in the local district. A group of parents got up a petition to have her dismissed because of her reputation, and the union wouldn't back her on it. She had been a girlfriend of Van's off and on and also been Royal's own first experience with a woman. She was a Guilder, one of the oldest local families, and had Iroquois blood, which she bragged about. She was still good-looking. You could see the Indian in her hair and black eyes.

Royal stood at the bar and waited for Alice to come over. People were rolling poker dice from a box, passing their dollars along to add to the pot. Royal saw the prison guard, Beam, and next to him—the tall and short of it—Jackie Pastor, the town cop, whose patrol car it was parked outside. Pastor was another who liked to wear cowboy shirts and boots and take part in the rodeos, bulldogging and whatnot, in the season. Now he was on duty, a glass of tomato juice in front of him. He was trim as a sailor in his pressed uniform. You saw the creases across the back of the taut blouse, the shine of starch on the collar against his shaved neck. He sipped his drink, a cigarette in the same hard little hand he lifted it with, pinkie out, put it down, took his time, rolled the dice. He let others call out his hand. There was a crumpled hill of the dollars he'd won on the stool next to him, but he didn't touch the money and wouldn't take it with him when he left since poker dice was illegal in the county. It would be kept for him.

Van was looking at Royal now, wanting to catch his eye. He'd made a gun of his hand. He pointed it at the policeman's back, worked the thumb, and moved his eyebrows comically. Janet was smiling, her bright lipstick wet. She shrugged, saying with her look, What can you do? Royal saw Van's dead-tired eyes, Janet's friendly smile. It was as if it wasn't himself there, as if someone else was watching out of his gaze, observing Jackie Pastor and Van and everyone else. He thought: To hell with this. When Alice got to him, mopped the bar, and put the beer pad down, he said he didn't want anything, had only come in to look around.

In the morning Mona called and said she was doing leftover turkey in a casserole, but he made an excuse, told Lou to go if she wanted. He didn't know if Van would be there.

The sun came out again, and it warmed up.

It seemed to Royal he had already walked everywhere in the county, but he kept on, crossing and recrossing the river by the old one-lane bridges. When cars came he stepped off the road. He did not want a lift, did not want to see people he might know. The rise in temperature made the wet roads steam. It was like early fall. He went out to the Daley place and looked around a little, though he knew Van would say it was the last thing he should do. Any sign they had been there, footprints, tire marks, was gone. He pushed the cover off the low wall of the well and looked down. It was deep, lined with mossy stones. He could make out gleams of water in the floor of leaves. There was no sign of the goods. He walked up into the hills behind the burned-out house, looking back and down on the river from time to time. He realized he'd been hearing the sound of guns all day. The hillsides leading up to the woods had once been farmed and were still clear, not like Mrs. Marquette's brushy pastures. The grass was a clean, bright brown, a little beard of frost on the north side of each blade that was in shadow, the melted drops falling, flashing blue in the sun.

He kept moving upward across the hilly shoulders of land. He had sneakers on, and they were soaked, his jeans wet to the knee and covered with seed.

He saw a deer.

It floated into focus like an instant film that develops as you hold it in your hand. It was standing inside the wall of trees above him, looking out. If he didn't concentrate, it disappeared again. It was an eight-point buck at least, a hundred and eighty, hundred and ninety pounds. It appeared to look right at him, its hard pale muzzle lifted, working through the smells on the breeze. Then it was gone. Royal went up, pushed in through the brush, and found two tracks in a patch of snow, blood in one of them. When he came out again he decided he recognized this situation. It was one of the deer escape routes to the river. He and Van had done stand hunting about a quarter of a mile south of this point the year before, hoping to ambush a well-known trophy buck. It hadn't worked, and they'd gone on from there. He wished he had his gun now, wished Van was with him. He thought: I can't get over it, not knowing what he meant by the words, sure they did not refer to the particular deer.

He thought: I feel good.

There was a line of trees along both sides of the road. He could see the river beyond them, smooth in the eddies, wrinkled in the channels. With stand hunting, even if you missed your kill, it was a pleasure. You sat back, drank your coffee out of a thermos, listened. You half floated on it. It was as if you invited your animal into your mind, tried to make it come to you that way. If it came then, that could be enough, even if you never lifted your gun. For those born to it, for the born hunter, it worked. The deer came. Though it hadn't last year, it usually worked for Van. It had worked for their father in his younger days. Royal thought it could for him the way he felt now. He thought: You don't get over a thing like this. Meaning what? All right: Van, this place, everything good that had ever gone down in his life, the things that worked right, as on a particular hunt on a given day, or with a really good car or an expensive gun, with anything that might give you real power, anything that worked right and made what you were seem right and in a powerful position in life.

A branch cracked somewhere far off, then the sound of gunfire again.

He walked down the hill and started home along the river. The good feeling fell away the minute he turned in that direction. When he was almost at Whitehouse a fit of shaking took hold of him. It stopped, then started again. He thought, scared: There's no bottom to this.

It scared him.

He started up into the hills again to get away from the smooth man-made road, thinking he would leave the fear behind, then, figuring it was all of it against too high odds—his chances, Van's—came back, and walked on anyhow. What were their odds on it? Wasn't it doom? It would not quit, this feeling that there was no floor to it. He said the seven-times-seven prayer. It was meanness in something when you asked it to quit, only to have it stamp itself on you, burn itself in all the more.

Seven-times-seven-and-God-in-heaven. Then he would find a wooden object and rap on it fast seven times. Anything would do. A fence post, a tree. If it was paper, that was all right.

He prayed: Leave me.

It lifted and shook him.

There was a cemetery by the river, the graves in it going back to the Revolution. Its church had burned forty years before and never been rebuilt. The farmer whose hayfields lay around it maintained it in a careless way, cutting the grass, raking leaves into a pile in a corner and leaving them. Tombstones were cracked or fallen, the limestone worn featureless in the oldest ones, a few good granite monuments standing up, one of his own ancestors' among them. The Wests and Porters, which was their mother's name, had people here, those who were Methodists. Also the Van Burens on their mother's side. One of the Porters was a veteran of the Civil War, and he had a marker and a little faded flag by his stone. This was the granite one. He had been a noncom of some kind and was killed in a battle. Royal leaned on the railing of rusty pipe and looked over into the old graveyard, seized with a remnant of the shaking now and then. He thought of the soldier, tried to picture him dying in the battle. Twisting around, yelling for help until he couldn't anymore. Then he was dead, looking up, dirt and whatnot on his face and on his hands, which had grabbed at the earth, his mouth open, clothes torn open where he'd tried to get at what was hurting him. The black hole of the mouth, the brown old-time teeth. Royal saw in his mind's eye a fly already at the wide-open mouth.

When the shaking stopped at last he remained, his wet clothes heavy on him. He thought he might have dozed off the way a horse does, on his feet.

He would think later that a voice outside himself had said, "Leave me," and that he was awake when he heard it.

Lou was on the porch coring and peeling fruit for canning when he got back. It was that warm. She and Mrs. Marquette sat in rockers, grocery cartons of apples and pears between them. It looked normal enough, but she said right away, "Van got arrested. Assault and harassment. He beat up Janet Colby."

Royal looked at Mrs. Marquette.

"She heard it on her police scanner first. Van came by himself and said to tell you it's a third-degree assault, which is only really disorderly conduct. He said don't worry."

"That's it?"

It was something to get excited about. Lou and Mrs. Marquette looked red and upset, staring at him to see if he'd yell or carry on somehow, get excited too.

"He was released in his own custody. They had the DWI on him at one point, but that was dismissed. He totaled his car. It was out of the shop two hours, and he smashed it up. He isn't even scratched, so don't worry. They gave him his appearance ticket for Tuesday. He came looking for you to tell you. He said Jackie Pastor right here in town was the arresting officer."

"Is he all right?"

"Well, he looked half sick or stoned. I don't know which. I believe he's in a nervous state right now, Roy. The breathalyzer was on the line, and they gave him the benefit of the doubt, but I think he was drunk or stoned this morning. He came up here on somebody or other's motorcycle and drove over that new grass right on the lawn. I don't know why he didn't hit this porch, just happened to remember to put on the brakes, I guess. Then he sat on the bike and said nobody was to worry, told me the story and told me to tell you. I'd say somebody ought to worry."

Royal said, "Shit," softly. "Don't I have enough to deal with? Why did he go after Janet?"

Lou shook her head.

"He drinks," Mrs. Marquette said. "That's his trouble. All you young people drink like there's no tomorrow."

It was too much for one person. Van was in command, said he was, yet it was Van caused this further trouble, drew attention. He said do one thing, but then he went the other way, did the wrong thing. It was like it was out of their hands, whatever they did. You can't struggle against your fate. It always came back to that, so let it go. You were not responsible in it, had no control, no matter what Van said. Royal saw what was happening. Everything was dropping into place. He had the truck full of Locust Grove convicts looking as if Royal was the one shut up and they were free. He had the wounded buck. The cemetery. They dropped into their slots, fit in. Now he had Janet Colby and an assault charge. It fit. It wasn't that you couldn't win, he saw, but that you were pulled the other way, to losing, like you pull a bull by the ring in its nose.

He saw Corbin's face on the front page of the capital-district newspaper.

He'd avoided looking at the papers, but it was as if this one came after him. It was two or three days old, and it was on the floor of Mrs. Marquette's kitchen under the sink. CRIME VICTIM'S FATHER TARGETS SOCIETY, it said. Louetta must have seen it, must have put it there, not even caring enough for his sake to turn it face down, maybe wanting him to see it.

The man with his long bald brow looked up at him, squinting in a bright light, proud, the cheeks furrowed, the chin stuck out.

There was the main headline, then smaller headlines in the body of the story under the picture.

"Urges Understanding," one said. "Study Crime's Causes." Then: "No Vengeance."

Royal read it, squatting, not touching it, then read it again. He could not make out its sense. He supposed Corbin thought the people who had done it were crazy, as Van said.

They gave the story of the event itself in capsule form, and Royal read that for the first time. It said the gun was at the site, that the perpetrators found it there and used it. It also said the boy died in the hospital outpatient, not on the porch of the house.

7

He walked over to the high school and stood at the edge of the football field to watch them warm up for the afternoon game. The Boosters Club had worked to have the league championship delayed by a week to give the teams a chance to get the holiday behind them and to practice. It drew out the season, which everyone liked. The weather was still fairly warm, and at ten in the morning people were already setting up picnics under the trees in the parking lot. Royal had showered and dressed neatly in pressed jeans, a white shirt, and his only suit jacket. He wore the boots with low heels Lou had given him on Christmas the year before. He thought, watching them run plays, remembering what he had to do: If need be, I'll miss the game. Van would be there, never mind his car and court appearance. Pauline. Mona would drive Wayne and bring a chair for him. Lou would walk over, join the family. If you could help it, you didn't miss this one.

One of the Boosters was there, and after practice Royal got a lift with him in his Cadillac the fourteen miles to Bradford.

The man, a familiar figure at the games, was an insurance broker, with offices in Whitehouse and Bradford. He had played for the team when he was in high school, was president of the Quarterback Club at the Lions in town, and, as he told Royal, talking steadily, gave money every month to help keep up the uniforms and equipment, the dressing rooms, and so on. Royal was supposed to guess how much it came to in the course of a year. He didn't give a shit. He said a thousand dollars.

"Three thousand. You believe it?" He asked, "Did you play, son?"

"I was second string two years. Then I had to quit and go to work after school. I wasn't so hot. My brother was All-Conference his second year. Van Buren West."

"I remember him. He was good. Quick. And he could hold on to the ball well. He ought to come to the Quarterbacks. It's Tuesday this time, give them a chance to recover. Van Buren West," he said. "He was in the war, wasn't he? In country, the way they say. He could answer the boys' questions. Never mind Ford says it's finished in Vietnam; they still face the possibility of going over."

He went on about a news story—a U.S. merchant ship the Communists had taken over when the war was supposed to be finished.

He said again about Van, "Ask him to come, why don't you? Ten A.M. Brunch."

Brunch.

"I'll ask. I doubt he'll be interested."

He wanted to tell the man Van had a court ticket and couldn't come on that account. He thought the man was foolish. It made him feel he was the older one, yet here he was hitching rides and the other driving the Cadillac. The man fished around in his pockets and found a business card. "Have him call me either number. I'm always one place or the other."

He drove too fast, not seeming to think about what he was

doing, came onto the limited access, and locked the automobile in at seventy with his cruise control.

"Nice car."

The man nodded as if that wasn't important. "Were you in 'Nam?"

"No, I didn't get into it."

They were headed north to the Bradford exit. Royal had his hunting knife in his boot, the way Van carried his. If he pulled the man over at the rest stop that was coming up, said he had to take a leak, pointed the knife at him to get his money, put him out of the car, and took it—the deep soft seats, the power it had, the cruise control—he could be over the border and in Montreal before night: change his mind and do that instead of going to Bradford. Let it all go and take his chances that way.

"I came up for the physical," Royal said, "and passed it. But then the war was just about done."

"I wish I could've been there. I'm only forty, but I'm too old. We didn't finish that the way we should have. It was a national disgrace. I don't believe it's too late yet."

Royal tuned the man out to avoid his hot air. They passed the rest area, which was half filled with cars. When he heard him again he was talking about the Corbin killing.

". . . terrible. It tarnishes our image, hurts the tourist trade, the convention trade. Summer people leave the area, real estate and employment go down. Those were fine people, the ones it happened to, the kind we want here. I believe the woman was from a local family, people with money."

He came off at the Bradford exit going too fast for the curve and had to brake hard. If you can't drive this thing, Royal thought, you should let someone who can do it.

He said, "It's too bad."

Royal wandered around Bradford Village for nearly an hour,

looking in the shop windows. Half the places were closed for the season—game galleries, ice cream and pizza shops, the little gift shops. The statue in front of the wax museum was covered by a tarp. There was a convention of motorcycle people in town, and the big bull-like bikes were parked everywhere, their owners, both men and women, sitting all over them talking to each other. Royal watched for a while. They were heavy machines, some with sidecars, stowage lockers everywhere, beautifully kept up and polished, maroon, silver. The owners were middle-aged-looking couples. They cruised up and down Quebec Street at about ten miles an hour, their radios going, or sat on the saddles that were like little sofas and talked, all in the leather clothes and scarves and earmuffs, looking cold though it wasn't yet. They met off season to save money probably. They looked happy.

People were strange. A little foolish. They pleased themselves like children. Dressed in leathers and helmets and big gloves, sitting astride these overweight bikes, grandfathers, grandmothers some of them, the gray hair showing under their helmets, wearing bifocal glasses: like kids.

He stood in the steep little city park and looked down at the lake. After the two warm days the temperature was about to drop. A wind from Canada brushed the water's surface. Where he was, exposed to it, it cut through his light clothes. Some fishermen were out after something or other, casting from an aluminum rowboat. The summer places on the other side of the lake were closed up, the hills above them thick with old state-owned timber pines no one was allowed to log. There were rattlesnakes up there. Van and their brother-in-law, Tom Bundy, had hunted them for the bounty until the price went too low to bother.

He was waiting, feeling a little sleepy, taking it easy, looking around at Bradford Village, what it had to offer, the people.

He went into Sports City off Quebec Street to look at the guns, something he had done often enough. He was in a kind of slow motion. The rifles and shotguns were in a rack, with a heavy chain running through their trigger guards. The handguns were locked in a case of thick glass. He leaned on his elbows to look them over. He had more than a hundred in cash in his pocket, so he asked the price of one, a heavy-looking .44 Remington magnum. Two hundred and twenty-five dollars, a twenty percent discount until Christmas. He asked about a couple of rifles too, not listening to the replies. He kept looking back at the .44. It made him feel strange to see it, contributed to the sleepy feeling. The woman in charge went behind the counter and asked if he wanted her to take anything out of the case. For a minute he could not get her meaning clear, not because he wasn't listening but because of his sleepy inwardness.

On the street he thought: I might as well go and do it. He wasn't worried, wasn't in a hurry. It was all right, good, to be between changes, events. You'd been through the one thing. The other hadn't taken place yet, but you knew about it and knew you would get through that too. In the meantime you were quiet, feeling the little fear that was really half a pleasure. You looked back, you looked forward, but you were quiet where you were.

The boy Michael had probably liked guns but was totally ignorant of them. That had been his problem right there, his downfall.

You don't put your trust in a machine or a tool you don't understand.

He walked back up the hill out of Bradford, the lake on his left. The Holiday Inn was a half mile out from the center, set against a low mountain, smooth black drives running up the slope to it. There were parking areas all around and tennis courts with puddles of rain on them at one side. Across a hedge at the other was a fancy restaurant.

The Oldsmobile with a Connecticut license, the one he'd seen on Coldspring Road, was in the lot. It had a college sticker on the back window and a Mets baseball cap inside on the sill behind the back seat. A newspaper was folded on the front seat. There was a blue windbreaker with a shield on it of some kind, like a club emblem, hanging by its loop from the hook on the doorpost.

He did not know how he would do it, but however it was, whatever went down, he was only defending himself and Van. He remembered the cons looking out of their transport, innocent as babies. Royal was not responsible, but he wasn't innocent either. Not yet. He thought: Let's go, inviting the man, though it was Royal making the approach.

The spring-action knife was tucked down where he had cut the stitches between the calfskin inner lining of the one boot and its outer shell. Let fate decide. Maybe it would stay there, maybe it wouldn't.

He went into the lobby. There were newspaper vending boxes by the entrance and a bulletin board with local churches listed, club meetings, whatnot. He could smell hamburger or steak cooking, and he heard a wide-open salesman's laugh from inside the bar lounge. A few of the big motorcycles had been parked outside, and now, glancing in, he saw their drivers at the dark bar, a blond woman, a couple of men laughing like fools, which was what he supposed they were. Behind a counter in an alcove near Royal, a clerk, a man, was on the phone. Posters, tourist brochures for the nearby sights: caverns, Highpoint Peak, where you saw three states, the dog racing.

He took his time, looked around. No one seemed to notice him. A clock in the lobby gave him the hour. He'd missed the kickoff. There were two marijuana cigarettes Van had let him have, in a cardboard cigarette box in the pocket of his jacket. He needed matches. The clerk was still on the phone, so he went boldly up to the young woman at the registration desk. She gave him several books of them and smiled. A pretty girl, probably just some nice local girl, no snob, so he smiled back.

He showed her the insurance man's business card.

"There's a fellow I'm supposed to see with a message. Mr. Corbin. I talked to him. He said I ought to go right down to his room."

She gave him the number after checking through a wheel of cards. If she thought there was anything wrong about it, she didn't show it.

A courtyard open to the sky was at the back of the place, with corridors to units leading off, each marked with a letter above its door. He located the one he wanted, lit one of his two cigarettes, and sat on a bench next to the tarpaulin-covered swimming pool in the center of the courtyard.

He told himself he wanted time to think it through, but he didn't think. The prickling, cooling inhaled smoke sharpened him, woke him up, but his thoughts stopped. The physical things around him moved in close: rainwater in the pool's sagging tarp; the tough-looking weave of the burlap on some shrubs nearby; a window rattling in its frame from a vibration, shaking the white sky at him. For a second or two he could look the world over as if it was in his power. Then, feeling for the edge of the drop, afraid of it, he said, "All right, let's go," addressing himself now, as if he had come to a decision. But it wasn't even that. What he wanted was more good from the smoke, which had stopped coming.

He didn't know what he would say. What do you say? You're sorry?

He would play it by ear.

In fourth, fifth grade, during the time he was with the court family, the kids called him Snake because he once picked one up in the yard at recess, wound it around his neck, let it slide under his shirt. It was probably a garden snake, Van told him later, harmless, but Royal didn't know that at the time. He remembered clearly the dry coiling movement on his skin, the little scraping of its contracting muscles, thinking it might be one of the east shore rattlers migrated over. It had been like standing in a road and shutting your eyes. Fuck it, let the car come. He did that too. Take bets: stand in the middle of the state road for fifteen minutes and not move, betting no cars will come. You stand and you do not move, a kid timing it, your eyes tight shut. To hell with it. If you got hit, you got hit. You were out of it. Now he made a movie in his mind of his brother Van putting his head down in the truck and, as if he could will himself unconscious, going out. Van in the movie grinned at him like a man about to do a stunt, folded his arms across the steering wheel, put his head down, and turned himself off as if he was no more than an electric appliance.

The man urged understanding. Let him understand then. If he didn't, there was the knife, and Royal could defend himself. He wasn't scared. He would have burned the man's house. He could do this without any trouble.

He went through the door under the letter he'd noted and down the carpeted corridor. It was two-thirds dark. A soda machine. An ice machine. The stub of the reefer was still in his hand. Anyone would know the smell. All right. Trays with the remains of meals had been set outside a few of the doors. He picked up an untouched roll, bit into it, took a last drag of the cigarette, and dropped it into some coffee at the bottom of a cup to surprise whoever came to carry it away.

Looked up and saw Corbin.

The girl at the desk had said, "Robert Corbin. Twelve-F."

That was his full name, and here the man was, coming out of his room and down the hall to him. Corbin paused.

He was taller than Royal remembered, thinner, darker, balder-looking, older than both the picture of him in the paper and Royal's memory. He had shadowed eyes and heavy brows, his dark hair white around the ears. There was a mole under one eye, a little scar like a hook at the corner of his mouth. He looked all right. He didn't look like a man whose son was just dead. He wore a suit with a blue shirt and a tie, carried a briefcase, a newspaper folded under his arm. In his free hand—Royal didn't recall he smoked—was a cigarette. He stared at Royal with that look as if he was going to instruct him about something: here was this kid stealing again. Bread rolls, left-over coffee, anything that wasn't locked up or nailed down. You almost laughed because it was like a joke, like fate.

Royal could see the man knew him. He could see the man recognized him and knew his connection with what had happened on Coldspring Road. He straightened and walked past Corbin out the exit at the end of the corridor, into the air.

That was it.

He had not remembered from that time to this what the sight of the man now brought back: he had been fired by Corbin because he was found lifting some little knickknack, some common thing. A letter opener with a face carved on it, which he'd liked. Something like that. He'd totally forgotten it.

He caught a ride and then walked. He could hear them from the high school field, yelling as he walked past, cheering some play.

When he started to make love to Lou that night she said, "It's my time of month."

He kept on at her like a bull calf, hardly speaking. She

said, "Don't be bad." But she could no more have stopped him than a heavy weight falling. At last she let him anyway, spread the towel, turned out the light. She would say he did it as if she was not there. Where are you, baby, and all that. He smelled her blood and felt as if he was going down to the end of the idea of her, that this was the end and there was no coming back or beginning again.

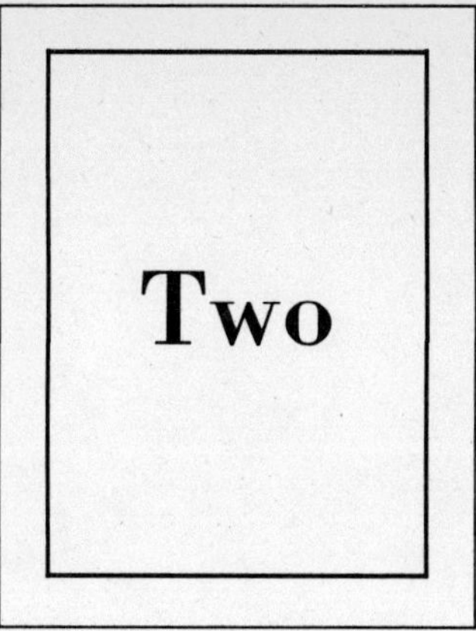

Two

8

"If you told me you could get away with a killing," Van said, "I'd believe it, but I'd say it's unusual. It's common enough in the military, where they make up their own rules. You kill your people now and then on purpose, a grudge or what have you, and I'm aware it happens in civilian life. It's just I'm a little surprised."

He was in what Pauline called a mood, down one time, high another, sore at everyone, Royal included, then all right again for a few days. Pauline was bothering him, he said, or their daddy. "They're out to enslave me, make me their servant, make me hang around them, the baby, all day and night in that coffin they live in." Then: "Listen to me. I'm being fucking paranoid."

"Keep out of my road for a day or two," he would say as if he was talking about somebody else. "I'll be frank. I'm in no mood for my family right now, you included. I'm just about paranoid on it."

He would drive over and pick Royal up, politely ask Lou's permission to take her husband away.

"Jesus, will you look at this?"

They'd be in town on Prospect, hanging out, or in some new

local bar, and he would give his exasperated laugh. "What's the matter with them? They're so dumb. Fucking zombies." Speaking of the people of Whitehouse in his loud voice to show he did not care if they heard. "They don't give a damn about anything. No concern." And suddenly he would drop, stay that way all day and night under his cloud.

Then once more he would be all right, cheerful, practical-minded.

"Manic-depressive," he said to Royal. "That's my diagnosis, and to hell with it. Only look at this. Look where we came to with it, sonny. Never mind the degree—what's mitigating, what's aggravating: I guess you could say we got away with murder.

"They're stupid, ain't they?"

It made him scornful, as if he had wanted a better fight. At the same time he was pleased and ready, as he said, to do whatever he had to to maintain their advantage.

They had gone into the winter carrying it. January. February. By mid-February they had six feet of snow, and it kept piling up. You were on Prospect Street, and all you saw on the other side behind the piled-up walls were the people's hats and caps going by. It was almost March, and there was nothing. Nothing had happened. No new thing came to light, no evidence. Royal hadn't said anything to Van or anyone else about seeing Corbin. He had waited at first for it to come down on him, then on Van, sure it would: the police, the trial, all of it. Prison.

There was nothing.

Talk died down. It was long out of the newspapers. The word was the Corbin house and land had been put up for sale. A few of the lakeside camps were listed with a Whitehouse real estate agency, it was said because of the killing, that the summer owners were afraid. For the most part, though, people seemed to have forgotten about it. All Royal was aware of was a little touch of coolness in certain attitudes. Here and there: a relative, an acquaintance. It was hard to pin down what it was. It looked as if the brothers were clear, nobody accusing anybody, but a few people were a certain way, as when you know a child is somehow at fault in something, some mischief, but it doesn't come out. There's the awareness the child feels, a little extra weight of suspicion: you keep an eye on that child, and maybe it feels it a little but not too much. Nobody accused anybody of anything, but it was as if it was more or less understood by a few people and, understood, was one more thing in the family or community, a possible flaw or danger to look out for.

Van shrugged it off.

"They don't know anything and wouldn't do anything about it if they did. Put it out of your mind."

Twenty-four hours after he'd gone to the Holiday Inn, Royal began to run a fever. The chills that started the day he saw the wounded buck came back. He tried to ignore it in the beginning, going about his business. It was the week he was supposed to begin looking for a job. He'd have the classified page, the opportunities circled, his high school record and record of past employment in his pocket. He'd get to the state road to wait for the bus, then the shaking would come over him, and it was all he could do to get back. He told Lou he was all right.

"Well, I'd hate to see you when you're sick."

Every morning in that first week Royal expected to find Jackie Pastor's black-and-yellow in the driveway. He imagined it there so well he was sure it was there in fact, the county sheriff's car alongside it for backup or pulled in behind the house in case he decided to go out that way. Jackie would be with his cousin, the cop whose name Royal could never remember. Each pair of men would be inside their own vehicle with their containers of coffee and cigarettes, waiting for him to make up his mind or just taking their own time coming in because they knew he wasn't going anywhere.

He went down in his underwear at seven A.M., bare feet, to look out the kitchen window.

Lou came and made him get back into bed. He lay under the quilts and shivered, Mrs. Marquette's thermometer in his mouth, Lou straightening the room, moving things from one place to another. He kept asking about Van.

"He'll be by. I saw Pauline in town."

Janet Colby had dropped the assault against him. He'd junked his car, sold it for twenty-five dollars in Sunrise. Pauline told Lou Van was hunting for work and had good leads. Lou had a lead on a job herself in Bradford, housekeeping for an old lady who had just come out of the hospital. The woman needed help from three to eleven P.M. and would pay a dollar better than minimum. Lou was getting ready to go for the interview and instead of worrying about Royal being sick kept talking about her letters of reference and wondering who would cook for Mrs. Marquette and him if she was out at night. She hoped he would let her take the job.

"Go ahead and take it if it's offered to you. I don't care."

"We'll have something for Christmas presents anyway."

He didn't care.

He lay in bed sweating and shivering, took his aspirin, then got stomach cramps. He didn't sleep well and didn't want Lou in the bed with him. "You'll catch whatever I have." He wanted to be alone in the room.

A man's voice, somebody, said, "Where's it at?"

Jesus! he thought.

They were here for him.

Lou was in Bradford at her interview, Mrs. Marquette shopping or visiting.

His heart started pounding like it could run away from him. Jesus!

"Royal's hiding out here someplace. Take a look for him."

Oh, shit.

The voice rose up the stairwell from below. First it seemed to come from the parlor, then the kitchen.

"Go around back and see he don't utilize that exit."

Royal went down at last. It was midafternoon, bright sun coming into the rooms, all the colors too bright, as if the old furniture was on fire, Mrs. Marquette's wall clock ticking away inside the quiet. No one was there. He looked out into the drive. He thought, shit, he was hearing things, voices, like in a ghost story. The next time it happened Lou was right in the room with him. "Take him down," a man's voice said. It was his fever speaking. Lou was working on a sweater for Van's son and didn't look up. He watched her from the bed until she became a blur, the knitting needles flickering like knives. Then he fell asleep.

Van didn't come, which was all right. Royal had never liked being with sick people either, hated being in the hospital room with their daddy after his stroke. All he'd thought about was getting into the air again.

The fever went away, so he didn't hear the voices anymore. He felt weak. Mona came and sat with him, smiled and smoothed his hair back. You could tell she was the kind of woman who liked men, liked to touch them. He thought she got fatter every time he saw her. She started to cross her legs, then gave it up.

She came back up the stairs out of breath after she'd said goodbye. "Listen. Go see Dr. DeLuca, Roy. Lou can use the truck to take you, and I'll pay."

He finally said he would.

Van came with the pickup. When he saw how glad Royal

was to see him he said he would drive them both and take them back. They all sat in the pine-paneled waiting room, Royal shivering inside his clothes. The office was in a yellow log building on the road south of Sunrise, a church and Christian summer camp on one side, the public golf course on the other. Royal looked out. A thin coat of snow was on the greens and fairways, but you could see grass through it, and the flags were up as if people were going to play. He had been in this building often enough as a boy, this doctor and the ones before him. It might as well have been on the moon today, it seemed so strange.

"Twenty minutes isn't anything in these places," Lou said when he complained about the waiting.

The room was crowded, kids coughing and running around, thc mothers trying to keep them still, old people sitting like stones. It was a cooperative, and you heard the drill in the dentist's office upstairs, a man grunting with pain, smelled the medicines. There was some kind of classical music being piped in.

Van looked out of it. At first he was quiet, wore his flat rodeo hat with its curled brim over his eyes, his boots stuck out in front of him, ankles crossed. If a kid ran by, he wouldn't move for him or notice him. After a while he began to talk about a smoke.

"Go out in the truck," Lou said.

"It's cold."

"Turn on the engine and heater."

He punched Lou on the arm.

"He just likes to suffer," Royal said.

She hit Van back, and they all began to poke at each other and make remarks. The people looked at them and away. Van kept saying, "We come to get my brother fixed up, so let's do it."

He said, "Here. They don't take you in fifteen minutes, I'll get my rifle and shoot this place up." There was a buck's head stuffed and mounted on one wall. "Look at that. You wonder how long he's been waiting." The young mothers in the place started to smile. "After a week they get to stuff you, sonny. Man's a taxidermist, not a doctor."

"Listen to that damn music," he said loudly. "Is that what you call classical? I hate that. That's taxidermist music."

He kept using the word. Everything was taxidermist. He stood and looked at one of the framed degrees on the yellow paneled walls, read aloud that it was from a school of taxidermy. He offered his tin of cigars to the old men waiting. They grinned and shook their heads.

Van lit one, took a few puffs while the mothers held on to their kids and smiled nervously, then ground it out on the vinyl floor under the heel of his boot.

Royal said he'd give it ten minutes from then. No more.

After two hours they still hadn't come near taking him. He'd told them his name, and that was as far as he'd gotten. It seemed they were taking people who came in after he did. The nurse kept disappearing in back.

"Well, I'm going to go for my hunting rifle," Van said. "Get some action."

He went out.

Royal got up after a minute or two. Lou followed him. Van was leaning against the fender of the truck, smoking. "Good for you, sonny," he said, serious now. "You had to make that choice yourself."

"Well, I guess you feel all right," Lou said.

He realized he did feel better.

Van said, "I'll tell you this. He feels too good to risk getting sicker hanging around in there with all those germs, those kids dripping snot and coughing and whatnot."

He dropped them off at the house. "He's all right, I guarantee. You tell Mona I cured him and saved her ten dollars."

Lou said over their lunch, just the two of them: "In that case I'll stop making my bed on the sofa and come back upstairs."

He really began to feel better. He decided it was Van who had accomplished it. The carefree way he acted, even the fact of his different moods. It was normal, Royal's normal world that Van brought home to him, and with it the sense of being safe. It had gotten through that in all probability the police weren't coming.

Lou had her new job. She went shopping in the morning, ran errands for Mrs. Marquette, came back, got lunch, then went to work. In the afternoons the widow walked down the road to a neighbor's for company, drank coffee, and watched TV there. Royal would wander the empty old house with its smell of kerosene and wood smoke and damp, poking into things. He was well enough to go out. He knew he ought to pull himself together and look for work, but since his people saw him as sick, didn't question it, he decided to wait awhile, didn't even pick up the classified. He gave himself a break.

Cars, trucks went by on the road outside, and he would run to a window to see if he knew who it was. Morning and late afternoon like clockwork the yellow school bus rolled past, the man driving too fast for safety as usual. Royal would stand looking after it. In the morning there was often a mist from the river, and he watched the red taillights of the big bus plunge into it, just disappear as if into water. He would hear the crows and small birds quarrel around the house. The snow froze and thawed, and he listened to the dripping from the eaves. Stood in his jeans, an old sweatshirt, slippers, looking out, listening, half in a dream. Once he saw a streak of reddish brown at the end of the pasture across the road and was sure it was a fox.

He got up before Lou, came down, looked out at the wall of river mist, listened to Mrs. Marquette groaning and talking aloud to herself. She was building up the fire in her wood stove. She kept saying, "Jesus, Jesus," not praying, just to make a sound. An International Harvester calendar on the wall above the stove was five years out of date, but she kept it for its old-fashioned horse race illustration. There was a religious picture painted on velvet she'd picked up at a county fair. Her scanner kept up its work whether she bothered with it or not, the red dot of light racing up and down the band searching for a signal. Every once in a while a flat police-sounding voice would give you something: an accident on the interstate, a fire, a call for the community ambulance to somebody's house. He went back up. Lou was curled tight, the covers thrown off, her narrow back with its bumpy spine to him. He looked at her, the smooth backside under the nightgown, her narrow feet resting one on the other, the soles pink and clean.

He hadn't done a thing with her in more than a week. She would come in at night from her job, lie stiffly in their bed waiting for him to make a move, her breathing quiet and awake. He thought, looking at her now, wondering why he didn't want to, that he ought to get onto the bed, fit himself to the familiar strong narrow back. She would wake up unwillingly, arguing in her usual way: Can't you be good once? Then allow him, get into the mood. He just didn't care to. She put him off. The look of her, her strong thinness, the morning bed smell in the room. He did not understand himself and did not try to. He thought: Let it go for the time being.

The thing was he felt all right now. Cured. He saw that all he had been was scared, and now that was past.

He'd accomplished what he was able to: gone to Corbin,

showed himself, invited an end to it, any kind of end, as if he'd said: You take it from here. What more could he do than that?

He'd done his best. The fear was gone because its cause was gone. It wasn't going to happen, the police and so on, at least not yet, not because of Corbin. He thought: Suffish unto the day.

9

Van began seeing Janet Colby again in March and found a job waiting tables in a restaurant on the old Bradford road. A week after he got the job he had what he called a misunderstanding with the manager and left.

"The man told me I could tend his bar after the first month. That was the job I was after when I walked in, and he knew it, the only reason I accepted being waiter. First payday, it turns out I didn't understand. He'd promised the bar job to someone who, I happened to find out, was a close friend of his. I didn't care for that and told him so."

They were in Janet's place, the three of them.

"I didn't show I was upset. I told him. I held up my hands: Peace, friend. All right? To hell with it. I told him this: I see your viewpoint. You have your friend and owe him loyalty, which is something I hope I can understand. Only there's this. It tells me, except to your good friends, your word's no use. You screw me on this, you'll screw me on something else. I don't want to work for you. The man's name was Dave. I said, Dave, I hope you understand. Somebody whose word is only half good is no good for me."

The waiters at the restaurant had parted their hair in the

middle and worn long mustaches Gay Nineties style. Van had let his mustache grow long over the winter, so all he had to do was wax the ends and twist them up. When he quit he shaved it completely, leaving a pale patch that made him look naked: younger.

He was searching for another job but not too hard. He was quiet, satisfied-seeming. The stories he told were mostly like this one. They were about his control, the people who crossed him and who he turned aside, taking it easy with them, being good-humored.

"I'm not fighting anyone right now. My war's over."

"Well, you sure fight me a hell of a lot for a man whose war is over," Janet said.

"That's the war between the sexes. That don't ever end."

He lived half his time with Janet, the other with Pauline in their father's house.

"The smell drives me out of Mona's. Never mind it's my kid. They never crack a window. Dogs, farts. They leave food around and it rots. The women don't notice, but I can't stand it."

Janet's apartment was the second floor of a house in Sunrise. There was an entrance on the side of the building, with an ice roof over its stairs. Royal spent a lot of his time there that winter too. They would drink beer, watch TV. It had three rooms and a bath, the living room with a good view of the mountains. It was warm but not overheated like Mona's. There were curtains with bows, pillows, patchwork quilts, stuffed animals. Janet cooked, and the place usually smelled of baking and spices or whatever soup she had on the stove.

She made the rules. "If there's some sin you can't commit before eleven at night, I haven't heard about it," she would say, pushing Royal out. "I'm a working girl and need my sleep.

You two want to go out and drink for the rest of the night, that's up to you."

The TV had a remote, and Janet would sit in her recliner, her long legs under her, the control in her big red-nailed hand aimed like a weapon. "That's a lie"—about a commercial. She would shoot it down with the remote control. She knew the products from the jobs she'd held. "I've sold that. Glycerin, alcohol, water, and color. You could make it yourself for twenty-five cents." She was selling women's wear now in the Space Center Mall in South Sunrise, making a good living, according to Van.

"Janet can take care of herself and us too if she wants to."

Van kept saying she was in love with both of them.

"If you're too drunk or lazy, lover, forget it," she would say. "Maybe Royal can get it on tonight"—kidding but giving Royal a nice look so that Van would wink at his brother: See?

She liked to refer to her Indian blood and said, except for the long legs, she was typical squaw. When he was sixteen and saw her naked the first time Royal had been amazed by the hair on her breasts around the brown nipples and the line of it running from the bush up her full stomach almost to her navel. Van told him she used a depilatory now. "That's her Dutch-English blood, the hairiness. Fox, which is her tribe, is near hairless."

The three went out to bars in Sunrise once in a while but generally stayed home. Van would bring a case of beer, sit on the sofa with his boots up, look through the *TV Guide*.

Now and then Janet was able to get some cocaine, and they would lock themselves in with it. She never said how she acquired it or what it cost. If Van knew, he didn't say. It was always the same small amount. She brought it in a little spice bottle with a plastic stopper, measured out two piles on the mirror top of her coffee table using a fingernail as a cup, straightened the hills into lines with a sheet of notepaper. Van took his using one of the half straws she kept. He did not let her offer Royal any, but if it was pot, he would share with his brother, take his own tokes, groan and sigh, lean back in the sofa with his eyes closed, smiling as if he had put down a ton of weight. If it was the coke, he got lively right away. He had a head for dope, he said, never lost himself entirely.

They asked Lou to join them when they went out or to come over and visit, but she didn't like to go to roadhouses and said she wasn't comfortable in Janet's. Pauline told Royal she didn't care what Van did or where he stayed right then.

"Whatever's on his mind, he has to work it out for himself." She and Royal ran across each other in town. "Janet's older, and I guess he wants someone more mature right now. Only tell her she shouldn't let him walk all over her, which I know is his instinct. He wants to dominate."

"I don't know how damn mature the woman here is, sonny," Van said when Royal passed this on. "It takes more than years. Pauline's got her hands full with our boy. That's why she don't care. Except when we fight, I get along with Janet, but not because she's mature. Pauline's right I like to dominate. She knows me."

Royal came up the outside stairs once and was into the living room before he realized his brother and Janet were fighting. They were in the bedroom, the door half open. He did not like to hear things he wasn't supposed to. He thought it was odd the way women like that who acted tough let you do them an injury. "Jesus Christ," he heard her say before he left. She was crying. "You won't give me any kind of a break ever, will you?"

Another time Royal had to get out of Mona's pickup to let them fight, Van yelling and Janet, her Fox Indian blood up, screaming back. They had stopped in the middle of town, Van hitting the brakes, shutting off the engine, and turning to yell at her all at once. Royal walked out over the bridge, looked down at the water. If you gave him a hundred dollars, he couldn't have told you what they were fighting about. When he came back he knew Van had slapped her. She sat turned away, her face to the window, the heavy dark hair a screen over it, tears splashing onto the big hands.

Van would explode about something and strike out, and she would hit back or, if her feelings were too hurt, cry until he cooled down and made his half apologies. Afterward, generally, he would take off and no one would know where he was for two or three days. Then when he came back he would sit as if nothing had happened, his beer in his fist, the hand-tooled boots he'd bought in Texas after his discharge on what Janet called the hassock.

"He's always talking about control," Janet said to Royal after one fight. "I don't see it. And it isn't that worries me anyhow. I can deal with his temper. It's the things he says. He tells me these things. He'll tell me something he did in the army, a crime almost. Or some local thing he was involved in. As if that's his self-control and I'm supposed to be impressed. I don't want to hear these things, Roy."

"He's only kidding you."

"I just don't want to hear it. You better tell him."

It made him do it all the more, that she had complained to Royal.

"We'll just walk in on Lou's night off, some night when there's no moon and the old lady's asleep. Rent a U-Haul, park it in the driveway, clean the place out."

He was talking about Lou's new job, the big lakeside house where she worked now. He was suggesting they burglarize it.

"You want to come in, Janet? Invest in our project? You

could rent the U-Haul in your name, say you had to carry some stuff."

"Just be quiet, Van."

He asked Royal, "You in?"

"Don't talk this shit in my home," Janet said. "This is where I have to live. I have neighbors. I'm law-abiding, and you know it."

"That's right, you call the law if someone gives you a love pat."

"Your love pats. Damn straight."

Van looked from one to the other. "Now, what do you think? Here I come to you with this proposed operation. What do you say?"

They did not reply.

"You really believe I'd do that? Involve Lou in a criminal activity? Involve Janet? I have to tell you that pisses me a little. You both piss me."

Janet would say she was sorry. Royal couldn't tell how serious Van was, how mad he was.

He talked about other things he'd done. Incidents of years before. How he had robbed certain summer camps. He said he'd begun doing it the first month he was out of the army, selling what he took to the service contacts he'd made. He would tell a story Royal knew was probably true from the circumstances.

"Did you know about that?"

"No," Royal said.

"No. That's right. Did I involve you?"

No.

"You see the point?"

But if he asked him about it when they were alone, Van would say, "I make up sixty percent. That particular story was true. All it is is to shake her out of her dream world a little.

That's my object. Maybe keep you from sliding back into yours."

It was hard to decide when he was serious and when he wasn't, when it was fact or fiction. He began telling his war stories again that winter, which he hadn't done since he came out. You knew they were more or less true but couldn't say how he felt about them. Whether he was serious.

"Yes, I was scared"—concerning an event, a firefight, some operation involving the villagers in a certain place. "I'm telling you for a reason, to demonstrate something, so you might as well listen."

He seemed to want Janet and, through her, Royal to know how scared he'd been, that he was not the hero, the fearless fighter. It was all right to be scared. You dealt with it. That was one thing. You were scared, dog soldier and officer both, maybe stupid and incompetent but not immoral like everyone thought, even the ones who supported the war. That was the other thing.

If it was something his people brought off halfway well, a combat assault, he was the proud noncom. His people were trained and knew what they were supposed to do and believed in it, though probably they were wrong to.

"I guess I told you this before"—looking across Janet at his brother.

"I like to hear it, Van."

Then Van would tell some story in which the people in his unit, however scared and incompetent, got the difficult job done. He did not spare details, but Royal remembered from times he'd told the story before different details.

"Can't we talk about something else?" Janet would say.

Finally, to cap it, to shake her, as he said to Royal, he told the story of his meritorious service.

He had blown the man up, it began. An individual whose

face he could see, so he almost knew him. As close up as Royal here. He'd even reminded him a little of Royal, he couldn't say how, but he did: his age, a certain look. He said he could still see that face. They had talked to each other first. He talked to the Dink, the Dink talked back in English, then Van moved away and blew him up.

Royal knew this story too, but not the details.

"Fuck you!" the VC had said. Cursed him. He stood there shaking, Van shaking too. "No prisoner!" the guy yelled in English. "Do it or I kill you!" Words to that effect.

Van kept building it, going back over it to add touches, how he had found the man in a shallow cave, an overhang, flushed him out of it, tracked and disarmed him. There was the remains of a tea party on a table there in the cave. Two chairs, teacups, even sugar in a bowl. The man was hurt in some hidden way. You couldn't see how, but he was the color of that newspaper on the table. "Fuck you!" the guy had yelled in English.

It was his first time so close to a Dink. He turned to look for a backup, anybody, and some deep instinct came to his rescue. The man had a knife out and was fumbling around with it, half dropping it like his hand wouldn't work for him. Van ran back out of range of his own weapon, turned, and blew him up with the grenade launcher.

"It was raining blood for about two minutes."

Janet went into the kitchen.

He yelled, "Don't you like that story?"

She was rattling pots, starting her dinner. He chewed fiercely on the skin around his thumbnail for a while, then yelled, "Listen. It was raining blood and bone on my fucking *hat* for about five minutes! I had to live through it, you can listen! Pieces of his bones and guts—you would never even want to look at pictures of things like that. I destroyed his *ass!* I don't exaggerate. Up the poor bastard goes and down he comes, shit, blood, bone, and all, in a fucking hail, splinters of bone, shit all over the landscape, including me!"

She called, "All right, Van, that's all. You can shut up about it or leave. I don't know why you like to do this to me."

"Well, I'm through now."

Calming down, grinning at Royal like a kid. Quiet: "God, that got to her, didn't it?"

Royal said, "I never heard it all."

Van yelled, "That's how I got the decoration, Janet. That was my meritorious service! You always wanted to hear it."

"I said I wanted to hear it to please you. You didn't need to torture me with it, Van. You didn't have to give the gory details. You do that to upset me."

"That's what a story is, Janet dear. You atomize a man, it's details. What you read in a newspaper's no story. I could give you fucking details. You don't know anything like what went on over there. Whatever you think it was, immoral or whatever, I'll tell you what it really was or what it also was. It was my fucking meritorious service, Janet, and I got my decoration out of it. And all I ever was the whole time it went on was shitless. And I'll tell you something else. I pitied that poor son of a bitch. That's the entire point of telling it to you, you dumb Indian. I pitied him. So you don't have to go and hide your head."

Later he said to Royal it was mostly a tall tale. "The blood and shit coming down. That don't really happen."

It got to the point that if he started any kind of war story, Janet would leave the room.

"I'm not coming in there until you're both gone!"—from the bedroom or kitchen.

On nights she kicked them out Royal and Van would stand on the sidewalk at eleven, eleven-thirty, stamping the cold out of their boots, too early to go home. The arguments seemed to give the older brother energy. He would jog up and down or dance on the sidewalk like a boxer and spar with Royal, slapping at him.

"Shit"—breathless. "Let's get something going. Anything."

They went to the Antlers, but it was quiet.

He ignored the few people he knew, looked them over as if he'd been asked his opinion. "They're all more or less like Janet, aren't they? Whatever their problem is, they'll never learn which end of it to pick up."

Royal said, "I guess you always know."

"Mostly."

Van looked over the place with a kind of anger—people playing pinball, the handful at the bar. He slapped his fingers on the table to the music, his beer to one side as if he was keeping it for someone.

Royal defended the people.

"Shit, you can have them then, sonny. Why don't they do what they're supposed to do?"

"What are they supposed to do?"

"Be something. Make their choice."

"You always want them to let you alone; let them alone."

"I do. Only they're sheep. I don't give a fuck about sheep. If they want to say they aren't sheep, they have to choose that. I am not a sheep! You have to be higher than animals. You decide that, then make something out of it. You choose and act, so you can be somebody. Otherwise the world will use you to wipe its ass."

"You can't always make a choice."

"That's right. Like the army. They wiped their ass with me for two years. If they'd told me to put you away for, to them, some good war-related reason, told me to kill you, I'd have done it. My own brother. I was their slave and robot."

When they went to bars in Bradford, Van watched the people

around them carefully. He would observe some stranger who came in, sat at the bar, and ordered a drink. "He don't care. Has his job, his rules to follow. A robot."

How did Van know what the man did?

"I don't necessarily. He looks to me like an insurance man. I don't say I'm right. If I am, then he's here to nail some poor bastard to the wall."

Another was CIA or a lawyer or a plainclothes cop.

"I saw his car outside"—concerning a man neither knew. "CIA. I'd bet on it. They always drive a late-model Plymouth or Chevy. Tan, dark green. Or he's FBI. But I'd bet CIA. They try to get people like me to go back in. They're on the lookout, hang around the small towns and depressed areas. They want guys for dirty wars. He prob'ly knows every detail about my life. He might know it all, Roy, but he'd use it for his own ends, not for justice."

They always went back to the Antlers to finish the night.

John May, drunk at four A.M., would be murmuring to himself at his end of the bar, his friend Solent taken home earlier by his son. Jay Cooney, the owner, a big man with white hair cut in a brush, stood ready, everything buttoned up, waiting for the three, the last ones.

"You ain't a robot, are you, John?" Van yelled at the old man.

"No, I ain't, West. Never have been."

"Good."

On and on.

Jay put them out. Van bought a pair of six-packs first. They took John along, drove to a lakeside beach, and sat in the chill of a lean-to.

Royal said he couldn't tell if he was drunk or not.

"You ain't, and John ain't either. If you're always drunk, you can't get drunk." He said, "Answer me this, John," sounding more country the drunker he got. "Is there anything to any of it?"

"There ain't, you ask me. What the hell are we doing?"

"Watching the sun rise, John."

When it did, its hard bright fire striking among the trees, May fast asleep, the brothers drank their beer and looked at the ice-covered lake.

"It's all there"—nodding at the scene. "All the morality and the rules you need. You don't need law or government, teachers or preachers to tell you what is true morality. You know it. You don't, you're lower than the animals."

"Why would you kill me if they told you to?"

"I was trained to it."

"Shit, Van."

Both drunk.

"It's wrong, I know. The same way the war was. But I accepted it, and once you do that you go down that road. Now I'm on my own and see it was wrong, a bad phase. They could tell me fifty different ways to do something now, take someone out, you or anyone, and I'd ignore them. I take someone out, it's my command. I'm my own commander in chief now and forever."

Royal walked the two miles from the farm to the Antlers one night late in March, then when he got there had to sit on the bumper of a truck until his wind was back to normal. His heart was pounding. He thought he might be coming down with something again. Van was somewhere, Albany or, for all he knew, New York City. Royal had told Lou he couldn't stand it if he didn't get out, but now that he was where he said he was going he didn't want to stay. He took beer nuts from a bowl on the bar, then forgot he had them in his hand. Paul

Beam, off his shift and halfway drunk, stood farther down the bar, nearly a head taller than anyone around him, telling some tale. Royal didn't want a drink but didn't like to leave. He had nothing to do. He looked at his daddy's trophy, a twelve-point rack, Wayne West's name and the date in 1960. They ought to dust the thing. Royal had been seven and remembered it as one of the few occasions he'd known his father to be happy and sober at the same time. Plaques and awards covered the pine-paneled walls. Van's name could have been there, but he would not enter competitions.

Beam was talking about some prison incident, the cons protesting conditions. They'd had a lockdown: the population shut up, taken out one at a time, and strip-searched.

Royal got change and played the game where you manipulate a claw inside a glass box full of gifts, picked up one of the plastic eggs, worked it into the slot, and redeemed the slip inside for a draft beer. It was his first of the day, and he stood at the bar with his glass, feeling dizzy.

Beam came over.

"Tell Van we got a friend of his and your brother-in-law Tom's up there now, your daddy's too for all I know. Armed robbery conviction. Tell Van to ask me about it. It's Roy, ain't it? Why don't you come on down and join us, Roy? Be friendly."

"I'm all right here."

Beam said, "Tell him though. He'll be interested. You ever been in a prison, Roy?" He kept his sweating face close, and Royal felt the man's physical power.

"No."

"Your daddy was in, wasn't he?"

Royal ignored it.

"I was just talking about how they counsel kids like you. That's what they call it." He stood close to Royal, as if the bar was crowded. "I don't counsel any myself, but some of the officers enjoy doing a man an injury." He said, "Roy, you keep out of the Grove. A kid like you, they'll break your ass down in ten days, officers and cons together. It's a game with them."

He kept after him. "Ain't that good advice?"

"I guess that's right."

"You guess? You better believe it's right." And then: "Don't take it so serious. You wouldn't do anything to get in there, would you? What's that in your glass?"

"I don't want another. Thanks anyhow."

He got away, got outside into the lot. He was breathing as if he'd been running a race.

When he saw Van he told him about it.

"Paul likes to talk. He's a hillbilly like all Beams, so he spins tales. Don't mind it. The State of New York tells Paul Beam to shit, and Paul shits. He decides to work on you, see what he can scare out of you because he fools around and wonders about this and that. He don't have anything and wouldn't act on it if he did."

But Royal could see he was thinking about it. Van must have been drinking the three days he was away. He looked pale, needed a shave. They drove around in Mona's truck and wound up at Janet's. She didn't want to let them in at first.

"I guess you're drunk," she said when she did.

"I wasted some money if I ain't."

"It's always wasted, because you don't really enjoy it. You get morose. I don't know why you bother."

"What do you think of Mr. Paul Beam, Janet?"

"I just know his name."

She sat in her robe and nightgown, legs under her, chain-smoking, magazines and a box of tissues on the sofa beside her, blew her nose every few minutes.

"A tall hillbilly with a mustache and long hair. He's one of the correction officers at the facility. Servant of the state."

He started to go on about Paul Beam, what he thought of the prison guard mentality, then about the attitudes of people who lived in Whitehouse.

"Van, I've been on my feet all day, it's late, and I don't care to hear your philosophy of life just now."

"You don't?"

"No, sir."

"Well, I care to tell it to you."

Royal saw she must have been doing coke before they arrived. She dabbed at her nose with a balled-up tissue, taking secret looks at the pink spots on it.

"You come here after three, four days, don't call first to let me get the place or myself presentable. You *know* I have to get up at seven o'clock tomorrow morning, and whatever your requirements are, I require my sleep, Van."

"I require to talk. Make a speech."

"Well, don't do it. Not now."

He looked at her and laughed. His narrow nose was pinched white. It happened so suddenly it scared Royal, and he could see it scared Janet.

Royal said, "Van, I ought to get back."

"I want to tell Janet more war stories first."

Janet said, "Why do you like to put your own people down, your friends?"

"I just put the women down." And then: "Is that a joke? Did I make a joke?"

"I'll tell you you sure don't seem to like women much. The way you treat them."

"The women around this town. That's correct."

"You'd put your own mother down if she told you to behave, wouldn't you? If she was alive."

"That's correct. If she was alive and told me any kind of shit like the shit you always give me. She was like the rest of you. She belonged. She was ignorant and proud of it, and bad-tempered on top of that. Roy don't remember her. I do. She never in her life had an idea or opinion or a thing to say for herself. Never read a newspaper or even a store catalogue. Ate and drank all day and all night. White flour, sugar, pork fat, and whiskey. And then acted like a madwoman if everything didn't go exactly her way, whichever way that was. I never could figure it out. She was foolish like all the Porters. Low IQ. That was our mother. She was here, what I'd do, I'd tell her to go straight back to hell."

"Come on, Van," Royal said.

"No. What the fuck is this?" He did not take the dangerous look off Janet. "Hell *yes*, I'm putting down my mother and you too and every other mistaken cunt in this town, male and female, who I *know* is in the wrong. Don't you understand enough to shut up when you see I'm into one of my moods? I have two, three separate individuals, various S.O.B.s working against me, trying to get me to act against my will. I have to decide if I'm crazy or not, because everybody says you better be crazy or you won't survive another week. All this fucking *pressure* I have on me right now?" He said suddenly, whispering as if he was embarrassed, "My *mother?* I mean, is that your topic? Well, I'll tell you what I want, Janet dear, since you didn't ask. I want you to shut up concerning my mother and about ninety percent of the rest of the shit you think you know something about and really seem to believe is worth discussing. Now, you consider the advisability of doing that, the mood I'm in."

To stop him and also because it was true, Royal said he didn't feel well. He ought to go home and get his temperature.

"Oh, baby!" Janet said.

She went for her thermometer, started to fuss over him, put the back of her big cool hand on his cheek. "Lord, he's burning up."

Van, who had been watching her, turned the amazed dangerous look on his brother. "He's okay. Leave him alone. He's not sick."

"Look at him. Take him home, sweetheart. Don't be so mean."

In the pickup on the way, Van said, "Dumb Indian cunt. I tell her there's no ethics, no one I know can tell right from wrong, she says, Well, what about you? You think you're so damn good? As if that was my point! Jesus! I never said I was better than anyone else or even any good. I was making a fucking point! She ought to see I'm in a down mood and act accordingly. She won't use her head."

He said, "Now what the *hell's* the matter with you?"

"I don't know. I guess I have flu."

"No, I mean what the fuck's the matter with you?"

He said loudly in the cab of the truck, "Don't be this way. Get yourself together. You're sick too damn much. You been sick three times this year."

Royal kept quiet, looked out at the road.

After a time Van said, "Shit. I'm in a mood. It's these people. They're after me to work for them. Not that they wouldn't pay pretty well."

"Why don't you do it?"

"I'm supposed to be their fink, do their spying."

"Who are they?"

"Never mind that, sonny. The less you know, the better. I'll say this much. You recall that man, that three-piece suit I pointed out in the Bradford bar? Well, you won't believe this.

He talked to me. I went in a few times alone, and he was there. Always sat in the same place, like he was waiting for guys to come in."

The one Van had called CIA. "He wants you to work for him?"

"I don't say he does. Someone does. There are a few possibilities." He said, "My instinct is to politely ask all of them to fuck off, tell you the truth. The only thing is, they may have me by the short hairs. Now, that's all you know and all you need to know."

"I'm sorry if you're sick," he said in the Marquette drive. "I didn't mean to come down on you that way. Don't let Paul Beam or any of the people around here get to you. Don't ever let them try to run you. They don't know shit, and anyhow you have the power in yourself to control them."

He said, "What is it—Janet? You're afraid I'm going to do her some injury?"

"No."

"Ain't that it? Well, I'll look out for her, Roy, and if there's a risk, I'll see to my own control. You just take care of yourself, since you're sick so much, and let me see to the rest of it."

Van talked to Paul Beam and came back to the younger brother.

"He was trying to fuck you over for the fun of it, like I said. He admitted it. Nobody's going after anybody, sonny."

Beam had told him the friend of Van's and Tommy's he'd mentioned was a Levi Walls, a man Van knew as a boy. Walls had moved away, and he and Van had run into each other again in the army. He was now in Locust Grove, carrying five to ten on his armed robbery conviction. He'd committed the crime in New York City, and they'd sent him to the upstate prison, which was fortunate, Van said, because it put him near his family. Van was excited. "We ought to pay him a visit. I haven't seen Levi since we were demobilized the same afternoon in Oakland, California."

"I don't want to go in there."

"We owe it to him, give him support. He's a hometown boy, home county anyway. A little older than me, nearer Tom's age."

"I don't know him."

"Well, you're full of goodwill, ain't you?" Van said. "You ought to know him. He's a decent man. Shit, I'll go with Tommy. As it happens, it ties in with that business proposition I was talking about. There's connections in a prison. People who know things about other people. You have to do what you don't like once in a while, Roy. Take a little taste of poison each day, they can't kill you with that particular poison."

Royal had had a mild case of influenza. When he felt better he started job-hunting, found a few leads, and saw them peter out. There was some night work available, watchman and so on. The entertainment parks in and around Bradford wouldn't open until spring and only paid minimum then. He wasn't qualified for most things that interested him, but he knew he'd find something sooner or later and wasn't anxious.

Pauline thought she was pregnant. She was going to get it confirmed one way or the other as soon as the weather improved. "I don't know how it happened, the little Van bothers with me."

Mona said, "Once is all it takes."

"Once is about what it was."

Mona lectured both Pauline and Royal in her easy-going way. They didn't take their responsibilities seriously. Here was Pauline probably pregnant and her husband never home. Their friends were always in trouble. One had just wrecked a car and put himself in the hospital, another was in custody on criminal possession, on and on. "You don't get an education, either you or your friends, that's the trouble, or use it if you have one. Van wastes what he has, Royal does, and you do too, Pauline. I'm no exception, wasted my few opportunities. Here I am a grandmother, still waiting tables and cleaning people's houses."

Royal didn't mind her criticism because she was pleasant about it, not really blaming anyone. "I guess it boils down to money as usual, who has it and who doesn't," she said. "But I'll tell you this: You have to come by it honestly for it to be of any use to you."

It was Van who worried them all.

He appeared once in a while, sat with his son on his knees, put his hat on the boy's head, held his cigarette away. He talked to the child as if he was grown. The dashhound considered Van its master and sat with its popping gaze fixed on him. Pauline said Van looked as if he didn't sleep three hours out of twenty-four.

One time he appeared with a purple bruise all over one cheek.

"A little tiff I got into. What you'd call a misunderstanding."

He would look into his redheaded son's eyes. "You mind your mother, hear? You'll end up like me."

Mona and Wayne and whoever else was there would make themselves scarce when Van visited, hoping he and Pauline might talk, but he took off after ten or fifteen minutes.

Wayne West said, "Let him go. You can't force him." He was getting around with an aluminum tripod cane now instead of his walker, and that was his chief concern and pride.

He said easily, "Van's just trying to find his level after all this he's been through."

Royal got a ride into Bradford one night and saw Van on Quebec Street with some men he didn't know, his brother with his legs straddling somebody's motorcycle, the others standing looking up and down the street the way men without work do, not saying much, as if they'd known each other for years. Royal couldn't have told the name of one of them. Van nodded to him, and that was it.

He would hear certain things about Van's activities, nothing very specific.

Their cousin, the one named Porter who had a criminal record of his own, stopped him on the street. "Why don't your brother let his life cool down a little before he gets involved again?"

The people he mentioned sounded from his description like the ones Royal had seen.

"They're from Troy and always into something, some criminal activity. I know them."

One day he took the bus into Albany to answer a want ad and saw Van with Jackie Pastor. They were sitting in the policeman's car on Broadway near the bus station. Royal had been in a factory office filling in an application. He saw them when he came out and turned away, walked away as if he had seen something he shouldn't. Another time, getting a lift on the river road with a friend, he observed the two of them, Van and Pastor, each one in his vehicle, parked so the driver's windows were next to each other, talking across.

Their daddy heard a few things. He spoke to Royal thinking it would get back to Van, since he did not like to talk to him directly.

"I've knowed many people like Van. If no trouble comes to them, they'll go looking for it. You get people like that in a family. Maybe it'll skip a generation, then show up again. He flirts with danger. That's why he runs with these people you hear about."

He said, "You two never did any time. I did. State's worse than county, but they're all bad. Van's been up there with

Tommy to see this friend of theirs, so maybe that will sober him. They got sissies in there, niggers. It's sixty percent black men. You got the black Muslims will knife a man just for being white. I'm here to tell you you two boys wouldn't like it.

"Luck won't stay with you if you don't treat it with respect. You got to be able to stand the idea of something good happening to you, and some people can't. Van got out of this trouble on Coldspring Road, then hurt Janet so she has him arrested. If he keeps it up, she'll get a peace bond put on him. He draws attention. I know men like this all my life. The world isn't to their specifications, they throw it away, throw away what they have and what you have too. I don't know if Van considers that. Considers you."

He said, "It's not that he ain't smart. Look at the way he did in the service. They don't give medals to stupid men or brave ones for that matter. They give you a medal because you can use your head in a crisis."

The women listened. If Iris was there, she would have some denigrating thing to say about Van, but she knew enough not to push it.

Her husband, Tom, said, "You hear things around. Nothing to upset anybody."

Tom was a tall, heavily built man with a quiet voice who had done work on the state roads most of his adult life. In winter he cut wood, drove a town snowplow and one of the school buses. He drank any time of day and would come into the hot room smelling of it, his big face red.

"That cop who works with Jackie Pastor, his cousin or something. He told me to tell Van he's got his eye on him. I told Van, and he laughed."

Wayne said, "I ain't worried. They don't have anything, not to this point anyway. It's how they keep you straight. He reminds you of his power. You note a cop on the road, you do the speed limit."

Royal was going to mention seeing his brother with Pastor, then decided that was Van's business.

Nobody seemed to know where Van was living.

Pauline said, "He used to be at Janet's a lot, but Roy says not recently."

"I believe he stays in Albany with some man he knew in the service," Tom said.

Tom did not have much to report about their prison visits. "Levi gets along. What Wayne says about conditions holds true, I guess. Him and Van talk about their army experiences."

"I liked Levi Walls," Wayne said. "His family anyway while they lived here."

Royal ran into Janet on a Sunday, and she took him up to her place. She said Van had called and told her to get hold of some coke: they were going to have a party soon.

"That was two weeks ago."

"He's looking for work."

"I'm not complaining about his absence, Roy. One thing, he owes me money. Another, I'm not dealing for him or anyone else. You don't say things like that on a telephone, not in the circles I travel in. Tell him the less I see of him, the better, that I don't give parties for the kind of people he sees fit to bring up here, and that I would like our account settled."

She said, "Now you listen to me. Van does not look well. I mean he is in sad shape. Job-hunting isn't an activity supposed to kill you. You ask me, he's looking in a bottle for his job, and that's no good."

She said she had a new boyfriend.

"He's a master mechanic just moved into the area from downstate. I'll have you in sometime when he's here, and you can meet him."

The apartment was clean, smelled of furniture polish and Lysol. He could see a corner of her bed through the door, the stiff skirt of the bedspread. When he went into the bathroom there were the guest towels, tissues in a metal box with flowers on it, soap tablets piled up in a dish like a seashell. There was no sign of a man, no sign Van had spent time in the place.

She was wearing her silver jewelry, her leather pants, a red blouse half unbuttoned so you could look at her breasts. She got bottles of beer, sat on the arm of the sofa next to him. When she leaned to put out her cigarette, bending her head into the light, her heavy hair slid forward and you saw it was about a third gray. He could see the lines in her face, the smoker's lines on the upper lip. She messed his hair, arranging it one way and another. "I wish you could see this gorgeous stuff in this light. It's red gold. You're a good-looking boy. I wish I had hair that color." He could feel her breast against his cheek.

"I don't mean to embarrass you."

"Well, it's just Van."

"Like I'm his property? I told you that's finished, honey. And something else you may not know. People don't belong to other people. And people don't or shouldn't use people, try their brainwashing on them. I'm nobody's plaything or possession. That's the reason I got my divorce, because some men think women are property to be used and abused. I like Van all right, I worry about him and feel sorry for him. But I don't belong to him or anyone else."

Janet's looks pleased Royal, the way she talked in her smoky voice. She told off-color stories so it didn't embarrass you. She would take her clothes off as if she was in a room with other women, talking, telling a joke she'd heard, being natural. He'd always liked the feeling in this clean place of hers. Never mind what else was going on in the world. Get the housework done, everything clean and fresh, beds made fresh. If it holds still, polish it. Let the world fall apart. Lou was the same. Work on the little things, and the big ones get in line.

She made him drink from her bottle, which had a smear of lipstick on it, then kissed him to taste the beer on his lips. He kissed her a few times. All she wanted to do was make a baby of him. He let her. Even when they were in bed she treated him like a child, leading him just as she had when he was sixteen. It was all right with him, the way he felt. He liked the familiarity of it, the ease on both sides. He liked the feeling he got from her that connected with Van. He knew it would be all right with Van if he told him about this or if Janet did.

Van kept trying to get Royal to go with him to visit Locust Grove.

"I don't want to persuade you against your will, but I'd like it. We'll see Levi, take him something. Tom says he won't go again. I thought the old man might come, but he's ashamed to be seen since his stroke. What are you worried about? Levi's the one doing time. You think someone's going to say you did a crime and keep you there?"

"No."

"I told you before, Roy. Look right at whatever it is scares you. It's never as bad as you think it will be."

He went with him on one of the regular Saturday visiting days in early April. Van drove fast, excited. Royal thought he looked all right, not too tired the way Pauline and Janet said.

Van said, grinning, "I guess you think your brother hangs out a lot with the local criminal element, sees too much of the seamy side."

"I don't care who you see." Then he said, "I know you see Jackie Pastor."

"I never see him. I run into him once in a while. What's this about?"

"Nothing."

"Nothing shit. Jackie's a joke to me, with his talk about law and order. Don't worry about Jackie."

"I told you I don't care who you see."

"You lie. You're always worried about something." He was cheerful, kept looking at Royal and grinning. "You're some kind of a watchdog, ain't you? Never mind."

After a while, he said, "Here you go."

They had come up over the mountain and down, and there it was just on the other side, across the interstate canal. It amazed Royal that he'd lived all his life forty miles from the place and never seen it.

The buildings were set among open fields, the canal on one side, freight tracks on the other, a village of guard and administration houses in front, with shops and a small restaurant. There was no grove of trees around, locust or otherwise. The tall cell-block wings were of yellow brick, narrow cross-barred windows running the height of them, so many it gave the place, in spite of the fact it was maximum security, a look of lightness and openness. The roads inside the perimeter were of neatly raked crushed white stone, signs fresh painted, the parking area as clean as if it had been poured the week before. Squads of guards going in and out of the main entrance, changing shift or in charge of work details, had on well-made uniforms. The cons were in pressed fatigues, looking as if they'd just stepped out of the shower. It struck Royal, this clean look, the open appearance, the organization. He watched trusties on tractors out in the weak sunshine, tilling carefully up to the borders of the fields as if they cared about what they were doing.

"Okay?" Van asked.

"I wouldn't want to move in."

"You don't need to. I'm saying it's like anything else. You have to give them some time, you'll survive it. Know your enemy. So long as you do your best to stay out, or get out once you're in, you're all right. The trouble with Levi is he halfway enjoys it. That or he's lazy."

He usually brought something with him. "I like the man, so I bring him a gift to show it. Something in his war experience weakened him, and one of the reasons I come is to work on that, build his confidence."

Van locked the truck. "Every one of these guards is a part-time thief."

"Do you ever see Paul Beam?"

"It's not his shift, and he don't do visitor duty anyhow. He's corporal, head of a squad of his own on one of the security blocks where they keep the in-prison crimes."

They knew two or three other guards from the Whitehouse-Sunrise area but didn't see them either.

"What about your business proposition you said the prison could help you with?"

"What's that?"

"The people who were going to hire you to work for them. You said you were going to develop contacts in the prison about that. The CIA and all."

"I was bullshitting you, sonny." A sign said: NO SMOKING BEYOND THIS POINT. Van was putting out his cigarette in a bucket of sand. "Suppose it's true. You think this is the place and time to discuss it?"

Royal said, "I guess I don't know what to believe half the time."

"Believe in your brother all the time." He poked him in the ribs. "You are full of shit. That's the only explanation for some of the dumb things you say."

They showed their identification, signed the register, emptied their pockets, and so on. Van had to open his paper bag to show the coffee and doughnuts he'd gotten at the restaurant across the road, slide out a few packs of cigarettes from the carton for the woman to look at. She inspected the gift he'd brought in without interest. It was a hand-tooled cowboy belt. She had a metal detector and used it on them, running it up between their legs, so that Van gave his brother a wink. There were other visitors pushing to get in. The guard looked upset with all she had to do.

They'd put down they were cousins of Walls, since you had to be family.

"That's what Levi put us down as on his list. They don't give a shit."

Walls was tall, had lank hair that fell over his cheeks, long arms, and big farmer-looking hands. He seemed older than Tom whose age he was supposed to be. He sat at the table with his family. The room was a gymnasium the rest of the week, and pieces of equipment had been shoved out of the way, tables and benches brought in. It was so crowded you were next to people all the time, brushing against them or touching them. They were always putting their hands on you to get by. The noise level was like gunfire, and you had to yell to be heard. There were blacks and other minorities with their families pushing up against you, yelling, taking picnics out of bags. Royal wasn't used to seeing so many black people together. Inside of ten minutes, with the noise and action, he had a headache.

Van had gotten to know people as usual. He circulated, had a few words with cons in their starched green fatigues. He would get himself right in there with the con and his family, put his hand on someone's arm, listen, grin at whatever was said.

Walls sat with his big red hand in some young blond girl's. Nobody introduced Royal to anybody. There were two older women in Walls's group, in flowered dresses as if they were in church, his mother and grandmother probably. Nobody spoke more than three words to anyone else. The girl and Levi would kiss each other and grope around, whisper a little from time to time. Royal couldn't see what Van saw in the man. He looked like the poor mountain people you meet, tall and stoop-shouldered, with long jaws and noses and bad teeth, like one of Paul Beam's cousins. Other cons were hanging on to their women, all but making out in public. It didn't seem to bother anybody. There were three guards, one at a little desk on a raised platform, a shotgun standing in a locked rack beside him. He was in charge. The others were unarmed. Even though you'd already done it at check-in, you were supposed to show the head guard anything you wanted to give a prisoner. Van went up with his packages, took the man's hand like they were friends, talked to him. The guard turned the cigarette carton over, looked at the belt, gave it all back, went to mark something down in his papers, then didn't bother. He seemed human about it. It was just the way Van had said, common and everyday.

Van yelled to him above the racket, "Crazy, ain't it? Just like home!" He looked the room over, grinning.

Royal remembered the convicts he'd seen in the transport and wondered if any of them were here. He watched the tall con standing nearest. He was black as coffee, had his head shaved, big shoulders. He wore prison pants, a black vest that looked like silk, and fancy shoes with stacked heels. The woman with him had one of those tall frizzy hairdos. You could see the nipples of her breasts in the tight thing like a sleeve she wore. He had her by the back of the neck, his face to hers, telling her some story, at the same time working his hips slowly with hers. He looked up at Royal once, right into his eyes, but didn't see him.

Royal watched Van's friend Levi. The man looked soft. There was a boil on his neck, a shaving cut with a piece of toilet paper stuck to the spot of blood. His aftershave smelled like he'd poured on everything in the drugstore. He never spoke to Royal, hardly spoke to Van, didn't mention the gift Van had brought. He kissed the blond girl. You could see his big tongue pushing into her mouth.

They all looked as if they had been in a hot bath for an hour, the cons. Some wore slippers, a few had bathrobes over their regular pants and T-shirts, like they were at home on Sunday. You could imagine they almost enjoyed it here, the way Van said Levi did. It was as if you were disturbing them by coming in. They ate the food people brought, held on to the women, had their kids on their laps, but it was like they wanted to get back to their cells and be with each other, as if the outside world disturbed them.

"You didn't talk to Levi any," Royal said on the way home.

"He was wrapped up in Barb. He's thinking about marrying her while he's still doing time. She wants it and his mother wants it, but I tell him he'll regret it. It puts her in an awkward position. The trouble is, they see each other in that environment and get emotional."

He drove fast up into the mountains, rapping the wheel with his knuckles to the music.

"I can't deal with Levi. He's lazy and won't confide in me. He can't see I'm trying to help him." He asked, "What did you think?"

"I guess there's worse places."

"You saw its good side. But it's like you say. There's worse places. My problem would be, if I went in on a sentence, I know too many guys, have too much on them. I'm not referring to these particular cons I talked to today. They're all good guys, though they're acquainted with some of the ones I mean. The fact is, there are men in that place will kill you for ten cartons of cigarettes, which is the going rate, and there are some of those would do it to me for half that."

"Jesus, Van, why?"

"Suffish it to say I'd as soon not go in, though I guess I'd survive if I did with my connections. They don't like Levi much better, and he don't have the reputation I have. He shouldn't be there at all. It's as dangerous as a battlefield for him in that place. That's what I'm working on so hard, Roy."

After a while, his mood different, seeming to sink, he said, "Listen. Don't be a worrier, not about Jackie Pastor or anything else. It's all under control."

A few days later Van telephoned near midnight from some bar. Royal could hear the commotion of the place behind him.

"You all right, baby?"

He talked like that when he was very drunk: baby brother, baby. "What's shaking up there? Down there."

"Nothing."

"Waiting for Lou to get home."

"I don't wait up for her. I'm drinking a beer."

"So how did you like it?"

Van meant the prison visit. Every time he'd seen him or talked to him since, he asked what he thought of it. Royal was tired of telling him.

"Hell of a place," Van said when Royal didn't answer.

He was quiet so long the younger brother thought he'd walked away from his pay phone.

The operator asked Van to signal when he was through.

"I'll let you know, darling," in the drunk voice.

"Give me the number, Van."

"There ain't any here. I'll tell you the truth, I don't know where I'm at."

Royal waited.

"I believe I'm in Albany, but it's uncertain." He began to laugh. "That bothers me. Where the fuck am I?"

"I don't know if you don't."

"I don't know where I am, and I don't believe I have a vehicle, so I can't tell you how I got here."

After another long silence he said, "I just asked a man. I'm in Troy. I won't get back home tonight. So, really, what the hell did you think of Levi Walls?"

"He was all right, Van. I liked him."

"No, you didn't. He's a prick. But he's all right too. Trouble is, I'm his friend, so I can't get out of it. He begs me to bring in coke and shit, and I do it from time to time. Make a note of that, Operator." He said, "I guess I won't get back tonight. I think I came down here to meet a business contact. If I did, I'm still waiting. What time is it?"

"After twelve."

Royal was sitting at the table under the wall phone in Mrs. Marquette's kitchen. His beer was on a counter, and he could not reach it. He could hear Mrs. Marquette through the thin walls, groaning in her sleep.

Van said, "You know how I carry the shit in? Well, I won't tell you, but suffish to say I can get any damn thing into that place I feel like. So where is Lou by the way?"

"At her job."

"Look out for her. You hear? Take care of her. You have to like Lou." He said, "Listen. I called to tell you this right here. Empty your mind and listen, baby."

Royal waited.

"Sometimes I don't mean what I say, and sometimes I will say things and forget what I said." He spoke in an interested voice, as if he was talking about someone else's problem. "I'm surprised at it myself, and I only know because people tell me. Now, I'm going to remember this here conversation. I don't mean this. But I'll have reliable people come and tell me I said some foolish thing, whatever it was, and I can't even recall it. I understand I'll do things too, make a deal, handshake, then forget. Do you understand?"

"You're okay, Van. There's nothing wrong with you."

"You hope. Listen. I'm saying this for your good, so you'll understand. Don't just hope. I'm tying up some loose ends here, and that's one of them. You can't strike a bargain and then forget it. You're going to get something, and they'll expect you to give something back for it. You can't get out of it because you forget."

Royal was taken on at the steel locker factory in Sunrise, where he had worked before. They had an order from a downstate school and needed extra help, so that though it was temporary it paid well.

Van and two men he'd been to school with were taking a few hardwoods out of Mona's lot, cutting and splitting them, and carrying the cords of firewood to the capital district to sell.

If he remembered the phone call he made from Troy, he didn't mention it. He seemed in good condition, almost too alert, Royal saw, like he was on something to speed him up.

"Watch you don't cut yourself on that sheet metal again is all," he said about Royal's job. "That's the hazard, those edges."

"Maybe they'll send me with the order to help install it."

"Good. You'll get away, travel, get out from under for a while."

Van would look around the Marquette kitchen sharply, tease

the widow, tease Lou in a sharp, alert way. Each brother had been best man at the other's wedding, their wives maid or matron of honor. They all flirted, but this was not flirting. These days when Van teased her, Lou turned away or even left the room. He would come stamping in directly from his work in his dirty clothes, hands banged up, sawdust in his hair, get his beer, give everything his sharp, serious look, go to work on Mrs. Marquette.

"I hope you're not one of those believe everything you read in that book," he said to her.

He would take the Bible out of her hands, turn it around as if he didn't know which way was up, read in a loud voice so she could hear.

"You don't believe in that, do you, Annie?"

"Yes, she believes in it," Lou would say angrily.

"You believe in miracles?"

"I surely do," Mrs. Marquette said when she understood him.

He was amazed. "Really?"

Lou said, "She tells you she does, Van, so don't joke like that. Nobody appreciates it."

"I'm not joking. I want to believe in such things myself, so I have to know how she does it."

"There's no trick in it. It's just faith."

"Maybe I want to learn faith."

On nights Lou worked late, he sometimes waited with Royal.

"You're past your curfew, ain't you?"—when she came in at last.

"That's for Roy to say."

"It's for somebody to."

"She had to work late, Van."

"I hope she's well rewarded."

"Don't be so damn funny, Van," she said.

"Is that what I am? And I feel so sad."

He kept the sharp, angry way with her.

He'd started a new mustache, this one growing down over the corners of his small mouth; Fu Manchu, he called it. There was a tuft of beard in the center of his chin: the goatee. It made his pale skin whiter.

"How do you like it?"

Lou said, "Don't ask me. What does Janet think? Just don't worry about when I come in at night, all right? Worry about Janet Colby and Pauline West and all the things you're into."

"Janet threw me out. I thought you knew."

"But you're not back with Pauline, I know that too. Since you ask, it makes you look like a little old man, the little whiskers."

"You never see any fault in him," she would say to Royal later.

"We get along."

"He leads you wherever he feels like. Takes you into that prison. What's all that about? He gets in trouble, you'll be in trouble, Roy."

"I'm all right."

"I seriously doubt it. Is this where you want to be? You're scared half to death most of the time."

The older brother said he wasn't seeing anybody, Janet or anyone else. He told Royal he'd stopped visiting Levi Walls. "Since that's worrying Miss Lou, I thought I'd tell you. I did a hell of a lot of work on that boy, but he won't try to do any good for himself, so I give up."

He was not talking anymore about enemies in the prison or the CIA, a lot of which Royal thought wasn't even half true, a smoke screen Van had put down for some reason of his own that no longer applied.

There was a late April storm, a freak, and Van stayed the

night because he didn't want to risk Mona's truck on the slippery roads. He made up Mrs. Marquette's sofa with blankets, charming her the way he could when his mood was right, and he and Royal sat by the wood stove drinking most of a case of beer and talking until nearly dawn—old family history, good things as well as bad. Royal could not explain it to Lou when she asked about it. It was talk, the way brothers talk: history, the blood that made them what they were. They were Van and Royal, and that was it. It wasn't a question of somebody leading somebody.

At breakfast Van had told the widow, teasing, that she reminded him of their own mother, giving Royal his wink: And you know what I thought of her, it said. Lou did not like it.

"Tell your brother not to worry Mrs. Marquette. She doesn't share his sense of humor."

"Tell Lou to mind her business, sonny."

He came out one midnight after he had been someplace, got his beer, looked around with the angry black-ringed eyes.

"Well, where is she now?"

Royal said she was working late.

"You better get you an affidavit."

"Come on, Van."

He'd had a new tattoo done. He had a rose that was almost faded out and a leopard with his battalion's number and the motto "Untamed" under it on a banner. The new one, on his right forearm, showed two links of chain, his name on one, Pauline's on the other.

"Where'd you get it done?"

"Albany, that street where they say they cleaned the whores out of, which they didn't. Why does Lou work late so much?"

"Never mind, Van."

Already half knowing what was coming.

"They say only a fool or a savage decorates himself. I suppose

I'll get hepatitis on top of everything else. I wanted to do something for Pauline."

He rolled up his other sleeve. "Look at this."

There were round raw wounds on the upper part of his left forearm, four or five in a row like red flowers.

"Cigarette burns."

"Shit, who did it?"

"I did it. I take bets. People say I can't hold the burning end down a specific period of time. Three seconds, five. The longer I do, the bigger the payoff. Do it in bars. I earned money on these. I don't say it's worth it. I ain't even sure it's legal."

"Shit."

The wounds were bright red, black at the edges, each about the size of a quarter. They glistened with what looked like salve.

"Antibiotic. I take chances but control the odds. I'm showing you this for your personal edification, show how you can make a living in a pinch. It's nobody else's business, so don't tell nobody."

He said, "What does she do—walk out from the bus this hour?"

Royal waited.

Van began to chew on the cuticle of his thumb, looking around angrily. He had rolled down his sleeves.

"Well, fuck it anyway." He said at last, "I saw Lou in Bradford the other week."

Royal answered, not knowing why, "That's okay."

"She was with What's-his-name? That man you know, I heard you mention."

"How the hell do I know, Van?" Get it over with. "Shit"—the feeling of sickness filling him—"Bobby Argyle, I guess you mean."

"That's the one."

Van had been in a bar called Trader John's, a tourist place usually empty, stopped in, and there was Lou with this man he'd observed around Bradford before. She'd seen Van too, he said, spoke a few words to him. "She didn't mention it?"

"They were just talking," Royal said. "Ran into each other." As if she'd told him about it.

Van said, "She's been waiting to see if I'll tell you. Rather, when. She'd know I have to."

"Well, you did."

"Hey, Roy."

"That's all right."

"They were drinking beer and talking, like you said."

The rest of it was he'd waited in his pickup, they came out after about twenty minutes, got into Argyle's car, an old Pinto, and took off, laid down rubber as if they knew someone was watching and didn't care.

That was it.

"You know I had to tell you."

He said, "You want my advice, get it into the open."

When she came in and he heard her downstairs taking off her shoes, then climbing up to undress in the dark, Royal pretended to be asleep. He kept to his side of the bed. He did not need this. It brought it back on him. Now he would have to pick it all up again, carry it. He was too tired.

"Are you awake?" she said.

He was the silent brother. That was the name he'd made for himself in his family, in school: quiet, kept his words to himself. He was Snake. He lay sleepless while she slept beside him. It was always when you needed sleep most you couldn't get it. He wouldn't think of her with Argyle yet, and maybe he could sleep.

In the morning he referred to it.

"That's Van," she said, mad right away.

She was dressing the way she did when she wanted to put him off, getting into her underwear with her nightgown on, turning her back so he could not see anything.

"I ran into Bobby, and Van was there. It's none of his business. It's my business and maybe yours."

"I guess it's mine. No maybe."

"He wanted to talk to someone, and I'm an old friend of his. It's about his wife, and he asked me not to discuss it. I'll say this in case you're jealous, which I guess is what's going on here, he's crazy about her. He had one beer and I had a diet drink of some kind, I forget, and he gave me a lift to the top of the road, and that's the end of it. I walked home."

"How come you didn't say anything?"

"It wasn't worth mentioning, and anyhow Bobby's entitled to privacy the same way you are."

"And that's all."

"That's all."

"Didn't you figure Van would say something?"

She said stubbornly, "It's none of his damn business, Roy. I told you. Get that part of it clear. Now excuse me, I have this house to do. And don't tell Van West about Bobby's problem either."

"I don't know what it is."

When he saw Van again he said, "It's all right. He was just giving her a lift, and they stopped off. They talked about a problem he has in his marriage."

"Who's that, sonny?"

Royal had to remind him of the whole thing.

"Well, that's good, ain't it? You're satisfied."

"We talked it through. There's nothing in it."

"Well, there, you see? All right."

Van was squinting as if he could not quite see him. They were in town in front of the Nook. If someone they knew passed,

Van did not respond to the greeting. It was as if he needed his attention for the one thing.

"What are you on?"

Looking hard at him, focusing: "I'm *on* the fucking sidewalk."

He said, "Maybe Lou ought to have a baby."

"We want security first."

"You wait for that, you'll never do anything."

A few nights later Royal heard a car's motor in the road outside the house, went to a front window, and saw it wasn't a Pinto. An old Plymouth. It idled, the muffler on it shot. After a while he heard the front door and Lou coming upstairs.

"I got a lift from someone I met," she said. "Works in town waiting tables the same hours I have. She gets through a little later because she has to clean up. I waited for her. It's her husband's car."

And a couple of nights after that, one of those phone calls where the person won't speak. Mrs. Marquette kept saying, "Who is this, please? I don't hear good." Until she finally hung up.

When it happened again she handed the phone to Royal.

"Who is this?" And then: "Bobby?"

Nothing.

He didn't say anything to Lou, and it did not happen again.

Van said he was working at a new job, skidding logs out of a woodlot north of Bradford Lake. They had to work fast, before the thaw got going. The lumber was for flooring, furniture, and TV cabinets. The business part interested Van.

"The hardwood market's at a high point. When the building trades are down you cut oak, birch, etcetera. When they're up you have the white pine. If Japan don't want it, Canada does. You're always in business. They're good guys to work with too. Tough but fair. I was running it, I'd hire these same men.

There's one or two hard-nosed ones you have to avoid or put in their place."

He would come from work scratched, his knuckles raw, not upset about it. He got into fights, showed up with his face marked, the skin around one eye yellow and shiny, the eye closed. He said he didn't mind. He still had the alert, sharp, unsmiling way Royal had noticed.

"I walked into a two-hundred-and-fifty-pound door. I couldn't begin to say what we were yelling at each other about, except maybe one of us said some denigrating thing concerning the other.

"I'm all right. I like the work. All that paranoid shit I go through? I'm better. I sleep. I'd say I'm really all right now, Roy."

"You look worn down to me."

"I'm good. Believe it."

He said, "Roy, what we could do is get a bank loan, lease some equipment. We'd get a skidder for maybe sixty thousand, that's the single big item. We'd buy the truck off Mona, two or three chain saws, start off farming her lot, give her her royalty. We'd leave her younger trees for growth investment, cut the shitty stuff out, the sick ones. They say you're working for John Deere and the bank, but it don't have to be that way. Be intelligent farmers, keep up the interest and principal so your credit's good."

Get the money, go into business for themselves: why not?

Then he'd forget about it, be onto something else.

He came out from his job, showed the bruises and cuts he'd earned, some from work, some from scraps. He seemed all right, putting himself down in his serious way. "I can't fight worth a shit, Roy. I'm just like a child to these mountain men. They straighten me out when I get too smart-assed. Some connection of Paul Beam's up there weighs three hundred pounds before he has breakfast and about three-fifty after it. He knows he can take me with one hand, but he also knows I'd make him sweat for it just a little. They like to brawl now and then, that's all. It's their fun."

It fascinated him the way the business part of it did.

"An Asian won't be that way. To him a fight means he's honor bound to kill you. Go home and get his knife and take you out, get a piece and come back." He did the Oriental accent: " 'What was that you said to me, please?' He's dead serious. It's honor but different to ours because the same things don't upset him. You don't put their ancestors down in any way, shape, or form. That's a capital offense. I don't say we don't have the same violence. Now here's something will interest you."

He said, "They have a man up there, I've met him, though he don't work with this particular company. He's a logger. He killed a man in Wyoming, a game warden, murdered him because he didn't like him for some I guess sufficient reason, and he got away with it. I'm serious as can be. He dropped out of sight, went to Texas or someplace, then a couple of years ago his friends told him it was safe to come back to that area, and he did. Later he came east to this place. He's got a wife and family now, lives a peaceful normal life, works regular. It was known to all the authorities, but there wasn't real evidence against him, and they couldn't touch him. What do you think of that? A little something for your files."

Each night during these spring weeks Royal waited to hear a car idling in the yard across the road from the house, for Lou to come upstairs. He didn't know if it was Argyle in the car or not. It happened three nights out of five on average. The car would stay ten or fifteen minutes, its motor going, then a door slammed, and it drove away, throwing up gravel. When Lou came in she would say something about her friend, about what they had discussed. He did not respond much one way or the other. After a week more of it she started to take the bus again and walk in from the state road.

Janet Colby began to call him. His brother was asleep on her sofa. She couldn't move him.

"I'm expecting someone, Roy."

"What do you want me to do?"

"I'll put the phone to his ear, and you say something."

It made him laugh.

"Yell at him, Roy. I'm not kidding."

She sounded all right, not really mad. He heard Van's voice, probably a little drunk. After a while he got on. "What do you want?"

"I don't want anything," Royal said.

"Then fuck off."

"Is Janet sore?"

"She don't like either one of us anymore. Strange but true."

He heard Janet: "If you're not going to be serious, hang that up, Van. I'm expecting someone, and I want you to leave."

"I guess you better leave," Royal said.

"I guess I better."

That seemed all right. Van wasn't especially stoned or drunk. It was the usual way they scrapped with each other. But Janet called one night late and said, "I'm sorry if I'm disturbing you and Lou, honey. I want you to come over here tomorrow morning before you go to work."

Her voice was odd.

"You stop by," she said when he asked what was wrong. "I've had more than enough of him, and we're going to put an end to it, by legal means if need be."

He found her with a man.

"This is Carl Thompson, a friend."

He was a little bearded man of forty-five or fifty. He smiled at Roy. If there was going to be trouble, it wouldn't come from him. He guessed he was the mechanic from downstate. He wore plaid golf pants and sat with his legs up in Janet's recliner, smoking a pipe.

Janet's mouth looked funny, twisted. There were brown patches of tiredness under her eyes.

"Well, he hit me for the last time, Roy. He comes up here with his friends, and they act like I'm the servant. They try things out too. Like if he can mistreat me, they can."

"Who are his friends?"

"Never mind that. I don't even know. This time I called Carl, and he came and chased Van out. Now this is as far as I'm prepared to go with Van West and his problems, Roy. What shall I do? You tell me."

Royal stared at her.

"Because let me inform you your brother's a sick man. I suppose you're aware of it. Everyone else in town is. Why don't I go to the police? That's funny. Maybe I can't, the position I'm in."

He said, "I know Van gets upset easy."

"Now listen, Royal. I'm in earnest on this. I am nobody's punching bag, and I don't want my mind messed with. I'm not his wife, and I'm not his girlfriend, not anymore. He can't seem to get that into his head. Do you think the fact he's been through a lot, suffered, is any reason he should put me through it?"

She waited for his answer like a teacher.

"No."

"Well, that's something anyhow. You tell Van I'm an old lady, damn near old enough to be your mother if not his, and I have had all I can take of the West brothers and their strange ways. Can you get him to keep off?"

"I guess I could talk to him."

"Yes, but can you get him to keep off? I doubt it. I know you will, but will he? I'm just about to get a bond on him, Roy, whatever the risk to me. Carl says I should do it. Tell me why I shouldn't."

She waited.

"Well, there it is," she said. "You can't tell me."

She looked at him.

"Come in here," she said. "Will you excuse us a minute, Carl? Give me and Roy a chance to settle this."

She led him into the bedroom and closed the door. She sat on the edge of the bed and waited until he sat down too. Her perfume was powerful in here.

"Do you know how scared I am of him and the kind of people he runs with?"

He said again, "Who are they?"

"Never mind that. Do you know I'm afraid for my life? My very existence? He scares me. If he's done half the things he says he's done, either overseas or here at home, then I have every right in the world to be scared, don't you think? Do you know he comes at four in the morning and yells and carries on until I let him in? Or he'll sit on my doorstep and cry? Then he comes in—I have to let him in so he doesn't disturb the neighbors—I say something, look at him a certain way, he takes offense and starts to manhandle me, Roy. Or he comes with one of his friends, I don't exactly welcome them, and he starts on me. Here."

She stood, lifted the skirt of her housecoat. He saw blotchy spreading bruises on her thighs. She pulled it higher so he could see the marks on her full naked stomach and, lower down at the edge of the bush, scratches, black-and-blue marks, yellow bruises.

She dropped the skirt.

"Now, not to embarrass you any more than you are, but so

you'll understand me and him too: He wants to get it on with me, and ninety percent of the time he can't, Roy. Eighty, ninety percent of the time he can't get it up. Am I clear?"

He nodded.

"I want you to understand. I'm telling you this to help you handle him, not to embarrass either one of you, because I like you, Roy. I'll go down in the morning to get my car and go to work, seven-thirty A.M., and he's sitting in that rusted-out truck, asleep. He's usually there at night, now it's the mornings too. He'll let me be for a space, then start again. Or he wants to humiliate me, brings his friends in. I won't go into it, but maybe you can guess. Unless I permit him in my apartment to do it, he refuses to wash or change his clothes. Am I starting to get through to you on some of this? Because I'm telling you, Royal, he needs serious help. Those blackouts. These fights he's getting into. He's a real war casualty, classic case, and he requires psychotherapy if he's going to get better. Does he quote the Bible at you?"

For the first time she had said something to surprise him.

"No."

"He does to me. He'll pick up that family Bible out there and be all over it. Quote from it. I don't have a thing against normal religion, but I worry like hell about religious fanatics."

He felt the same sickness he'd experienced when Van told him he saw Lou with Bobby Argyle. He didn't know why. This particular thing was the least of what she was saying, yet it made him sick.

"He's no fanatic. He never mentions that."

"I'm telling you he sits and reads out of that Bible and not in any rational way, not even like he knows what it means, yet he'll go on for half an hour at a time, throwing out these words like they're magic. I call that fanatic, and I don't like it."

She watched him.

"Honey, listen," she said in a softer voice. "Talk to him. And if you can't, get your daddy to. He's doing himself an injury, and he's going to injure others on this road he's going down."

Royal said nothing.

"If he touches me again or does some trick to humiliate me, I'll go to the state police, and this time I'll take his stories with me, his tales of violence, and let them make out of it what they will. I'm telling you this particular aspect of it because I trust you. You tell him I said it, and God knows what he'll do to me or have done to me. Look right into my eyes and you'll see I'm in earnest."

"Did she say I'm crazy? That's okay. You think I don't know what people say where I'm concerned?"

They were at Mona's and their father's place for a cookout on the Sunday of Memorial Day weekend, everyone polite to each other, joking. There had been a parade earlier. The high school band, vets marching, baton twirlers. Royal had seen Van on the sidewalk on the other side of the street, the first time in almost two weeks, and his brother made one of his goofy faces, bugging his eyes, letting his jaw drop. Look at these fools, he meant.

"One time I brought in a friend of mine. One time! Man I knew in the service. It was late, we got her out of bed, and she had to make us some coffee because we were a little tight. She's still sore about that? Shit!"

Lou was helping to barbecue and serve. She was in a good humor, affectionate to Royal. She brought him his beer, put a hand on him whenever she passed. It was a good day, the sun with some warmth in it for the first time. Other parties were going on in the mobile home park, and they spilled into each other, everybody's kids running around and getting underfoot. Van had helped organize a softball game, then walked around for awhile carrying his fat redheaded son and yelling at people, being funny. Now he stood on the back porch he had helped his father build onto the house before Wayne West's stroke, the sun in his face, squinting at his brother through the smoke from his cigarette.

"Except for that one time, I never bring my friends around. She makes up shit to worry you and get back at me. I hit her when she calls me crazy because that's what she does it for," he said. "I don't really get mad, and I don't hit her hard. She wants me to do it and prob'ly wants other people to do it. It's those people are marking her, not me. I read the Bible as a joke, for Christ's sake! She has absolutely no sense of humor if the joke happens to be on her. She looks at you like a dumb squaw: 'What's that?' She never caught on to a joke in her life."

"She sounded like she'll go to court and get a warrant."

"She won't. All she wants is you on her side. She'll say any shit to impress you. You think she's scared of me? She goes on at me to see what I'll do, how far she can push it. It turns her on when I get mad at her. She's close to this guy Thompson now, and he's a nice guy, straight, so Janet's feeling clean. When she's in that mood she can't admit to herself she was ever in any other kind of mood, can't admit her wild side. I know Thompson didn't beat her up. I don't know who did. She's Fox Indian, Roy. One person drunk, another sober, and she lies like a rug both ways. You have to understand that to deal with her. I know she had you in her bed a couple of weeks ago. What do you think that was for?"

Royal didn't say anything.

"That's all right. She made sure I knew about it. She saw I didn't care, and that made her mad. She did it to gain control over me through you, use you like she's doing right now, because her mood's changed and she wants to be a straight arrow." His voice was quiet. "She ain't *afraid* of me, Roy. Who do you think started all this clowning with the coke and all? Me? Van West and that cocaine are the only excitement she has in her dull life, and she can't afford to let it dry up. She's come to realize that over the months. Never mind Thompson. When it gets down to it, it's all your brother."

He smiled into the sunlight, watching his family.

"Now, don't tell me weather don't make a difference. I feel like a new man. You rise up in the spring. Winter's just like death."

His hair had been cut. He was clean-shaven, had new clothes on. He spread his arms and hands.

"Do I look like I sleep in my truck, sonny?"

There were still scabs on his cheekbones and the backs of his hands, but they were small now; the bruises were fading. You couldn't see the cigarette burns.

"You look okay."

Van yelled, "Hey, momma!" to Pauline, who was carrying a tray of things down the back steps.

"Did I tell you I opened an account in her name? Every cent I got logging and selling firewood went into it. Over fifteen hundred. I kept back ten percent for these clothes and a few expenses."

The logging was finished. Royal had been laid off because the order for the school lockers was filled.

"No matter how bad I need that money I can't touch it. It's my gift to her and this child she has coming."

He said, "Listen. I won't give Janet any more trouble since

it worries you. I won't see her. That's all I need to know, that it worries you. I don't see her, she won't have cause to complain."

Later Tom Bundy took Royal aside. Each had a hamburger on a paper plate, a beer. They stood under one of the trees at the edge of the trailer park. Bundy was drunk, happy with family around, his pink face close to his brother-in-law's so that though no one was near he could show his story was a secret.

"You ain't gonna believe me."

He started to laugh and couldn't get going. It made Royal laugh.

"I'll believe it!"

Here it was: They had been back to Locust Grove one more time to see Levi Walls, and Van had smuggled a toy gun in to see if he could.

"Jesus!"

"Ain't it crazy!"

Tom stared into Royal's eyes, delighted. Royal glanced at Van, who was on the other side of the yard listening to his stepmother talk.

"He walked in, took this fucking thing in in his bag of stuff, food, and then before the outside guard got to him he said he had to go to the john, had diarrhea. It was all worked out beforehand. Jesus, Roy! I didn't know the first thing about any of it until it was done, or I wouldn't have let him do it. He had the thing wrapped in Saran Wrap or something. He was pretending to himself it was a real gun and he had to protect it, like there were bullets in it. He goes in, puts it in the toilet tank, comes back out. They do the body search, look in the bag. He says, 'Oh, Christ, here I go again,' runs back into the toilet, and gets the gun! Are you listening to this? We walk in. The other guard's in there who you're supposed to show stuff to? Van holds the bag up across the room, the guard just nods. It's okay. He already knows Van, so it's all right! He had it all worked out like that. Shit!"

Tom looked across at his brother-in-law, starting to laugh again.

"Levi practically fainted when he saw it. Turned pale. He looks in the bag. Van says, 'You take a good look in there, motherfucker. I brought you in a piece, now you can escape from this shit-hole you're in.' Jesus! Levi just turned white as paper. You could see it happen to him. 'Go on,' Van says, 'take your fucking fate in your hands for once.' 'Holy God, Van, please carry that right back out. I can't take that upstairs. I'll lose my fucking good time!' I thought I'd die. I mean it looked real, Roy. Like a police Colt. Levi thought it was real! Of course, even if it wasn't, he's fucked if he's caught with it.

"We get out," Tom said, "I turn to him. 'Jesus, Van!' I just about killed him right there. He says, 'I did it to show I can take anything in there I like. Get him an assault rifle, blast him out of that prison.' "

Van had looked up, hearing his name, smiling at Tom's big laugh. He probably knew what story he was telling. Royal gave his brother a look, shook his head: What can I do with you? But he was smiling too. Afterward people kept asking what was so funny. Van went around, and when he caught Tom's eye or Royal's, they could not help laughing.

Royal said, "I sure like the way you're careful."

"That was then. This is now," Van said. "I turned over a new leaf today. Memorial Day."

Royal just wandered after that in a kind of happy daze, ate his dessert, a cake Iris had baked, watched the kids play their games. Wayne West got down the steps of the porch into the yard without help and stood blinking in the sun, his hair on end, ash from his cigarette spilling all over him. He didn't smile, never did, but Royal could see he felt good. Royal watched Van talk to him, serious, the father and son. He looked at Lou playing with the little kids. She smoothed her skirt under her and sat on her heels. He knew now there wasn't anything between her and Argyle. He thought, watching: Maybe we ought to have a kid. You could just about see Pauline was pregnant.

He thought: This is the way it should be. No matter what went down, there was the family. Never mind anything else—the stories, the things Van got into. Against all reason he felt happy.

One of Iris's children had been given a rabbit for Easter. She had it out of its box, and it was hopping slowly this way and that in the warm ground mist the sunshine had raised. Kids and grownups stood around, Lou among them, everyone quiet and restrained so as not to scare the timid animal. It was a good size, with big black and white blotches all over it. Royal saw it wasn't really scared. It hopped a few slow steps in each direction, probably looking for a treat. It made him feel an ache of affection in his shoulder, which he guessed was what they meant by the heart aching.

He'd only had a few beers, but he felt drunk. He sat on the bottom step of the stairs that led to the porch. You could see the cemetery through the trees, most of the stones at this end gray with age, mossy, a few new hard-edged monuments rising farther off against the sky. You could see the fresh Memorial Day flowers that had been set out, the little flags. He thought of the dead there, past caring. All right. He would come to that too. It didn't matter. He thought of that Porter in the old river road cemetery who'd died in the Civil War, whose death he had imagined. They ought to have gone out, put some flowers down. The family didn't pray as far as he knew, except Iris, but you could be quiet out there, think things over. He leaned back on his elbows on the step above him and looked up the length of the big trees, their leaves just starting, into the soaring sky, felt the more or less weak warmth of the new sun. Tears filled his eyes.

He went into Sunrise that night by himself and, already half drunk, drank beer. The mood of the afternoon persisted. It had rained a little. He stared drunkenly at the lights making their long legs of color in the wet street, saw into the pharmacy with its pink light, the bright bins full of things. The bars, people standing up two, three deep. He watched the kids on the curbs on both sides of the street, yelling at each other over the jacked-up cars that moved past, the guys in the cars looking as if they didn't care. It was like watching himself, he thought.

Finally the beer and the kids made him feel both randy and a little sick.

He thought: Let's talk to Janet, be sympathetic. When he got to her street and looked up, he saw lights. He also saw a man climbing her outside stairs. No score for Royal that night. It wasn't Thompson. Two men. He saw one was Van, recognized the hat, looked around but couldn't see the pickup. There was the Mustang, though, Pastor's car. Jackie Pastor going into Janet's with his brother. No real surprise after all, yet shit. . . .

He thought: To hell with it, the good of the day draining out.

10

Early in June, Van said he and Royal were invited to a wedding in Bradford. There was going to be a bachelor party on a Friday night, the wedding in a Catholic church in town the following noon. Van had rented his outfit and had money for Royal to rent his. The groom was a friend who had been overseas a couple of years before Van's tour and was a WIA. "He lost a leg. Greg Prevost's his name. He's a good guy." The bride came from somewhere in the south, a nurse, he understood. He didn't know her. "You have to come, Roy. I got him to ask you."

He'd brought an invitation. It had both their names on the envelope.

"I never heard of him."

"Now you heard of him. I've known him off and on since he came out of the service. He's a good guy."

He led Royal to the window in Mrs. Marquette's kitchen. "I have it for the week."

A new Chevrolet Monte Carlo.

"What did you do, steal it?"

"Come on. I leased this car."

They went out and sat in it. It was green, had deep bucket

seats of cream-colored leather or a material as good as leather. The windows were watery green. Van started the motor, turned on the radio, the air-conditioning. "I had it up to ninety for about a minute on the limited access, and I was doing seventy, seventy-five on the state road. It hangs onto curves like it's glued."

He got the rental contract out of the glove box and showed it.

"Where'd you get the money?"

"Why do you want to know? I have money, for Christ's sake. I know where to get it."

"Shit."

"Mona and Pauline think I won in the lottery. Our daddy figures whatever I say I'm into something crooked. Like you, only you do it because you're such a miserable bastard."

He let Royal drive to Mona and Wayne's, showed him his outfit, the tux, the studs and cuff links in their plush-covered box.

"You go to the same place, Danny's, in South Bradford, give Prevost's name. He wants everybody in the groom's party the same. I'll give you cash, you take the Monte Carlo and go over. Take the car. Your only problem may be shoes. You can dye old brown ones or get it done. I may buy a pair yet, patents. I don't know."

"How come I'm in the groom's party?"

"I asked him."

Royal said he guessed it was all right. He would go. He studied the suit, which he liked. Lou would think he looked good in it.

The party met at the best man's place, an apartment in a village on the eastern shore of the lake with marinas and tourist motels. They all drank but didn't seem in any hurry to get drunk. They didn't horse around or play tricks the way they had at Royal's party or Van's. One of the things they did was tell stories about other parties, as if this wasn't one of them. They also talked quietly about war experiences, which made Royal feel left out. The best man's wife had gone somewhere for the evening, so they sat, all men, in the darkening apartment talking and watching the sun set over the water. Around eleven they got into cars and drove around the south end of the lake into Bradford Village, and by midnight they were still drinking in one or another of the bars and still fairly quiet.

Prevost was a tall heavy man of about twenty-eight, already losing his hair in front, which made him seem older. He told stories that made the others laugh, then looked surprised, as if he didn't know what was funny. You could see the mechanical leg work under his jeans as he dragged it forward, its shoe uncreased and new-looking. Royal liked him, the way he handled himself, slapping at the leg when it didn't do what he wanted, talking to it.

Jackie Pastor was there. He came late, shook everyone's hand like a politician, and started right in with jokes. He looked at Royal and asked Prevost, "You sure this one's old enough? I got a few ripe stories."

Van was wearing pieces of his uniform, which he had not done since the night of the event the previous Thanksgiving: his tunic with its stripes, the camouflage pants tucked into polished combat boots. Royal supposed he did it because they were all vets there, though his brother was the only one dressed that way. It embarrassed him a little. Nobody else seemed to care except Pastor. "We going to have a war, West?" Pastor told his jokes but, like Prevost, didn't laugh, just lowered his eyelids or looked away. Royal had not mentioned to Van seeing Pastor go into Janet's. He guessed his brother had something on him, but you couldn't tell what it would be. In the car going to Bradford he told Van he didn't like being in the same place with him.

"That cop's okay. He won't shoot unless you draw down on him first. No, him and Greg are good friends, and that's why he's here. They were in some airborne division together and rode helicopters. Except for the fact he feels he has to arrest me every once in a while, Jackie's all right, just sort of boring. He'll put you to sleep the way he talks. Watch him drink. A man who can hold his liquor, usually you see in his eyes how much he's had, but Jackie won't show even that. The iron man."

The policeman was several years older than Van and Greg Prevost, short and narrow-waisted, with big shoulders. He looked like a quarterback, which was what he had been for a time in high school. He had dark hair with gray in it already, a sharp Irish nose. He had been married but was divorced now and lived alone. His wife had the kids. He told his raunchy stories in a monotone that made you feel tired like Van said, lowered his eyelids instead of smiling. When you talked he listened hard the way you'd think a cop would, as if he wanted you to trip yourself up. If he liked what he heard, he nodded, said, "That's good." If an anecdote surprised him: "That's different." He dressed like the part-time cowboy he was, even on an occasion like this—the western clothes and heel boots. If there was a gun on him, you couldn't see where it was, unless he hid it in a boot, which was possible. He kept quarter horses on his place south of Whitehouse, used them in the rodeos, and talked a lot about getting into racing.

The others were friendly. Nobody out of the ordinary. There were eight altogether. Royal tried to pace his drinking because he saw it was going to be a long night, but soon he felt the buzzing cloud that was his signal to lay back, take a break.

Van, like Pastor, was drinking Scotch. He would take half a glass down, then, as he did when he was serious about his drinking, shove it away on the table and study it as if it was something he had to tame. They'd pooled their money to treat Prevost. The little policeman was the banker, keeping the bills in the breast pocket of his starched, embroidered shirt. They'd also given the groom a Japanese sex manual one of them had picked up on the West Coast as the joke gift. They passed it around for a while. It looked as if this was as wild as it was going to get.

"Here's to my final hours." Greg would lift his glass. "To the end of the free world as I know it." His poker-faced kidding. "You know what's on my mind, what worries me in this?" What? "You can't, the way you do on your own, just cut one if you have to. Cut a fart. What do you do, Van? You're laying in the bed, what do you do, just lay there and suffer?"

"Hell, I just let go. Pauline don't care."

"Did you ever ask her?"

"Hell, she cuts her own. It's marriage, that's all. You'll see."

Van embarrassed Royal telling about his younger brother's bachelor party.

"Here's my brother, the last time I see him he's fifteen, I was taking him trout fishing, taking him to some county fair or someplace. Now he's getting married. I advised him: I hope to hell you know which end is which, Roy, because if you don't, it's a little late for me to start in and tell you. I said, But here's what I'll do for you. I'll take her and check her out, then tell you the best way, what she likes best, all right? I told him, in case he's worried, it's okay, it's the West family tradition, goes back four, five generations, the older brother, especially if he's best man, which I was, takes the bride to bed first to make sure she's up to the family standard. So he says, 'Van, give me a break. I can't let you do that. Lou wouldn't like it.' "

"Shit, you know I never said that. Why do you tell it that way?"

"You believed me, sonny!"

"What I did, I told you to lay off me."

"I said, 'Lou wouldn't *like* it? Man, you better believe Lou would like it!' You were mad as hell, and you were worried too."

It embarrassed Royal, but he laughed with everyone else.

Van also told about how the two brothers drove people home from that same party in a truck whose owner was passed out in the open bed in back. They got to the man's place last, and when they looked he wasn't there. Searched the pile of feed sacks he'd been sleeping on, looked under the truck, both drunk as hell. They decided he must have bounced out when they drove up the bank to go down his street on everybody's front lawn. But when they walked back they couldn't find him. Finally Van knocked on the man's door and told his mother they lost her son out of his truck but could they borrow it to get themselves home?

Van went on, building it up. The way he told it had everyone laughing. The woman kept saying, "Where's Russell? What the hell did you do with Russell?"

The way it happened, Royal remembered, they didn't go into the house at all, either no one was home or only the boy's father who he lived with and who was probably inside drunk himself. No mother. It was a classmate of Royal's, Russell Emerson. He got the name right, but Van didn't really know him. There was no lawn, just mud and scraps of junked cars and a broken-down house in scrub woods. Russ came up at last and said he'd jumped down on purpose to be sick, then had to walk the last mile. He was still drunk and happy, told them to take the truck, went into a shed to sleep it off.

Van's stories matched Pastor's raunchy ones, which were just standard, Royal knew, out of some joke book. Van told his well and they were original, which was to say mostly funny lies. He was drunk, starting to show it a little. He and Pastor weren't paying particular attention to each other except in the stories, as if they were in a competition. They never addressed them to each other, but you could tell that was the intention.

Prevost was drunk, and the others were getting there. Van grew quieter after a time. They'd moved from one bar to another in the little resort town, not settling in any place. There were local people in the bars, some known to their group, and a few summer residents who had come up to open their camps. Greg's party didn't get offensive or try to take over places. They tended to include people they came across, were free with money. Van had reached the stage of being superpolite, lighting people's cigarettes, bringing drinks, getting the money from Jackie to do it. After a while he began to work on the policeman a little, giving Royal a look first: Watch this.

"I'm glad we have a cop holding the money. You sure as hell can't trust me with it."

Greg said, "Hell, I trust you, Van."

"There's your mistake. You shouldn't. Jackie don't, do you, Jackie?"

The policeman just listened as if he was interested.

Finally he said, "You want an answer? Well, I don't, to be honest."

"You're right not to. Shit, I don't trust myself."

"Well, you know yourself, I guess."

"Shit, look at this right here. I put the change in my own pocket by mistake."

"Keep it there. That's all right, Van," Prevost said.

"No, here, you take it, Jackie. I don't trust myself with it."

He kept referring to the car he'd rented.

"You prob'ly think I couldn't afford that in my situation, that I'd have to boost it."

"Is that what you done, West?"

Pastor put all the money out on the table and left it there. He watched Van as if he was amused by him. "There you go, Van. There's the bank. Help yourself when you need it."

"I don't need it. It's for the common good."

As Van had said he would, the policeman took two drinks to everyone else's one and was just the same. He held his liquor.

"Shit, why waste it, risk your liver, Jackie? I never saw such a waste of expensive Scotch."

"You seem concerned with money, Van."

"I am. Money concerns me. You don't live in this country and money don't concern you, unless you're on the public tit like you are, Jackie. Or like Greg, who gives it all up for the sake of love. His opportunities."

"We don't need to keep getting into that one, Van," Prevost said mildly.

"Okay with me."

Van had told Royal the story.

The veteran had been set up in an appliance and small-machine repair shop in Sunrise. It hadn't gone either well or badly, just getting started. He used his lump disability to take out a second loan. When he got engaged the girl's parents told him being self-employed was too uncertain and that having debts was against their principles. He had to get a regular job—the hours and the overtime, the benefits and whatnot. "The day he got into the union and was taken on at the paper mill was the same day the family gave its blessing and the girl set the date.

"So much for free enterprise," Van had said.

He'd discussed the issue with Prevost off and on all evening but in an easy, humorous way. Now, his mood changing, he began to show the irritation.

"Only it seems to me you threw away a really golden opportunity."

"I don't have a head for the business end of it, Van. It was the right decision for me."

"Okay. That's what you keep saying, and I hear you."

But it was as if he'd been letting the thought of what Greg had given up work inside him.

"I tell you I'd let those old people know what I think about getting permission to marry somebody. I would."

"She'd have gone ahead on any basis I said, Van. It was what *I* wanted."

"Okay, I won't say no more."

But later: "If I was in that same position, I wouldn't let older people I hardly know dictate to me out of religion or some such irrelevant thing, tell me to quit my own independent business, go to work as some stockholder's slave on salary. Jesus, I mean, you tell me. Isn't it better to be independent and go a little hungry, the two of you, if that's what's needed, to get your business on its feet? Now you have to join the union, so you're a slave to the union and the man both. What do you call that? Shit, I know I'm out of line on this."

"Hell no, that's okay. Say whatever you want. I just don't agree."

Greg was happy, easy. Jackie listened, kept his neutral look. The others shook their heads at Van.

"Go ahead, Van," Greg said. "I don't care."

"No, I've said suffish already."

They shot game after game of eight ball at the table in the rear of the particular bar they'd settled in at last. By two-thirty some of the party had dropped out and gone home. Van stopped drinking, saying he wanted to be in shape for the wedding next day. He had a sack of home-grown pot and, while Pastor, who was good, was running the table again, sat down and made himself a cigarette in one of the corn-colored papers he carried. He twisted off the end, wet it, let it hang between his lips.

"Is that what I think it is?" Pastor said, glancing at it.

"What do you think it is, Jackie?"

The policeman said, "You know I'll pick you up or any man who looks like he's breaking the law." He moved around the table making shots, not even looking at Van now. No one else paid much attention.

"I guess that means I better not offer none to my friends, get them in trouble. So you'd pick me up, would you?"

"Yes, I would."

There was nothing in Pastor's voice, no particular tone. "You or any man."

"Only you pick me up more often than you do anyone else."

"That's because you get overheated, Van. In my opinion you ought to cool out. Go for a walk."

"Smoke it outside."

The policeman didn't answer.

"Well, you're a hell of a law officer, ain't you? Shit, you wouldn't know a crime from a birthday party if it happened in front of you. You'd pick me up for nothing at all. You don't *see* anything, Jackie, not that's worth seeing. Everybody in this county's blind, deaf, dumb, and incapable. You call what you do working for a living?"

"You work?"

"I do, Jackie. I work. I do a man's work. Independent labor. I cut timber."

"You cut shit. You cut farts, like Greg here was talking about. I heard you worked out there for two days on that woodlot on the river, got in some little scrape, and quit."

"*That's* a lie," Van said. He grinned as if he didn't care.

"Somebody was beating up on you, but it wasn't no loggers. Who was beating on you, West?"

"Fuck yourself," Van said mildly.

"You say so. You know all about that."

"Yes, well, you're a hell of a lawman, ain't you?"

"And you're a hell of a freethinker and a communist in your U.S. of A. uniform and boots. I'll bet you have your combat knife on you, right?"

Neither one raised his voice. If one glanced at the other, he looked away, Royal saw.

"Well, you don't understand shit, do you, Pastor? Why I wear this? What it symbolizes? You don't know shit, that's all."

He and Royal went out, sat in the Monte Carlo, and smoked the joint.

"Hell, Van."

"Never mind."

"What was all that about the logging?"

"That was nothing. He runs his mouth."

Royal said, "Why don't we go home? I believe I've had enough."

"You mean you think I had enough. Well, I tapered off, and I'm coming down right now. I'm sober." He was silent. "Fuckers. They're a lot of fucking sheep. It's Greg bothers me. I can't stand that."

They went back in after a time, leaving the car windows down to air it. The others had finished their tournament and were setting up shots. Everyone had switched to Canadian ale to finish off. The bartender was starting to close down. Van was quiet at first, almost apologetic.

"Listen, I want to say something here, and I don't mean no offense. You're my buddy, Greg. I respect you in every other way except in this one thing. I'm speaking my mind honestly now."

"Do us a favor and don't, West," Pastor said.

"Roy, this man, Greg Prevost, should have had the Medal of Honor," Van said to his brother. "If there was any justice in the world, he would. He don't because the world's fucked up, blind, deaf, and dumb."

"I didn't earn no medal, Van."

"Well, of course you'd say that. I don't mean to embarrass you. Suffish to say he's Medal of Honor material as much as any man ever was. Except. With all due respect, my friend, you fucking shouldn't have given in to the family concerning your store."

The others groaned.

"Okay, it's none of my business, but I'm no friend if I don't tell you what I think. You still have the lease on the place. Open it up again. Why the fuck should you knuckle under to anybody?"

"I was kidding myself, Van. I couldn't handle the hassle with taxes and record-keeping and all that shit. I couldn't stand the idea of debts. I still have a big piece of that to deal with. It keeps me awake nights. This is what I like. Let them do the paperwork, I get the security and the benefits. The day I went into the mill I almost doubled my income."

"I can't believe I'm hearing it," Van said. "Shit, don't you know you always have to give something to get something? What you want, what any real man wants, is independence. You have to give up security at first to get it, you make the sacrifice, sweat a little paperwork. A loan. The bank's risking the money, let them do the worrying. Suppose you lose your beauty sleep, for Christ's sake? What do you want to give up for? Just think about it, Greg. Why the fuck, if you have a chance, which you have, why should you knuckle under to some supervisor or boss or some union?"

"Maybe I don't want independence."

"Oh, come on! Shit, Greg! I can't take this!"

Pastor was watching, saying nothing.

"You can take it." Prevost was beginning to show his own irritation. "Just let it go, Van. I made my decision."

"I can't just let it go. I mean what about it? Are you going to knuckle under to those bastards—what are they, hard-shell Baptists from Georgia or someplace? Give in to her family once, you're stuck the rest of your life. Take my word for it."

"Why don't you drop it, like he wants," Jackie Pastor said at last.

"I'm asking a plain friendly question here, Jackie, so stay out of it. Greg, why do you give in? That's the question. Why do you run with people like these in-laws of yours? They're just weak-willed and proud like so many of the country poor. The whole system wants you to give up your shop, your independence, for Christ's sake, go to work for the man. You ought to be the one in charge, and they just run you like you're some kind of a machine! Why?"

"Everybody knuckles under to somebody, independent or not, Van. When I run a business I knuckle under to the banks, the customers, the tax man, the insurance man. You can't run loose no more like some frontier outlaw."

"You can give them a fight, for Christ's sake, Greg! You just quit!"

There were two left in their party besides Royal and Van and Pastor. They were setting up shots, trying to ignore the argument. Now they stopped. The few left at the bar, strangers, had turned to listen. Van looked at them. "You tell him. He won't listen to me."

"Come on, Van," Royal said.

Van said to Prevost, louder, "Why the hell *can't* you run loose? Be an outlaw. All you need to do is do it! Just cut free and do it! They won't encourage it because they want you in the mill working for wages while they shuffle papers and take the profits! Maybe we *need* a little communism here. I don't care what you call it. Jumping jacks. A fucking Chinese lottery. Call it fucking fascism, so long as you get your piece of it. I mean I talk to you frankly because you're my friend; I wouldn't bother with no one else. I don't say share the wealth. Keep it! Only, when you have the chance like you have it now you take it, run with the ball. Run loose like you said. Take your shop back. Don't *ask* anybody. Learn how to fix the fucking TVs right this time or whatever it was you fixed, *do* the paperwork any little kid could learn in ten minutes, because, shit, you better run loose and take what you need and not subsistence either. Take his wealth and let *him* go fight. And don't give up shit! They got your leg, didn't they? Now they want the rest. Right? Come on, what the fuck's the matter with you? You know I'm right."

Suddenly he yelled, shaking, "You fucking know I'm right! What does it cost to say so!"

He picked up his beer bottle in a shaking hand, put it down. The bartender had come halfway around and into the room. Jackie Pastor was quiet, watching.

"Because what I *can't* take is for somebody I know, respect, a fucking hero for his country, to see him knuckle under and kiss the man's ass, that's all! If that's all you're going to do, why did you go to war for him? You're going to go to war, do it for yourself one time!"

One of the men at the pool table said, "Why don't you shut up, West? That's just fucking stupid. You said all you need to say tonight."

Van stared at him. It was as if he couldn't come back, as if he was too far away to come back. He said loudly and vaguely, "What's that?"

"Come on, Van," Royal said again.

Greg Prevost had turned away, pale with anger. "I don't kiss nobody's ass, Van. Fuck you."

They were all silent.

Van said, "All right. Okay."

Royal could see the anger raging lower and lower in his brother. His nose was pinched white and narrow. He looked closely at the men at the bar and made them turn to their drinks. He gave Pastor his stare, which the policeman gave back. He said to Greg, "I didn't say that."

"Fuck you," Greg declared. "You said it."

Pastor asked him, "Do you deny you said it, West?" As if he was only curious.

Van looked at him again. It seemed to be Pastor he wanted to address. "If I said it, I apologize," he said to the policeman. "I don't remember if I did."

The party's money, crumpled fives and tens and ones, wet with beer, lay on the table.

"Don't forget to take your share of that," Pastor said, indicating it.

"He don't want it," Royal said.

For what seemed to Royal only the second time that night, Pastor looked at him. "Is that right?" He kept on looking at him.

"Take your money," Greg said to Van.

Van said, "I'm going to leave this place." He said, "I don't mean this bar. I mean here. I'm getting out of it all." He said to Greg, "You take that money because you need security. I don't need it. I can get money if I need it."

"Ain't that your trouble?" Pastor said.

But Van's anger seemed to have run out all at once.

"I won't see you all again."

Greg would not look at him.

Jackie Pastor hadn't stopped watching Royal. He seemed interested, as if he'd never seen him before and couldn't make him out. When Van was gone he said, "Well, you get out too, young West. You think you're big, but I believe you ain't nothing but a piece of shit."

"I'm about gone from here," Van said.

They sat in the rented car in the parking lot behind the place. Royal could see into the bar through a window, people moving across. Van was still shaking a little.

"Let's go. We'll use the heater."

"I ain't cold. I'm scared." And then: "I don't know what came over me."

Royal said, "I believe Greg's going to come out. He's trying to make up his mind to fight you."

"He's a good man. I like him. That's the whole thing. I like him and respect him too much. Did I say that to him?"

"I guess you did."

"I can't believe it." He said, "Well, that's all. Yes, he'd fight me, never mind his leg." And again: "That's all. The end of an era."

Van drove them out of Bradford and onto the state highway into the foothills, the road beginning to twist almost at once to accommodate the steepness of the climb. He drove erratically, speeding around a curve, slowing on a straight stretch. A car behind tried to pass, and he crowded it, sped ahead, so it had to drop back. Cars coming against him flashed their high beams to get him to lower his.

"I guess we're uninvited to that wedding. I am anyhow. To say the least of it."

"I won't go."

"Jackie's full of shit. You see him? He just sits there and looks at me, like I'm the thief and he's not. He makes me laugh."

He said, "What the hell are we going to do with those tuxedos? Maybe we should put them on and go sit in the Antlers with them, give Alice a shock. Jay Cooney."

He laughed, then shook his head. "Shit. Poor Greg."

It was nearly four and, with the moon down, black outside. Royal didn't think about where Van was taking them. He dozed in the comfortable car with its big loose springs. They came down a mountainside into a crossroads village, a dozen old houses and a couple of stores, no lights. Royal felt the lift of both of the car's right wheels and opened his eyes.

"I believe I hit a dog."

"What?"

Royal looked back and saw a pale heap on the edge of the road. There was a grocery store gas station with old-fashioned pumps in front of it.

"That could have been anything. A pile of rags or something."

They came out to the access and overpass of the freeway, big over-the-road trucks on the three-lane roads running north and south under them. There was a diesel stop with a restaurant lit up. Van pulled in, got out, and looked at the front of the Monte Carlo.

"You didn't hit anything."

"I'm the one liable to the rental people. You were asleep anyhow."

He sat up on the hood of the car and blew on his hands. Royal got out too. He saw that his brother was holding his hands together tightly as if to control them.

"Where are we headed, you don't mind me asking."

Van said nothing.

"I don't believe you hit a dog or anything else."

"Yes, well, just shut up for two or three minutes if you can. All right, sonny?"

Royal looked away at the truck stop restaurant. There were several big diesels parked behind it.

Van said at last, "You want to go to Florida?"

Royal, angry, gave a snorting laugh.

"I'm serious. We get in this thing, get on that road there, and drive south."

"What do we use for money?"

"I have money."

Royal didn't know what to say. "You really want to go?"

Van shook his head. He didn't seem to be saying no. "Shit, I'm just scared. I'm the way I was when I first came out. Everything scared me like I was going to die in ten seconds, like the air I was breathing was poison and I couldn't take a breath. It lasted about a month, six weeks, then I was okay. Better anyhow."

"You'll be okay now."

"I hit that dog on purpose. It was laying out in front of the store. It must have been old to be out there like that. They can't sleep, the old ones, wander around all night. I caught its eyes in the headlights the way you do, they light up red? I looked over before I did it to make sure, like I didn't want a witness, and saw you were asleep or your eyes shut anyway. I just turned my wheels in a little and went over it. It had its head almost in the road, but it wasn't asleep."

He said, "Prevost did that same thing when he first came

out, only not on purpose. He was like me, scared of everything. They gave him this special car he could drive, with most of the controls at hand level, and the first thing he did with it was kill a dog. I heard he broke down and cried, and was so worried and upset by it he never drove the thing again, sold it. He don't drive yet, as far as I know. I'm not that intimate with Greg, so I don't know the details. I do know that's part of it—what they did to him to make him so weak and ready to give up on everything. I was thinking of him when I did it. Like a dedication. I said to myself, Fuck it, and killed the dog. I'm just telling you."

After a while Royal asked, "Are you going to Florida?"

"I don't know where I'm going to go. I'm going to go in that place there right now, get a cup of coffee, and try and pull myself together."

They went in after a few minutes. Van put a lot of cream and sugar in his first cup, drank it fast, then had a second, black. He nodded. After a time he lit a cigarette and looked around. The place was big and open, buzzing with fluorescent light. They had taken a table at one end. Some tired-looking drivers sat at a counter eating, an old man waiting on them.

"We ought to be in the Teamsters," Van said. "Keep the goods rolling and let the other guys fight the wars. All you do is go on strike once a year and complain about the road tolls and taxes. Hey!" He tried to raise his voice across the big room, but it fell short. One of the men half looked around.

"How's the road conditions, boys?"

They didn't hear him.

"They don't look so tough," he said to Royal. Then, unheard, his voice weak in the white buzzing space: "Hey, boys, how's the conditions over the road?"

He said to Royal, "They can't hear me. I'm going to go over there and talk to them."

The older brother looked as if he was concentrating hard on something, trying to remember.

"Why don't you stay here, Van?"

"You think I want to fight them? I want their advice on the road conditions down to Florida."

"Let's drink our coffee."

He gave his brother the deep concentrating look. "That's right. You don't like to scrap, do you?"

"I generally lose when I do."

"Shit, if all you ever do is win, you're undermatched, you're picking on the losers. I feel better after a scrap." He turned to the truckers again, watched them as they paid and started out, three older men talking among themselves. "Good luck to you." Then, in the deadened forceless voice as they left, unheard: "Fuck you all."

He said, "They'll prob'ly be waiting for me outside to settle this thing, Roy. I'll take care of it. You do the accounting work here and get in the truck."

He gave Royal the keys and a twenty-dollar bill and went outside. Royal found him a few minutes later in the middle of the almost empty parking lot, about twenty yards from the car. One of the diesels was cranking up, another running, its lights on. Van wasn't looking at them. He said, "Where did you get to, Roy?"

"I was paying inside."

"What's this here?"

"It's the car you rented."

"I forgot. I thought we had the truck. I thought someone stole it."

Royal got in behind the wheel. After a moment Van got in too. He said, "We'll just go down to Florida, the Keys maybe. It's supposed to be real nice there. We'll work out the details as we go, telephone home to our wives and whatnot. What we need most now is to lay out on the beaches for a week or two, get ourselves together."

"Are you serious?"

Van was silent.

Royal said, "I'll drive us home."

The older brother said nothing. Royal waited. At last Van said in his usual voice, "Drive out to that place, Roy. I want to go there." And then: "Do like I say. I'm going to rest."

He let his head drop back and passed out.

Royal sat for a few minutes more, then took the way they had come, going west. He had had a lot to drink, but all he felt was a gritty tiredness as if he'd been awake for twenty-four hours. His legs and shoulders ached. When he turned onto Coldspring Road the first daylight had begun to brighten the rearview mirror. He switched off the car's headlights a quarter of a mile from the house and was able to see.

"Van?"

"I'm here."

He glanced across at him. Van sat as he had, head back, eyes closed.

"I'm coming out of it."

Royal pulled up across from the house. You could tell it was empty. The yards and garden were grown up. Though it was warm, the storm doors and windows were still in. The glass glittered emptily in the early light. There was a chain and padlock on the barn door.

Their arrival had surprised the place into silence. Now the sounds started again, the crickets or whatever they were, a night bird. A flowering bush was open, and its smell hung heavily.

Van said in a normal voice, "That leaves a taste in my mouth like I was sucking on a gun barrel, which I don't recommend you to do. The doctor over there said it's some kind of epilepsy. I never told you that, did I?"

He stepped out of the car, went a little way into the tangled garden, and was sick. Royal's vision sharpened. A door was hanging loose on what had been a small chicken house. Weeds grew up everywhere, some even pushing up through the surfaced driveway. It wasn't as bad as it would be later in the summer, but the neglect showed. The long clapboard-sided house had a white, blind look.

Van came back, leaned his elbows on the sill of the open passenger window, looked in.

"You ain't drunk, are you?"

"No," Royal said.

There was no particular smell from Van of sickness or liquor. He said, "I just have this headache myself."

"Don't the police patrol this road?"

"It's the end of their shift. They're somewhere getting breakfast."

"We hope."

Van looked around. "You see? This is all there is to it." He banged his hands on the sill, got into the car, opened the glove box, and took out a pint.

"Wild Turkey."

He drank from it and handed the bottle to Royal.

"All right, dreamer?"

"What? Shit!"

"That this is all there is to it. It's no dream."

"I never said it was a dream. Jesus!"

"Because you're on your own."

Royal was silent. The whiskey burned in his chest and stomach.

"You see, you're still a little cowardly, Roy. That's not good or bad, it's the way you are right now, and you have to deal with it. I got to leave you to deal with it."

Royal said, "You told me he was dead when you came back to the truck."

"We couldn't have done a thing to help him. You have to trust me I know about something like that. Now, why didn't you ask me that when you read it in the paper? You see, that's where you're cowardly. You want to dream your way through it all. If you have to lie, lie, but don't fuck with your own mind, don't lie to yourself."

He said, "Now, here's this. You went to see that man. Corbin. I know because I know the girl who was behind the desk there in the Holiday Inn. She recognized you and told me she saw you and you asked about him, said you said some dumb thing about being an insurance agent. June Kellner, her name is."

"I just saw him and walked away."

"You wanted to quit, tell him what went down and quit, drag me down with you."

Royal said, "I was going to carry it myself."

"Carry what? Bullshit! June said you looked just like someone who was going to faint. You went in there and came right back out. You looked sick. Shit, you were going to quit on me, give it all away and take me down too, then you didn't even have the guts to do that. All winter you're sick here—influenza, whatnot. Ain't that another way of dreaming your way through it?"

"I'm not dreaming, Van."

"I hope not, because I'm telling you you're on your own now, so bear this in mind. You have fucking got to come all the way back up, you hear? For everyone's sake. Now I don't remember what else I wanted to say."

He chewed at the skin of his thumb, looking up over it at the house.

"All right. Here's one you didn't know. Jackie Pastor used Janet's assault charge that time I totaled my car to cover an interrogation. You never knew it, but I was officially questioned by the police on this thing up here way back then. Two other cops were present. Jackie didn't want to pick me up in any way that would put a cloud over my name, because we were friends, or he thought we were. That was before he got on my back so much, the way he is now. I made a statement, signed it, and that was all. I didn't tell you because you were so scared in those days it prob'ly would have killed you."

"How is Jackie on your back?"

"He just is, or was, with all his lies about me. Not that it means shit. Tonight finished it, as maybe you understood if you're observant. I came out from under tonight. I won't bore you with the details."

Royal told Van that he had seen Pastor going into Janet's place with him.

His brother seemed to think it over. He didn't ask what he'd been doing there, whether he had been spying or what.

He said, "That didn't mean anything, Roy. He knows Janet, that's all." And then: "Maybe there's more to this than meets the eye and maybe not. Just try to keep away from it. Don't bother about it." He kept nodding as if he was still thinking it over, chewing on the thumb. "Shit. Here you go: He had me by the short hairs there for a while, or at least I let him think he did. He used me to get at Janet, they didn't hit it off, and that was that."

After a time he said, "Now this is what I want to say, so listen. I'm on a little downhill slide now, prob'ly temporary. Right now I'm more concerned about my control than at any time since I was in service. Janet's right. If I stay, somebody's going to get hurt and not some stranger. I told you it didn't have to be that way, that I was in control. Now I see I was wrong. Someone's going to be done an injury, and I don't just mean that prick Jackie Pastor, who from now on every extra day I stay here he will have to look out for his ass. I don't want to hurt anyone, not even him, and I don't give a shit about him. Other people, people I know and like, are at risk, and that's important to me. Janet and Pauline, to name two. You, Roy, are at risk. That's correct. I don't want to analyze it, but believe me it's no dream. I have those other people on me again—still, I should say. I stay, I'm going to be forced to betray certain individuals who trust me now, a whole network of very good people. I don't want to hurt them. So that's where I'm at with it. If people are going to take my honor, I don't have a choice in the matter. Pastor's looking at me again, trying to get me to do some dishonorable thing, get that on me, into my jacket. You saw him trying out things tonight, seeing how far he can go. That's typical.

"This car and the money? I won't make you accessory, but I did something you wouldn't like. Someone got hurt. Not by me, but there was violence. Suffish to say it was bad, and I'm sorry it's done.

"I fucked up at this house here six months ago, got my own brother into some desperate shit, and I'm sorry for that too. But understand me. I never once . . . maybe I'm a killer, maybe I'm some kind of whore in some way, but I never pretended things were different to what they really are and never told myself a lie that I knew I was doing it, so don't you tell yourself lies either."

He said, "Look in on Pauline from time to time. You take my new rifle and use it. You'll be all right. No one's going to bother you. No one knows shit, but even if they did, I got things on people, and not just Jackie Pastor. That's my power, and now it's yours."

He said, "Don't you judge me. Don't no man judge me."

Van touched his own cheek.

"Give me a kiss here, sonny, and that's that. It's over."

Lou woke up as he got into bed with her. There was light coming in around the windowshade, the early-morning birds making their racket. He lay there and looked at the Beatles and the Rolling Stones.

"Well, he's leaving," he said.

The rented tux and the blue ruffled shirt hung from the top of the closet door.

"He don't know where. He might go to Florida or head west. So that's it."

"Maybe he doesn't mean it."

He told her about the fight with Greg Prevost, a little about the way Pastor leaned on Van. He said they would not be going to the wedding.

"What about your tuxedos?"

"We can't go. Not after that. It's money down the toilet. I'll have to return it."

"It's a shame, Roy."

"He said if he didn't go away, he might hurt somebody. Hurt Janet."

"I believe he might. It's better if he leaves for a while. It's only Pauline's pregnant again. I know you'll miss him."

Royal said in his regular voice, as if this was what they had been talking about, "Well, you might as well tell me about Bobby Argyle. It's as good a time as any."

He heard Mrs. Marquette shuffling around in the kitchen under them, putting coal in the stove, trying to be quiet.

She said, "What worries you and worries me are two different things, Roy."

"Well, I worry."

"Don't."

"You say so."

"Roy, you ought to get some sleep." And then: "I think you have enough on your mind. I don't want you worrying about me and Bobby."

"Because it isn't true?"

"There's nothing there for you to worry about, concern yourself with."

It was as far as she would go.

"Shit, if it was anyone but Bobby."

"I'm married to you."

You could smell Mrs. Marquette's breakfast starting. It made him sick.

"Baby?"

She touched him. He was wild for her right away.

When they were finished with it she would tell him he had cried right through. He hadn't been aware. Her nightgown was pushed up around her chest, and she would show him how it was wet with his tears.

She said in the midst of it, "Oh, babe, I'm coming so well!" He'd heard that. After a wait, he took so long, she went on to try to make it again.

Royal was picturing Lou with Argyle. He saw her naked with him, and it was with that picture in his mind he was able to come after a long time. He knew she had made it with Bobby Argyle as surely as if she had told him.

She said, "I feel weak as a kitten. You are so fantastic, babe."

Cold as ice.

Coming down, lying in the tangled sheets, getting their wind, tuning in the sounds from below: it was over between husband and wife.

That was it.

He walked the two miles to the mobile home later. Mona said Van had packed and taken the rental car into Bradford. He said he was going to turn it in and get on a bus, he didn't say where to. Maybe Pauline knew. He'd said goodbye to Mona, his daddy, his son, talked to Pauline for half an hour in their room, and left.

The end of an era.

Three

11

Royal slept on the sofa in his father's house while he looked for work and someplace to live. He found the job first, waiting tables in a Bradford restaurant, and after a week rented a furnished apartment on top of an old house in South Bradford. The widow who owned the house said she could have gotten a higher rent from transients but didn't like the kind of people who came, bikers and hippies and so on, she called them, who partied and broke her things. She charged Royal half high-season rent because he said he would stay the winter.

The furniture was a double bed, a table and a couple of wooden chairs, a chest of drawers. The kitchen had enough in it to do some cooking. You could see Lookout Peak from the back windows. The bathroom was downstairs, but he didn't share it. There was an outside staircase like Janet Colby's.

"I guess it's okay," he said.

The woman said, "Don't make noise after twelve-thirty. I mean it. The police are friends of mine."

She held a wet cigarette in her mouth like a man, her head back to get away from its smoke, her old eyes sharp behind her bifocals.

It made him smile.

Her name was Wilcox, and she seemed sour but wasn't. When he said he couldn't afford the deposit or month in advance, she told him she'd wait for it until he'd saved some. He could see she didn't mind him. He gave her the kind of smile older women liked, the way Van would.

He was working four to midnight in a restaurant on the lake. The place had a deck with umbrella-covered tables, flowers in pots, and a view of the water. The owners were Italians from Queens. The waiters, waitresses, and busboys were mostly college kids on summer break. Some of the waitresses had given him encouraging looks already, one in particular, a girl whose family was thinking of moving into the area from Long Island. She had gone to school at the local state university and dropped out. Her name was Pam.

He felt all right.

Van was gone, but he didn't have much time to think about it. He saw Lou because they both went to Mona's on Sundays. They were friendly when they met, didn't talk about personal things. Neither one mentioned Argyle. It was known they were separated temporarily and that Van had left. Events like that were common in the town.

There were cards from Van, one to Royal after a week, the others addressed to their father. They were the kind you buy in the post office, with the stamp already on them. Royal guessed he would stop in, buy one, use the post office pen, and mail it. The first postmarks were Maryland and Virginia, some ragged words and his name or a "V." The messages were mostly normal—that he was all right, that the weather was good. Some made Royal think of what Janet had said about Van reading from the Bible, only you could see he was joking too: "Be good, stay straight and keep the faith," one to Wayne West said. Others were scrawled, and you could only make out a few words.

"Keep on keeping on"—another. He told them to say hello to Levi Walls if they found time. "Tell him I'll spring him loose yet."

"Something's loose," Iris said. "He has a screw loose."

She would bad-mouth Van if he was there or not. Royal, who normally defended his brother, didn't bother.

They had four or five of the cards in July and a few in August.

Everyone in the family seemed a little quieter, a little easier with him gone.

"Maybe it's as well in one way," Iris said. "I love Van as a sister and as a Christian, but he wasn't a good influence on you, Roy."

Nobody seemed especially worried that Royal and Lou had parted. They were interested in Royal's new job. They liked his anecdotes about the landlady who smoked and cursed and bet on horses at the harness track, about the Italian family, his bosses, half-wild people, he said, who wanted to adopt him one day and fire him the next for something he'd done: he dropped a cup or something. He liked them, the money was good.

Pauline was expecting at the end of October, and she and the baby were healthy. She didn't seem concerned about Van not being there. Everyone was relaxed the whole summer, Royal especially.

He would lie out on the beach with Pam, watch the power boats and skiers on the lake, the hills and private camps on the other shore dancing in the heat haze. Sailboats ran around. He watched the thick summer clouds build up into castles, then storm, rain, burn off. He liked the damp lake heat, the way the sun blinded him. He let it break into stars under his lids, watched the colors it made. It was really a vacation, the first he'd ever had. He took it easy, leaning back on the old blanket, breathed the way you do when you're almost asleep. He could drift for whole afternoons before work. Sometimes he did sleep. Pam was dark and fairly pretty, tanned. She wore gold chains and little gold studs in her ears. He would lie there and see out of the corner of his eye her shape shining with the oil she smeared over herself. He would hear her say something, answer, then almost forget she was next to him: just lie there, feel the sun and the extra heat from her body. Sometimes when she said something it would come to him later, and he would answer only after a minute or two. It made the girl laugh. She didn't seem to take him too seriously, which was the way he wanted it.

They would go up to his room, make out, lie under the roof in the heat, or go out and walk around the town, look into the shops. They'd change again, pick up towels, go back to the beach. Parachute skiing had come in that year. Power boats pulled the man along until air currents filled the chute and lifted him off the water. He hung thirty, forty feet up, looking around like a gliding hawk. Royal thought: I have to try that once before I die. But he wasn't about to do anything to make it happen.

If the girl, Pam, asked what he was thinking, he would say he didn't know. He didn't. There weren't even pictures or the usual kind of dreams in his mind. It was an emptiness that was like the clouds he saw. The realest thing he knew was the heat reaching down through him.

Sundays he went to family cookouts, which Wayne West had decided to start that summer. His daddy was overcoming his disability, used a light cane now instead of the three-footed one, and went around with his spiky gray hair standing up, pushing hamburgers on his family, beer. He himself took one gin and tonic after another, and it didn't seem to bother him. He was in a good mood. There was the smell of charcoaled meat from grills all over the mobile home park. Neighbors dropped by to trade gossip. Wayne West drifted to other groups to tell his stories. Everyone yelled back and forth and carried on. The children especially seemed wild with happiness this summer, into trouble every second. Louetta would arrive, really to see Pauline, nurse her beer, watch the kids for a time, the fun, then leave. She'd heard about Royal's job, and he dropped hints about Pam, which he saw she picked up on.

He had observed her with Argyle in Bobby's car once or twice in Bradford. When he said so she only nodded as if it was a fact of life she could not alter. He knew they were making it. He could tell by looking at her, but he knew anyway that if it wasn't true, if she and Argyle weren't lovers, she'd have found a way to make that clear.

There was a twist of pain when he thought of it, not too much. In fact, he couldn't understand why he didn't care more.

The whole family was a little that way, he thought, as if they were on a long vacation.

"Let it go," one or another would say of some problem, whatever it was. They seemed to be saying in the hot summer, the rest of the world on a holiday: Don't we deserve a break too?

Royal bought a pair of dumbbells and a jump rope and worked out in his room. He began to do more on the beach than lie in the sun. He would jog, swim. He was a good swimmer. In spite of the fact he'd been lazy in recent months, he was in fair shape.

There was a library at the end of the town where the better houses were. He hadn't been in it since his class trips in grammar school. A red brick building with polished red columns on either side of the entrance and names carved into the stone above. Plato, Virgil, Dante, Shakespeare. He remembered looking up at them when he went in with the class.

They'd read a Shakespeare play in high school, *Macbeth,* and he had memorized a speech.

He began to drop into the place now and then. Even without air-conditioning it was cool there. He read newspapers, looked through *Time, Newsweek.* Bad news sold papers, he knew, and it made you sober to read it, but it was worthwhile to know what was going on. Pam kept up with current events, and they talked over some of the stories as they lay on the beach. It was a sad old world, she said, as if she cared. To his knowledge no one in his family except Van ever read a paper's front page or watched a news show.

It was the bicentennial year, and there were articles about it every day. The stores in Bradford had flags out, and they'd had two parades on Quebec Street beside the big one July Fourth. There were patriotic exhibits and essays on the bulletin boards in the library, things schoolchildren had done. He read a few of these. They were bright kids, he thought. He looked around at the thickly filled shelves of books, saw the people pick them over. He watched a little girl take one down, look at it. It was all there, he guessed; just open up those books and there it was, if you knew how to use it. A few men but mostly women and kids: they pulled the books out, looked into them. Sooner or later he would begin reading some of them himself, he thought. Start with the news of the day and work your way up into books.

It was also the summer they decided the country would go back to capital punishment. All the men who had been waiting on death row thinking maybe they were safe—now they would put them down. Royal thought: if they could pin it on them, on Van and him, now they would be allowed to kill them. It would be a legal killing.

He thought about it in the same easy way he lay on the beach with Pam and watched clouds build or the parachute skiers float along—not hiding from it, not dreaming the way Van always accused him of doing, just easy, unworried.

Say they were picked up—it was Jackie Pastor—and got a poor lawyer who missed out on pleading the lesser offense, the manslaughter.

Some lazy court-appointed lawyer who didn't know his behind from second base. They were put in a position where after all they had to kiss everything goodbye, the world.

Die.

It made his head light to think of it, but it was all right. He was not in any bad, worried way about it. He was easy. He thought: Put it this way:

Number one, they couldn't do it. They were clear. Free.

Number two . . .

Unworried, for the first time in the six or seven months, he looked at the thing, the event, on his own, went through it step by step in this new light, in light of the idea they could now take it all away from them if they wanted to. All right: if they were going to entertain the idea of doing that, then he would play it their way. It was like you had discovered your enemy.

He thought: Shit.

He sat with *Time* magazine in his hand, looking out through the windows at the blind lake, the tree-covered islands, not seeing them, his mouth open as if he could drink his idea. He thought, as in the daydream where you win something big, a million dollars: I'll last. And Van would too. They would be free of it forever because now they could name their enemy, this death the people suddenly wanted to throw at them. You don't have to give anything to death.

Later, ready, he read on, avoiding lightweight items now, sports and so forth. Carter and Ford: he read that. The Russians. From now on he would be serious. He read opinion, editorials, obituaries. There you go. Everything fit in, whatever you read, looking at the faces of the dead in the photographs, an actor, a senator. They set that against you—death—and you had something to deal with and something to throw back at them, at your enemy.

As if it was another photograph in a magazine, he saw on his mind's screen, plainly, solidly, the boy on the porch with the gun in his hand, waiting for them to come out.

He was getting into shape. He worked out, used the salad bar at the restaurant when he ate with Pam and the staff after they'd cleaned up. He was tanned, his red hair bleaching. He felt right. Women glanced at him. Tourists in their outfits turned around and looked, as if, since they were on vacation, they didn't have to be polite. Men looked too, gave him that second glance.

He and Pam did outdoors things together, healthy things.

He borrowed Mona's truck, went to the Marquette place when he knew Lou would be at work, got his casting rod and lures, and took Pam to a beach at the edge of a pond he and Van used to fish for largemouth bass. He didn't bother about the license because they were just out for an hour's fun, and as it happened they didn't catch anything worth keeping. The girl was easygoing, made Royal think his jokes were funny. At the same time she kidded him, his pronunciation. He said "pand" instead of "pond," she told him. "I never heard anything like it."

"You sound like Brooklyn."

"I lived in Brooklyn until I was ten."

She referred to her darkness, said she was a gypsy. One day she said she had black blood. Her black hair had a kink to it. She watched his surprise and laughed. "Guys up here are so bigoted."

She said she was kidding, of course. She was like that, kidded him like a friend, was carefree, halfway a hippie, wore the odd clothes, the loose old-lady dresses, sandals. It all went well with the mood he was in. He liked her.

She said her father was a retired New York City policeman and watched him take it in with her pulled-down, wise smile.

He thought, being funny inside his own head: Great. All I need.

"I better keep away then," he said.

Was he some kind of a criminal?

"Hell, yes, I've done everything. Arson, rape, and murder. I'm also a druggie."

"Well, my old man's too worn out to arrest people anymore."

He did not think he had mentioned Van or anyone else in his family, but he must have said something, because she told him once his whole family sounded prejudiced.

"Against what?"

"Anyone different."

She called him a country boy, teasing him.

"What's Long Island? That's country."

"Well, you have a lot to learn," she said with the smile.

He looked around the streets of Bradford, the tourist town. There was something to learn all right. You saw the different types, heard the languages, saw how they dressed themselves, the Canadians and the others in their outfits. Royal himself wouldn't be caught dead in clothes like that, but it was their privilege. The Italians who ran the restaurant where he worked. Jewish people. You could distinguish different types. He read articles in the library about equality and justice that sounded half religious and were always next to the news stories about the exact opposite: the wars and murders and race riots and whatnot. You would think one would affect the other, but it didn't. Maybe the articles were just wasting their time.

Some things he couldn't read at all. He would pick up the nonfiction books, look into them. He knew two thirds of the words or better, but if he looked one up to be sure, then tried to fit the meaning in, it made no sense. He couldn't even guess what it meant half the time. It was the way the man or woman had put it together. The philosophy of it was too deep for him. He would look at these pages, at the words like stones sitting there, and it gave him a stomachache, made him cramp up. There was frustration in it. He would feel this angry twist of frustration in his private parts because though he understood the words he couldn't see how they fit in.

Time was all right, *Newsweek:* you could read those.

He read about Jimmy Carter.

The man sounded all right. A peanut farmer, for God's sake. He sounded like he cared about people anyhow.

The new capital punishment law. It was all right too in its way. He believed in capital punishment: the child-rapist, the traitor, any mean killing done on purpose. People should pay for their bad crimes. It happened he and Van were in the clear because there had been no bad intent. But if it was murder first degree, you should pay. Manslaughter was something else. Reckless endangerment. There you needed a good lawyer to show the difference. Then, when Royal came to that, he thought: poverty. It made him think about the poor, how one man could afford good legal help and another had to take some boob from the bottom of the law class, appointed by the court, who would get his man strapped into an electric chair due to his ignorance or indifference. Wasn't that a kind of murder too? Or someone just born stupid: what about that? Could he help his crime? The rich and the poor.

Royal sat in his deep library chair, gazing out at the lake, nodding. He thought: these were things to learn. He thought of Levi Walls, in prison on the other side of the mountain he was looking at. He should go see him for Van's sake, take him something. He should help him break out of there the way Van would, carry a real gun in to him. He smiled at his reflection in the glass. Get some friends, hire a helicopter the way he saw it done in a movie, hijack it, put it down in the prison compound, and just lift the man out during his yard time. His family, that blond girl, staring up into the sky as they got smaller. Shit! Freedom!

He thought: you had to learn what freedom was.

He had his job waiting for him. Pam. Not that he cared so much for her emotionally, but he enjoyed her company. He liked the town, which he was really getting to know for the first time.

He had found that people took to him. He could joke with the customers, be smooth the way Van was, show how he enjoyed them, their jokes. They liked him for doing it. Royal had his families that came in, got to know him, called him by name. He would kid the son, flirt with the daughter a little. They would say goodbye at the end of their week's vacation, leave a big tip, twenty, thirty dollars or more. Once in awhile you had some rich old bull with his wife, and the man would watch Royal, say he wished his own sons worked as hard, though Royal wasn't doing much, leave a generous tip and his business card: look him up in the city if he wanted real work.

Other women besides Pam were interested, he saw—customers, women walking on the streets. He sized them up, thought about approaching them. He could probably have any one of them if he took the trouble.

He felt free and happy.

Pauline West made her own pass, which he'd half expected for some time. It didn't amount to much.

She said to him on the particular Sunday, "You look good, Roy." People sitting around half in the bag the way they usually were. A muggy August day. “I wish I’d tan like that. All I do is freckle and blister.”

“Come on in here a minute,” she said. “This is something I want to get done. It won’t take us five minutes.”

She didn’t try to keep the heat out of her voice. It was almost like a joke someone would tell: five minutes.

There were a few of Van’s things in the room, the guns in the rack, his shelf of paperback westerns and mysteries.

“He told me to say he wants you to use any of this you need.”

“I might borrow the deer rifle in November, Pauline, if he isn’t back.”

You could see she was pregnant, but since she was fat anyhow it didn’t show much. She sat on the edge of the bed while he looked around. The room didn’t have much more of Van in it than Janet’s rooms did. He said, “I guess he ought to think of you more.”

“He’s the way he’s always been.”

“He’ll be back before the baby, I guess. He’s prob’ly working somewhere, saving his money.”

“We talked it through, Roy. I don’t think he’s coming back soon. Maybe six months, maybe more.” She took hold of his hand, made him sit beside her. “Honey, you are so sweet. I’m as sorry as I can be about what’s happened between you and Lou. Do you want to talk about that?”

“We’re all right.”

“I hear you have a girl in Bradford. I hope she treats you well, but you know that can’t be anything more than a romantic interlude, Roy. Your future’s with Lou.”

“Don’t worry about it. I don’t.”

It was only her way of clearing it with her conscience, since she and Lou were friends.

“Well, I won’t tell you what I sometimes wish, because it

might shock you. You are so good and sweet-looking. I never knew two brothers could look and be so different. Will you give me a kiss, dear? It doesn't have to be any big thing."

He kissed her pretty mouth, which shone with gloss. She used her tongue and put a hand up high on his leg, ready to get to the point right away. He thought: Van's wife.

She said, "I shouldn't do this. Excite you. I'm sorry, sweetheart. I'm being crazy. I thought we could go someplace some night, but I know it's out of the question." And then: "If you're concerned about Van, we'll forget it." She said, "Forget it anyway, hon. I just wanted to see if I could make you care a little. I'm in such a mood."

"I guess you made me care a little."

"I'm sorry. I'm so sorry. I'm not this way really. We better go back out. Oh, Lord, I am truly apologetic, honey. If you can, will you forget it?"

"Sure."

It didn't amount to much, but it tended to keep him away, keep him in Bradford.

They went into September the way they were.

Pam cooked spaghetti dinners, or they brought Chinese food to his room. They drank wine, watched TV on the little black-and-white he'd picked up. Later, like a settled couple, they would go to bed. She kidded him. She was going to work through the fall, save what she could, and return to college for spring term. They'd get married when she graduated. He asked: What about his present wife?

"You just made her up to protect yourself. If you didn't make up a wife, the women would be all over you." He ought to be a movie actor, she said. With his looks and her brains they'd make millions.

He said he'd like her and Lou to meet. They'd enjoy each other. She reminded him of Lou.

"Thanks a lot. I'd as soon remind you of me."

She had her dry slow style. It was the way she said things, not what she said: talked in a Brooklyn way through her nose, made jokes. She was half Jewish, it turned out. Her mother was. "That makes me all Jewish. In Israel under Hebrew law it's through the mother. If the mother is, you are."

It interested him, and he kept coming back to it. He remembered Van saying Corbin was probably Jewish, the boy Michael a Jew, as if it explained something.

"I have a bad temper too. That's the Irish side."

"Yeah? The Jews don't lose their temper?"

"Not so much. In my experience."

It fit in. It was intensely interesting to him, something to set against any enemy that would come against them. He wanted her to talk about it.

"What is there to say? Basically, people are the same. There are cultural differences. Maybe Jews learn to keep their temper because of the way they've been pushed around in the past, for survival."

But if you did something to one, hurt him, he wouldn't necessarily be out for revenge?

"Revenge?" She thought about it. "Maybe, maybe not. I think in some cases it's a strong probability he wouldn't."

"Isn't that cowardly?"—sounding like Van.

"I don't think it is. That's just a word. I wouldn't be."

They talked about capital punishment because he raised the subject, and she said she was against it.

That fit in too.

Whatever else she was, she went to Catholic mass every Sunday and knew about saints. He thought maybe she was kidding him concerning the Jewish part. Among other things, their women were supposed to be good in bed. It was what you heard in school. But Pam wasn't particularly good or bad, just quiet. She could take it or leave it, would as soon baby him the way Lou liked to do or—he remembered the recent time—Janet.

They rented a paddle boat and went out. He told some old fishing stories. Illegal stuff. Going after trout out of season, dodging the game warden. Ice fishing. "You drive a truck out here where we're at now in this boat, chop a hole, put the shed over it you carried with you, build a fire inside it right on the ice. All the comforts of home."

"Just to catch a trout?"

"Naw, you go river fishing for the trout, I meant to say."

He'd once caught six of the fish, laid them out on the river ice, and watched an eagle carry off five of them one after another, scared him to death, the giant bird flapping at him.

They sat back paddling in the hot sun in their bathing suits. He told his hunting and trapping stories. Stories of near-fatal accidents, drunken country boys in pickups doing eighty on back roads that twisted like snakes, boys fifteen years old in their daddies' cars, drunk as skunks. He had a list as long as her arm of friends, schoolmates, dead or maimed, throwing their lives away half as a joke. Guys dead in the war. He never mentioned Van to her but used Van's local adventures and war stories as if they'd happened to him or his friends. He had his own stories but used Van's too.

They got off the paddle boat on an island at the eastern shore of the lake.

She knew country things better than he did, the names of things. She told him what the tree was outside his bedroom window at Mrs. Marquette's because he was able to point one out that was like it on the island. A spruce.

Her father had taken her for walks in the woods on Long Island with a book when she was a little girl. Then she'd been curious and studied on her own. That's how she knew the names. There were different kinds of the same tree. One the Indians used for their canoes. There was another they'd made root beer out of. She showed him a plant the Iroquois used to make chewing gum, flavored the thick white sap with mint, set it beside the fire to harden overnight.

"Who told you that?"

Her father.

It amazed him, learning the names, looking at whatever it was. That plus the glassy hot September weather made him sleepy, brought on the easy-breathing sleepiness.

Indian chewing gum. He halfway wanted to meet her father.

"He's the best man I know," she said.

Well, you could learn something from him anyway, he thought, and from her.

A spruce.

She kept telling him there was no emotional involvement between them, that she'd had enough of that to last a lifetime. There had been a boy who hurt her badly. Royal said a little more about Lou, not much.

"We've both been burned, Roy, so we'll just stay cool here."

All right with him.

She kidded. "You're just like a brother to me."

For about a week after Labor Day things were quiet. Then, with the lower prices, office workers started their vacations, and there were more Canadians coming in. The restaurant took people on to replace the college help. It was a different mood without the younger vacationers. Secretaries came in twos and threes, shared their rooms, fussed over the bills, who would pay, the tips. They were all right. Quiet. Older people arrived in October for the foliage, and they had more to spend. Royal was making under minimum wage but between a hundred and two hundred a week in tips. Good money.

Pam borrowed a car, and they took a drive into Royal's part of the country around Whitehouse and across the river, so he could show her some of the things he knew about. It was the first week in November, and they heard the hunters' guns, saw the cars pulled off, a buck's carcass in a pickup's bed.

"I'll take you out, you want to go. You can just walk along."

No, she couldn't stand the idea.

"It's the greatest thing in the world. It's just the animal and his super instincts, your own trained instincts, and a good weapon. That's all there is to it. Men are born to hunt, I believe."

They argued but not in a bad way.

They passed an old farmhouse on the trip back, half a dozen skinned, dressed carcasses trussed up in the branches of a tree in front. They hung at different levels, naked, yellow-pink, split down the front.

"Are they deer?"

"I believe it's pigs. They'll smoke them, I guess."

She said they looked like men they'd hung, stripped naked and hung. "I hate it."

"It's just life."

Looking over at her, he thought he could see tears in her eyes.

He was aware of the way she watched him when she thought he wouldn't notice. He half liked it, half didn't. This time when she dropped him off she finally said something. She said it jokingly, like she was kidding again, but she wasn't, he knew. It turned him on. At the same time he told himself that by this time in a certain way he didn't even like her much, let alone love her. She let it go right away, changed the subject. She asked: What did he want to talk about? "Anything but love, right?"

He guessed that was right, embarrassed.

They went on that way from day to day, the general good mood of the summer persisting into late fall.

Pauline had her baby in November, a girl. Iris called him. She sounded bitter about Van not being there but said Pauline wasn't too depressed. "She keeps saying Van wanted another boy, as if that mattered a damn since he isn't here." There had been a postcard, she said, this one from Texas. "He's hurt her bad, Roy. I only hope we're going to see some more of you now."

The baby's name was Shelley. He sent flowers to the hospital, bought a toy for the child, went over when they were home, stayed for an hour in the stuffy house, got out fast.

The middle-aged bikers returned to Bradford for their annual convention and were everywhere, holding up traffic while they rammed up and down the state roads in columns. They came into the restaurant, took off their helmets, and there was some grandma in bifocals, some old white-haired dad.

It made you laugh. At the same time he couldn't believe a whole year had passed since the last time he'd seen them.

He saw Pam observe him across the tables when she should have been working. It was time to break it off, he thought. Or he would watch himself in the mirror in his room some morning while she dressed and think: It's time, wondering how to put it to her. He looked like Van in the mirror, with his boots up on the unmade bed crossed at the ankles, the cigarette going. All he needed was the hat.

The way life goes, it's always the last thing you expect that happens, though in another way, in this case, he had been expecting it all along.

The day he was going to tell her, finish it, his mind exclusively on that, was the day he got the call Van was dead.

What took place immediately was that the one picture disappeared, and there in its place was the other. Van kicked the door straight out, stepped onto the porch on Coldspring Road, and without considering whether there might not be another way, shot the boy down. First degree. Nothing mitigating.

12

He thought he would be all right about it. He felt no reaction at all.

Mrs. Wilcox called him downstairs. She said, "I'm sorry."

It was Iris. She had already phoned about Pauline, so he thought it was that: something had happened to the baby. "We got word Van has passed," his sister said.

He still didn't know. He thought she was talking about taking a test. Van had taken the civil service and passed. He was in school someplace.

"I'm at Daddy's. Mona's hysterical. I can't believe the way she's reacting. Pauline's all right, thank the Lord. Daddy said you should take the bus and come over, tell your people at work you need the day off."

Passed. Shit.

The landlady had stayed around watching him on the phone. She said, "The woman said your brother died."

"That's right."

He waited in his room, then went out into the damp day to walk around town. He couldn't get his mind on it.

He thought: Jesus. But there was nothing there.

He went over to his father's house at last, looked around

the familiar living room. It was past six, but no one had turned on a light. Mona sat with her back to the room, looking out a window into the early darkness. He couldn't tell if she was crying or not. His father was in his recliner, leaning back, seeming to stare right at Royal from under his brushy brows. Iris was in the kitchen. She was making coffee or something, being careful not to bang the pans and pots. He didn't see Pauline or the kids. The little dog was there, curled up in a nest of sheets on the unmade daybed, where someone must have slept the night before. There was a little aluminum Christmas tree on top of the TV, a couple of packages under it.

Wayne West said, "Well, he slipped past us. We lost him." He said, "It's a heck of a thing. Just too hard to believe. In many ways he was the best of you, the best of the lot."

He'd had a letter, and about an hour after he got the letter there was a phone call from somebody who didn't know the letter had been sent. Both the letter and the call were from someplace in Texas. "They were supposed to telephone before, give us a chance to think about it, I guess, get used to it. But they got into some red tape and the official notice come first."

Royal put on a light and sat down with the letter. It confused him, just as the call from Iris had. It was written on county sheriff's office stationery. A place called Meadesville. There was a Meadesville north of Whitehouse about fifty miles, and he thought for a minute his brother had been up there all this time. But it was Meadesville, Texas. From what he could make out, Van had been waiting for a trial on an indictment for armed robbery and grand larceny. There was a note attached from the sheriff and an autopsy report. There was also the name and address of a funeral home down there. It looked to Royal like they were supposed to let the people know their wishes in regard to the remains.

Iris had come in with coffee. "Four hundred dollars. Can

you beat that? Nobody consulted us. They just went ahead."

"Well, what could they do?" Mona asked. "They had to act on it, prepare him and all."

"They want somebody to go down if possible."

Wayne West said, "When I speak to them I'll say they can send him up on the train to North Lawrence or Tyson by freight. What's the use going there if he has to be sent anyhow? You'd have to fly down."

Royal said, "I have the money."

"The money's not the point."

"I think somebody should accompany the body," Mona said. She had begun to cry. There were Kleenex tissues all around her on the floor.

"Here we go again," Wayne West said, his own voice breaking.

Royal asked, "Where's Pauline at?"

"Tom took her and the kids to her mother's for a couple of nights," Iris said. "She needed to get out of this place. He said he'd bring pizza when he comes back."

"That reminds me," West said. "I want you to pick up a bottle and some six-packs, Royal, you get a chance."

Royal was still studying the letter, unable to put his mind on it. He didn't know if he was supposed to make a decision about something. The note from the sheriff was handwritten, the autopsy report half a sheet of closely typed smudged carbon, unsigned. He didn't really try to read either one.

He said, "Did anyone let Lou know?"

"I did. She's on her way." Iris took the note from Royal. They must have been passing it around all afternoon. She said, "The man who wrote this sounds halfway decent, though he's a policeman."

"He says Van was a good man, that everyone liked him," West said. "Read it out loud."

"If I do, I'll break down."

Royal got the keys, took Mona's truck, and went to the liquor store for a fifth of gin for his father, then to the market for the beer. He used his own money. He was afraid the man at the register, someone he'd known all his life, would ask after Van, but he didn't. In the truck he kept saying aloud, "Well, Van's dead," trying to feel it.

Tom was there with the pizza when he got back. He saw Royal, and his eyes reddened.

"Roy, can you believe this? Jesus Christ!"

When Lou arrived she went to Mona and put her arms around her. "You feel just like his own mother, I know. I'm awful sorry."

She said to Royal, "Baby, I'm so sorry about your brother."

She gave him a kiss, then bent over Wayne's chair and kissed him.

"Well, we don't have Van no more, Lou. He made his getaway. It's the completion of a cycle. He was a good son and a good man. There was no bad in him."

She sat by him, and he stroked her hair.

Royal noticed how his father turned to women, had little time for him and Tom, barely acknowledged them. He had probably always been that way, but Royal had never taken notice of it.

Wayne West was silent while Lou held his hand. Finally he said, "I know I won't sleep tonight."

"We'll get some pills from Dr. DeLuca," Lou said.

"I have a phenobarb I can give him for tonight," Mona said.

West would be still for a time, as if he was thinking of Van, then come back to the subject of the arrangements, the expenses. He said there was Van's GI insurance and maybe some other benefits, but by the time you collected you'd advanced so much of your own money you could find yourself in trouble.

"That's the reason I don't want you to go down there, Royal."

Looked at Lou and talked to Royal. He guessed he'd always done it. Never looked at a man, even if he talked to him.

After a while Lou asked, "What did he die from?"

There it was: the first time he'd heard the word that night.

Iris said, "Autopsy says it was stroke."

"Like me," West said.

A cerebral hemorrhage.

"That's the thing I can't get over. Like father like son."

"You have to wonder if they didn't beat him down there," Iris said. "All you hear about those Texas jails."

Her father said, "I talked to the man. It wasn't like that. Every lockup will have a pet, and apparently Van was it. They liked him. We all know Van had his physical and mental problems since the war."

Wayne West had had a call in to the sheriff's office in Meadesville. At ten their time, the man telephoned.

"I appreciate it," West said. "That's perfectly all right. Yes, sir. I'd as soon send you the money order and you get it over to the funeral home where Van is at now. That way we have some authority we can trust controlling it. If that's all right. I'll let our people here know, and they can contact your funeral people and arrange the freight. Now I'll tell you. We've been talking it over, and the feeling is we don't need no one to go down to accompany the remains. The expense . . ." He listened. "Well, now that's another reason against it. We're not in what you'd call affluent circumstances here, and any help . . . Very well. We appreciate that." He listened, his family watching him. "I thank you, sir. Please pass my thanks on to everyone down there who's done so much for us in this time . . . Well, you're a gentleman."

He listened for a long time. He had a plate of pizza on his lap, a glass with gin and ice in it.

When he got off he said, red with anger, "Can you beat this? Now we have freight on top of everything else! Two hundred dollars! He springs this on me!"

"I'll pay it," Royal said. "I have it from work."

"I ain't worried. I know it'll get done. It's just these people are so hooked on their own authority, the way they talk to you! It's a disease with them! They have to dominate you!" Then, as if Royal had angered him too, he said, "Well, maybe we'll just let Roy advance it since him and Van were so close."

"I said I would."

When he calmed down he said, "The man told me Van stole a car from a shopping center and used it with some other fellow to hold up a convenience store. There was an off-duty officer in the store. The second fool had a gun, which he didn't use it, thank Jesus. That one they already tried and convicted. Van's trial was scheduled two weeks from today. My God almighty! Those crazy postcards kept coming, and he didn't say a single word to us, that he was arrested and facing trial or anything. It's hard to believe it."

He said, "The man told me they came into his cell four days ago when Van didn't answer the morning call. You have these county jailers get upset like mother hens, they're running around because they thought he hung himself. He was dead all right, laying in his sack dead, a cigarette burnt down so it scorched his fingers. That's what he told me right now on the phone. He said the guard who found him cried when he saw Van dead."

"Poor old boy," Lou said, tears filling her eyes.

After a time Tom and Iris drove Lou over to Sunrise so she could be with Pauline. Royal stayed, used the daybed. The dashhound slept across his feet until he pushed him off. He thought: Well, this dog's going to miss Van. Never see him again.

He fell asleep almost right away.

Woke and saw his father standing over him. He didn't have any idea what time because he couldn't find his wristwatch: two, three in the morning. A little light came from the refrigerator, its door standing open. He could hear the motor running. West stood in his underwear, a beer in his hand. "Roy, I'm scared. I was just laying there thinking about Van, and I thought I was getting another stroke myself. Fucking pill's good for about two hours, then you're awake again. I dreamed I was back in jail. That's because of Van, thinking of Van in the lockup in east Texas. Shit."

"You all right now?"

"I guess. I can't sleep."

There was sunshine in the morning. It rains the day of a death, sun the next day, Royal remembered someone saying.

Mona would start to sing in the kitchen, stop as if she'd suddenly recalled what had happened. Wayne West got up at seven as always. He looked as if he'd slept all right, ate his breakfast. He said to Royal, "We got plenty of things to see to. We need a couple of cases of beer because people are going to drop in. You'll have to go to Mosley's. When you know the exact amount involved, Mona will give you the cash to get a money order."

"I'm going to pay it. I'll write a check."

"No, Roy," Mona said. "You save your money. Wayne and I talked it over."

"I said I'll pay it."

"Don't get upset, honey."

He was not upset. He wondered when he was going to get upset.

West was eating—eggs, bacon, biscuits. Sun came in through the curtains, cars were starting, voices, people in the park getting ready to go to work. Now and then West would toss a scrap to the dog, see if he could catch it: two out of three.

"He's getting fat."

"So are you," he told Mona. "But you don't see us cutting you off."

For the first time since his stroke two years earlier Royal's father seemed exactly the way he had been before it.

The phone started around nine, people just hearing the news about Van. By noon they were dropping in, family mostly.

Royal ran his errands, got more beer, cake, and so on, using his own money. The people at Mosley's Funeral Home were ready for him. Mosley was a booster, a Monday Morning Quarterback like all the commercial people in town, and he was always running for office. Royal knew him, and he knew Royal.

"Just leave it to us. We'll arrange it, get Van back here, then work out what to do about the money. We don't even need to discuss it now. I'll call your father, let him know when the remains arrive, and we'll work it all out then."

He said something about Van's football, his army service.

"I can't tell you how sorry I am, Roy. I'll be conveying my sympathies personally to the rest of your family."

Royal drove to Pauline's parents' house in Sunrise.

Her father was retired from the paper mill and spent his time in the gardens he had around the place. There was an orchard of apple trees, and when the crop was good he put out a sign offering apples for sale. They were quiet, community-minded people who got along with almost everyone but had never approved of their daughter's marriage.

It was a week before Christmas, but the temperature had already dropped below zero half a dozen times. People said it would be better if it snowed, but it didn't. Royal's nephew, Van's son, was running around in the front yard bundled up in a snowsuit and a big cap.

Lou had left, Pauline said, but would be back later.

"I just thought I'd say hello."

Pauline said, "Come in, Roy."

She was dry-eyed, serious-looking. She said, "I'm as sorry as can be. I know how you must be feeling it."

"What about you?"

She didn't say anything. Her parents weren't around. He knew they didn't like anyone in Van's family, himself included, and had probably made themselves scarce when his truck pulled into the drive.

"I'm not going back there," Pauline said. "Lou said she'll bring the rest of my stuff and the babies' things."

She looked unfamiliar, already into her old life. He had never seen the clothes she was wearing, as if she'd opened up some storage chest in her parents' house and found them. An old flannel shirt, a long wool skirt, high-school-looking loafers, a necklace with a little heart on it.

"You want me to bring it? I have the truck."

"She'll get Bobby to use his car. Let's leave it at that."

She was cold to him.

The TV was on, sound off. There was a big standing clock in a case, and he heard its tick. He was sure her parents were somewhere around.

"How's Shelley?"

"She's all right, Roy. She's upstairs asleep."

He didn't know what to say or do. When she turned away and bent her head he thought she was crying. He put his arms around her.

"No. You had your chance," she said.

He said, "I wasn't trying anything. I just thought you'd want a hug."

"Well, never mind. You don't understand. I could have used some comfort once upon a time. I could have forgiven you."

"What's the matter?"

"What's the *matter?*"

She said, "You got him into it. That robbery and that homicide out there. He told me it was your idea to do that. That's what drove him away and led to all this."

She said, "Now Shelley doesn't have her father. Van wasn't worth much in that role, but that's what he was whether he was here or out somewhere in Texas. Now little Van doesn't have a father. That's what's the matter, Roy."

13

The ground was like stone because of the cold, so they couldn't bury Van yet.

Royal and Tom had gone down with the Mosley hearse to Tyson, the nearest railroad junction, thirty miles south of Whitehouse, and come back with Van's body behind their heads. When they got the bill months later it would list the trip as part of the funeral service and charge for it. West raised hell, and Mosley took his pen and crossed it off.

"I ain't going to argue with a friend on a thing like this. No one advised you about it, and they should have."

Now they stood in Mosley's basement doorway while the coffin was unloaded, their breath making clouds in the cold. A broad drive surfaced with blacktop led up to the street. It was a place Royal often passed as a boy walking to school, looked down and wondered about what kind of a job it was to do that—funeral work. There were always kids who said they'd be undertakers, there was money in it. He saw a big refrigerator door, baskets of wilted flowers. Van's coffin had been set on a pair of trestles padded with carpet. It was of dark wood polished like a mirror and had brass handles. A yellow form had been taped to the top of it, with Van's name, Wayne's name and address in Whitehouse, the date of death on it. Next to "Cause of Decease" whoever it was had written in "Natural causes."

Mosley came down and shook their hands, first Royal's, then Tom's. He didn't seem too serious or too interested.

"I was going to ride to Tyson with you, Roy, but something came up and prevented me. I guess we better take a look. All right?"

Tom said, "You think we should?"

"I recommend it. You won't be satisfied otherwise."

Royal stood back from the coffin, turned so he could see both it and the street at the same time. Tom hung around, then suddenly walked up the ramp to where their car was. Mosley took a big T-shaped key out of a pocket and started to loosen the brass screws inset around the lid. Royal watched the man's bent head, the silver in his hair.

Suddenly there was Van.

The coffin had a divided lid, and the man had opened the top half, pushed it up on a sliding hinge, and tightened the wing nut to hold it.

Royal was looking at Van.

He kept glancing away and back, but he looked.

He thought: I'm looking at Van dead.

His brother's skin was darker than it should have been, as if he had been in the out-of-doors a lot. His head was on a silver-colored pillow. It looked heavy the way it pushed the pillow down. There was silver satin in pleats around the inside of the coffin. They'd put his glasses on, and his hair was shiny with oil, combed back on the sides with a twist that fell over his forehead so he looked like pictures of Elvis Presley. There was a scar on his cheek. That was new. The ears seemed smaller, and the hands too, than Royal remembered. They looked like a ten-year-old boy's hands. He was in a gown tied around the neck and the waist. His stiff clean little hands, one on top of the other, lay heavily on the material. Royal looked for marks on the fingers where the cigarette had scorched his brother but saw nothing.

"You need to decide if the coffin should be open on Saturday, Roy. I'd say yes. He looks fine."

"All right."

Royal could see Tom on the sidewalk at the top of the ramp.

"Shouldn't he be in his own clothes?"

"You can send over whatever you want him to wear."

"He never combed his hair that way."

Mosley said in his neutral voice, "You tell us how and we'll do it, Roy. Whatever it is."

"He sort of combed it straight back."

"You going to faint?"

He heard Mosley's voice coming from a distance as if he was yelling at him.

It was a cool, half-stoned feeling, like hiding somewhere and looking out.

Tom said, "You fainted."

"Shit. I didn't."

He had not been unaware. He could still see Mosley, Tom.

"Man, you were on your knees."

Mosley and an assistant Royal had not seen before were standing over him, the undertaker with a little green bottle of smelling salts looking as if he couldn't decide whether to use it or not. He didn't seem excited or worried. Royal found himself in a chair. When he saw Royal was all right, Mosley handed the key to the assistant, who shut the coffin and tightened the screws.

Tom said, "Jesus, I heard the man say something and came right down. You were on your knees, Roy, passed out cold."

He had never fainted before.

They held the service at the funeral home. Except for the chapel, it was an old place with big rooms and dark wood trim. The chapel, a cinder-block addition, had church benches and a window with blue and yellow panes in it. There was organ music turned low. You forgot you were hearing it after a time. The coffin was in front, the whole lid up now. Pauline had picked out his clothes: jeans, a white shirt, and a tie. He had on his tooled belt with the Lone Star buckle, good boots. His hair was combed in a more natural way.

Royal went and looked at him. You got used to it.

Mosley had brought a minister in because the Wayne Wests didn't have a particular church, and the man talked about Van's childhood in the town, how he liked fishing and hunting and cars, his football career, the military service, his Bronze Star, and so on. Information he had gotten from Pauline and Wayne West. He was half humorous, said Van wasn't much for church, his or any other, but he had the reputation of being a good, kindly man, and God was ever alert to goodness in his children. He talked about Pauline, that she was a fine wife, about Van West III, Shelley. "It was Van's misfortune, being away on a trip at the time of his passing, never to see his beautiful little baby, to hold her. . . ."

The immediate family was packed in up front, the women crying and carrying on, Mona's voice above the rest. Pauline had a handkerchief to her eyes. Royal and Lou sat together. Lou was crying.

They stood around afterward drinking coffee and eating cake Mosley had provided, quiet, a little stiff in their good clothes. There were the relatives, and then the people Van had known in one way or another, friends, the men he'd run with before, during and after his service, those remaining in the neighborhood anyway. There were some people Van had not known well, some he'd only shot eight ball with a few times, people from the Antlers he'd had some conversations with. They considered themselves friends and said so to Royal. There were two old teachers of Van's Royal hadn't seen since he was in their classrooms himself. He talked to them. Janet Colby was there in a black skirt and a black ruffled blouse, without her usual silver jewelry. He saw her watching him from across the room, so he went over.

She held his wrist in her strong hand, her Indian-looking eyes dry.

"Just look at it that Van has found peace."

She seemed angry. She said, "It's you I'm worried about, honey. I want to be sure you're okay."

"I'm okay."

"You think you are." She said, "I guess you know I'm hurting. Do you believe that?"

She kept looking into his eyes.

"I loved him, and I also know how you felt about Van, Roy. He was your role model. Now you have to forget all that and live your own life. The way you ought to look at this is he's gone, has his rest, so that pressure on you is eased and you can rest too."

"Well, there wasn't any pressure, Janet."

She nodded. "You want to come over, don't hesitate, honey. We'll just talk. You know what I feel for you. That don't change."

He got away from her, talked to some others. He felt all right, just as he'd said. He even went back once or twice with people, late arrivals, to look at Van in his coffin, returned for another cup of coffee. Wayne West was the center of attention. He had a suit on Royal didn't know he owned, a tie. Since burial had to be postponed and there was no graveside ceremony, he was reminding people to drop in at his place later for a drink.

They would not have to pay for the funeral until the burial, which would be in the spring, when the ground thawed.

People were talking about it.

Lou came up to him. "They should have buried him down there and been done with it," she said. "Save us this circus. Anyhow, he loved the southwest. I saw you talking to Janet."

"I think she's stoned or drunk."

He told her what she had said.

"Well, I think she's right, Roy. There's been pressure on you. I also believe Van was her only love, so this would cut her up."

Lou kept giving him her own signs: a hand on his arm, the tone in her voice. She would ask his advice. She acted as if they were together again. She had come with Mrs. Marquette. Bobby Argyle had driven them and was going to pick them up later.

"How's Bobby?"

"He's all right," Lou said. "How are you doing, babe? I mean really."

"I guess I feel bad about Van, but I don't know. I mean I don't know what I feel."

She said, "If you want to come and stay at the place, you're welcome."

"I have the room in Bradford."

He saw Jackie Pastor and Paul Beam. He hadn't seen them in months. They hung together, gazed around the room, held their coffee cups and paper plates of cake. Pastor wore dress ranch clothes. Royal went over after a while, and Pastor told him, as if the younger man might be interested, that he was already starting to work the quarter horses on his place, getting ready for the summer rodeos.

"You have to keep them up, or they lose it. You lose it

yourself, your edge, you don't work out. Took some falls too." He showed his knuckles, which were skinned and puffed.

"You know what I call that, messing with horses?" Beam said. "Horse shit."

Pastor said mildly, "Well, you know about horse shit, Paul."

The little policeman said, looking around the room, "Van's drawn a crowd, ain't he? I'll tell you something about Van West anyway. He was well known."

"And well liked," Beam said for Royal's benefit.

"He was well known. He had a reputation. He was a good grade of man in his way. But he wasn't especially liked. That's my opinion." He looked past Royal as he talked, sipped his coffee. "Van was all right when he wasn't into his criminal shit. Him and me got along. But he had a criminal mind, that was his trouble."

"So do you, Jackie," Beam said. He said, "Shit, there's enough stories about Van West to fill a book."

That was all. The two left after a while.

Jay Cooney, owner of the Antlers, came in. Alice Daley was there. Two of Van's old employers stopped by. Greg Prevost came with his wife, and Royal met her for the first time, a thin blond girl with a worried look. She held on to her husband's arm.

Prevost said, "I'm sorry Van and I had that misunderstanding. I believe it was liquor talking, the fact Van was under a strain and I was too. If I was out of line on my side, I'm sorry."

Janet came to say goodbye. She was going on about something: the world needed love. She kissed him on the mouth, so that he had to go and clean off the lipstick. His face in the bathroom mirror was all right. Normal.

"Everyone's after you, Roy," Lou said to him. She had watched him with Janet.

She herself kissed him.

Later, at the Wests', he went out and looked over at the cemetery where Van was going to be put. The older part was closest to the mobile home court. From there it sloped up to the newer section on the other side. Concrete pathways made a gridiron across it all. You could see wreaths on graves and here and there a carved figure rising or a pillar. It was multidenominational Protestant, and most of the town got buried here eventually. From where he stood shivering in his suit jacket he could see the brick house where Van would be held above ground until spring, and sure enough—it was an hour and a half since the service—there was Mosley's hearse, the people apparently just finished putting Van into the building and locking it up again. They were shoving their folded dolly back into the hearse. Three of them. One had been to school with Van, Royal knew, and had spoken to him, expressed his sympathy. Even at this distance Royal could see they were kidding each other, laughing the way you do when a job you don't like is done. One lighting a cigarette. Another with a container of coffee or tea. He could see them in their black clothes, throwing joke punches at each other, dancing out of the way.

He went back into the Wests'. There was still a lot of family around, lots of drinks and noise.

Pauline was there, the new baby on her lap. She watched Royal, gave him her special looks again as if she had never been mad at him.

Mona was the same, only she was all over him. His stepmother. Made him sit beside her on the sofa, put her arm around him, kissed him. She had her drink. She was drunk, but not so much as she wanted to look. She kissed him. She put her tongue in his ear. She put a plump hand on his thigh.

She didn't care who saw. "Jesus Lord, I love that, the way men are. That's just like a piece of iron, that leg. How do you get that way?"

That was Van's funeral.

Royal thought: Let him die.

He would be in a burning field, sparks flying up in showers as the wind veered around. He wasn't trying to get out of the fire, but he knew it would kill him after a time. He would wake the way you do, lie under the roof in his room in Bradford taking breaths to get calm, thank God it was a dream, and so on. The room seemed bigger in the dark. Then light came in around the windowshade, and he saw things—part of a car, a dog standing and looking at him. Jesus. What the fuck is that? Then the room came down to size, the shoe became a shoe, the stain on the wallpaper, which had been the dog, became what it was.

He'd wake up, find someone was really there.

"Who is it?"

Wake Pam, scare her half to death.

He dreamed of animals burning, people. They would look at him like they were begging for his help. Kill me. They held up their raw fingers, the skin burned off, blood and grease, the fat of the man running down, fire coming off his fingertips like candle flames. The blood bubbling hot. Holy Jesus, only let me wake up!

Then: Thank God it was a dream, the way you do, his heart pounding like he'd run five miles.

"What do you dream about?"

He didn't want to tell her. He said, "I dream about fire."

It was because of Van, he guessed, his way of reacting to it.

There was a bird trapped inside a burning house. It flew from window to window, crashing against them, while Royal watched from the street. Then he saw it was Lou in there, trying to get out.

Just after Coldspring Road it had been a drowning in sleep, a slippery, floorless falling. Now it was fire.

People in the dreams yelled, "Help me." Or: "Kill me."

Get it over with, they meant, help me to get past this death. He would wake up with an erection like wood but could not turn to Pam with it, to the woman in his bed. It was as if someone else needed it more, and he had to save it for whoever that was. When his breathing got quiet again he would try to sleep, though he had just tried with all his power to pull himself out of it. He wanted to get back, find whatever it was in there needed so badly, as he saw it, to get fucked.

He would go to Whitehouse, see his people, look across at the cemetery, at the little brick building with Van still in it, snow piled high on its roof. They called it the charnel house, Mona said.

"I can't stand to think of him in there aboveground still," she said to Royal. "That's not right." It gave her nightmares, the way it did Royal. She would sit in her chair with her coffee, a sack from Dunkin' Donuts, look through the icicles like bars over the window. "Ain't this a hell of a climate?"

"It's like it's unfinished business," West said. "They ought to do it somehow. Dynamite the ground if they need to. I'd do it for them."

He was feeling good enough to talk about getting on the town snowplow team, work he'd once done.

Pauline had a job as a clerk at the high school. Lou was still with her invalid. Mona was doing sewing in the house, running up curtains and clothes for people, which she was good at. The sewing machine and the bolts of cloth and patterns added to the confusion in the place. She would work the machine and look up, or sit in her chair eating and duck a look at the cemetery.

"Poor old Van."

They were getting through the long winter.

Royal had gone back to his own job, thinking it would be good to be busy, but he wasn't there a week before he knew it was going to take all he had to keep it up. It made him mad to lift a tray, set a table. He couldn't speak a friendly word to anybody. His boss, a peppery little man, thin as a stick, had always kidded him. That was their basis. Royal had seen from the start the man liked him and wanted to act as if they were friends. His wife, who was tall and plain, treated him, as she was always saying, like a son. They had only half a dozen customers a night. When it snowed heavily in February, March, the place would be empty for a week at a time. Most of the staff including Pam had been laid off. He couldn't understand why they kept open and said so. He said a few things to the woman when she gave him her orders. If they were going to treat him like one of their sons, he'd act like it. The boss would ask him to do some little thing, but it was extra, not his regular job. If people hadn't been laid off, he wouldn't have been asked.

"Come on, Roy. Gimme a break."

The man wanted him, for example, to take his household garbage out to the Dumpster. When Royal said no, the man thought he was kidding. The busboys had always carried the household stuff out with the restaurant's. The family lived in an apartment above the establishment, and it was taken for granted.

There were no customers in the place at the time. The man's wife watched nervously from the register.

"I'm your waiter, not a busboy. And if I was a busboy, the house garbage isn't part of the work. Let your sons take it out."

The thing was, he had always done whatever the man asked, so the guy thought he was joking.

"I can't figure out why you don't take out your own garbage," Royal said wonderingly.

They had two sons to carry garbage. The fat prince who came back from school and played the baby-foot or sat at the bar drinking Cokes. The other in his ice-hockey outfit, yelling at his parents. Why the hell should Royal do it? If they had a union in this fucking town, which who knew, maybe they ought to with guys like this, a waiters' union, there'd be a representative with something to say about employees carrying the boss's garbage, though Royal didn't care for unions any more than Van had. One had you coming, the other had you going: boss, union. Fuck it.

Even with all this, it took a while for it to get through that Royal was serious. When it did, the little man went off like a firecracker.

Royal untied his apron, hung it up, and said he'd come for his paycheck on Saturday. The staff that remained, the bartender, one other waiter, stared. They were cleaning up for the night. The boss shaking and yelling. "You get the fuck out of here! Nobody talks to me like that. We treat our help good!" His wife wringing her hands, the guy yelling. "Look how you upset her! Look!" So on.

Then he chased Royal down the street, caught up with him. "All you have to do is apologize!" Apologize to the man's wife and he could come back.

Dagos, he thought, raging in himself. City people.

He went to his room, had a few beers, watched TV. He looked at the bed like an enemy.

When he slept at last he dreamed about the burning. Trees were going up the way a sheet of newspaper does when you light it.

He had money in his checking account, so he could take his time about a job. Pam had found temporary work in the state employment office on Quebec Street. He would hang around with her, look over the few opportunities in the files.

"You should apologize to her."

"I won't work for some New York City greaseballs who act like they own you."

"You're not like that, Roy. Don't try to be that way."

He was just like that, he said.

They would sit in the late-winter morning arguing, no one in the office, snow piled up outside, the sun glaring on it. She disagreed with everything he told her. She kept saying he was better than he acted or the things he said. All he had to do was show her a little of what was really inside him and she said he wasn't like that. She didn't want to hear the truth, just wanted to argue.

That was the Jew in her, that wanting to argue.

"It's because of your brother, isn't it? The way you're unhappy. The dreams."

They went to bed, but it wasn't much. If she showed interest, it turned him off. If she said no, he was interested. She pointed this out.

"It's the way I am," he said.

"It isn't."

She had to argue about it, of course.

He had meant to break it off with her the day he heard about Van. That had stopped him. He should have done it.

He wanted to hurt her. In fact, she said, everything he did hurt her one way or another in the long run. When they made out, it took him forever to come. He would beat against her, sweat pouring down, until she cried out, tried to push him off.

She told him the way he used her was the same as rape.

She'd gained weight over the winter. He would take the flesh at her waist and twist it, hurting her but acting as if it was meant in fun. He had slapped her several times because of the way she insisted and argued, then said he meant that in fun too, they were love slaps. Okay: if this was love country style, where you beat up your woman or something, to hell with it. She wasn't going to be anybody's statistic or victim.

But he saw she wanted to be a victim.

He would go out to a bar with some friends, some men he had gotten to know from his job and just hanging around, come back, and find her waiting on Mrs. Wilcox's porch.

"I thought you weren't going to see me anymore," not caring. "You're going back to the community college, get your degree."

"The state university," she said. "I will."

Shit. Let it go.

He would meet his friends after they were off work, sit in the bars, watch them go through the mood changes you get between two A.M. and dawn, all of them staring at the lake and the hills, talking about women, their divorces, their jobs. Two were bartenders themselves, and there were serious discussions about mixing cocktails. That was as deep as things got. Royal didn't care. He just wanted to stay awake. As a joke he kept an eye on the night depository bag one of them carried every Saturday after work. They ought to rip it off, he said. The man could pretend he'd been robbed. It would be late at night, some criminal hanging around the bank's side-street door. They could bang the guy up a little like he'd been mugged, take the bag, meet later, cut it open, divide the contents.

No one was surprised when he suggested such things. He had his own reputation.

He would sit until dawn looking through the picture window of some bar at the frozen lake, drunk, scared to go back and fall asleep.

Go to bed at ten in the morning, shades up, thinking light would give him clean dreams, and there was fire like in a furnace waiting for him. Sleep just opened the door to it.

He went through the winter that way, kept it up with Pam off and on, stopped going to Whitehouse to see his family. When spring came it was early, the warmest in ten years. By the first week in April, Mosley said it would be practical to inter Van.

They had to work out the day since coffins had been piling up in the holding house, seven or eight by then. They had to locate the man who'd done the original service. Wayne was starting to worry about the costs that would come due.

Their date was mid-April. Only the immediate family. No announcement. Mona cried, but that was it. Everyone was somewhere else in their lives. It was as if they had gone past this point long before. Two or three burials were taking place in their sight, hearses here and there in the warm sun, the striped tents set up, the bright-green fake grass. They walked back afterward, cutting through the broken fence to their own place, had coffee, sat around.

"Well, that's that, old man," West said, rubbing the dog's long ears. "That's the one you liked best, and now that's finished with."

All right.

Royal slept in Van's room for two nights without dreaming, so it looked as if the burial had cured it. The fire. It had been unfinished business, as Wayne West said. Now it was done.

When he got back: Pam.

"That's the end of the story as far as I and you are concerned," he said. "I don't want nothing to do with you now."

She had plenty to say, and after fifteen minutes of it he hit her the way you hit a man in a fight, knocked her down. When she got up he hit her again and knew he had cracked a rib, heard it. She sat on the floor with her eyes closed, yelling for help.

He went down the outside stairs and walked over to Quebec Street. For all he knew she was still yelling. There were a few tourists already, it was that warm. Patches of snow in the deep woods, and here were the Canadians, men and women in the foolish short shorts, their asses hanging out of them. He looked into shop windows for a while, then went and looked in the window at Sports City, at the rifles and target pistols, big heavy-looking automatic weapons with marbled grips and scopes. Take one, run wild through the town. Do it. Let them get him on something he wanted to do.

He thought about Pam: Let her get her cop father with his books. Let him take care of it.

Mrs. Wilcox came to his room in the morning. She kept her cigarette in her mouth and looked at him in a hard-eyed way.

"I want you to pack up and leave. I told you the police in this town are friends of mine. If you're not gone in twenty minutes, I'll call them. That little girl won't press charges, but I ain't scared of you. You're trespassing right now."

She sat there while he packed, ignored his grins, the country charm he turned on: What about his side of the story?—not really giving a shit himself. She didn't want anything to do with him, she said, didn't want the rent he owed.

She said, "Get it all. I don't want one thing of you left behind. That poor child. She told me what you did to her. I'm sorry I ever knew you."

He went over, put the bag in a locker in the bus depot, walked to the limited access, and used his thumb.

* * *

Lou came out into the driveway.

"Bobby's living here now. I'm just telling you. You want to come in and say hello to Mrs. Marquette? She's missed you, keeps asking what's become of you."

"I thought we could talk."

"I don't want to get into anything, Roy."

He said, "I can't see his car."

"He's at work."

"Well, can we talk?"

"Oh, babe."

They stood in the drive, each looking in a different direction.

At last she said, "Well, come on in."

Mrs. Marquette was in her chair, the police scanner crackling, TV on. If she'd missed him, she didn't show it. She asked about his family in Whitehouse. It was the same place, smelled of linoleum and kerosene and Mrs. Marquette's musty old-age smell. Lou offered him a beer, and he said no. She asked if he wanted to go upstairs.

"I mean to make out."

They both watched Mrs. Marquette, who did not look up or react. Lou was half smiling.

He said, "Okay, I guess."

"Yes, thank you, you mean."

He laughed, said it.

The room was different. A new bedspread and curtains, a chair he didn't recognize. There were a few new concert posters. An army jacket was over the back of the chair.

"I guess that's his."

Bobby's.

It had a row of ribbons on it, the PFC stripe.

She'd turned down the bed. Now she looked up. "I just wear it around the place here when it's cold."

He said nothing.

She said, "You want to do this?"

"I don't know."

"Make up your mind."

"I don't want no favor."

She said, "Roy, the only thing there is is favors." She waited, watching him, smoothing the sheets of the bed. She said, "I don't think you have any idea what you want anymore. It's like you're looking in a mirror this whole year. Year and a half. You don't see anybody but yourself and your trouble. If you're upset about something you did, never mind how long ago, go to the police with it. Get rid of it."

She kept smoothing the bed.

He said, "Well, never mind. We'll let this go."

She said, "Roy, I talked to a lawyer Bobby knows in Bradford."

"Okay. That's okay."

He walked into town, hung around. He had taken his old aviator wraparounds from Lou's, and now he looked out from behind them. As he had before this, he noticed that at least half of the people he saw on the street he knew or was related to. There were some who even looked like him, some who looked like Van or Lou. A few spoke to him. The surprising warm weather had brought them out after the long winter.

You saw a Van walking away from you. A Pauline getting out of a car, going into the grocery. There was his old court mother, who he knew was dead. Two squares down at the little Lions Club park where the tennis courts were: his brother-in-law Tom. You got closer and saw it was someone else, but you nodded. The man did too, because he knew he knew you somehow.

Wandered around.

He did his seven-times-seven, the first in over a year.

"Leave me," he said, knowing it wouldn't.

He had a memory. Summer light burned under the church door, burned in through the squares of colored glass. Whatever heat came in hung up in the rafters, so it was cool below. The place had seemed big to him then, though it was a small church. It was three of them. Mrs. Gladys Tower, his court mother, moving around, busy, smiling. She ruffled his hair each time she passed him. Dr. Carl Melvyn, the pastor. He knew she liked the minister, but it was Royal she went to. Came and smoothed his hair, combing it with her thin fingers. All around were cartons of their neighbors' clothes for the rummage sale—clothes belonging to people who had died recently, outgrown stuff, none of it worth much.

She took him by the hand, told him she loved him. He also recalled that she said the same thing to the man, the Pastor. It had never occurred to Royal it was odd or wrong. He'd never questioned it, her saying that to the man too. Royal was what then—seven, eight? For the first time, questioning it, hearing her say the words to both of them, the memory opened itself up. He had loved her for saying that in her soothing woman's voice, saying it to him and to the pastor both. He thought now: Well, that woman was in love, had a love-affair; and he had been in on it, in her love-affair. And he had been loved himself.

He went to the Antlers in the late evening, didn't talk to anyone. After a time people left him alone. It was a slow night. He thought about eating something, hamburger or hot dog, then forgot about it. He closed the place. Cooney put him out. He found somebody's pickup outside one of the rental cabins behind the tavern, climbed into the front seat, and slept for a few hours.

When he woke it was about four A.M. Cold again. He started to walk to get warm.

He cut down to the river and walked out.

After an hour he thought: Shit. He could have taken Mona's truck, saved himself.

The sun came up, lit the trees on the other side of the river, and the water caught the light, showed sky and clouds and the opposite bank. It was odd how the thing reflected in the water looked clearer than the thing itself.

You learn something new every day.

He thought: It's going to be warm again.

A car was running up slow from behind. It pulled in, crowding him, a county black-and-yellow. Jackie Pastor on the midnight-to-seven DWI shift. He was alone in the car.

Royal walked on, the cop following, his radio making its static.

"You all right?"

"Sure."

"Where you going?"

Royal didn't answer.

"I'm surprised you're still around. I didn't see you since the funeral, so I figured you left the area and joined the service or something. Somebody said you were going into the air force."

"Not me."

"You should. Serve your country and get an education."

Royal didn't say anything. He did not look at him.

"That's my advice."

Pastor said, "You know what you want? You want the shit kicked out of you. I believe you'd really like that. You're the same as Van was. He'd push and push until somebody had to put down whatever he was doing and go do it to him. He just liked it."

Royal said, "Fuck you."

"I've did it myself, beaten on Van. He enjoyed it. He really did. He liked to beat up people too. Women mostly."

He said, "Well, I'll come see you, Roy. We'll visit, talk."

After a while the cop pulled ahead, accelerated fast to spin his wheels. He showed Royal his finger out the window.

Fuck him.

It got warmer.

He turned away from the river into the hills, took a lift with a local farmer, then another, then started to walk again. Around nine-thirty: the day everyone had been wishing for, praying for all winter. Spring sunshine, record-breaking heat lifting everything, starting the leaf buds before they were due, the flowers. You walked in the cool shade, then up over the crest of a hill into the hot sun. There was a broken-down sugar shack in the woods, the buzz of chain saws from the side of a mountain where they were cutting. Cars went by, and Royal waved to them. Another memory: When he was little he used to daydream about walking a country road like this with his brother, just the two of them. It would be hot like this. They would stop at some farmhouse for water. An old stone well in the front yard. She would come out of her kitchen door, the woman, with a pitcher of the water, the frost of water on it running down. You heard the screen door slap shut behind her. They would stand around on the dark lawn, little flowers all over it, drinking, the woman shy, cold air coming up out of the well like a breath. They left her after a while and went on into the warm summer evening. Then night. Van would talk about the woman. That was the kind of woman he wanted to marry. Maybe he'd marry her. Royal wondered now: did he daydream that or did it happen? He no longer knew.

He walked out Coldspring Road.

When he got to the place there was a car in the driveway. Everything was as dilapidated and deserted as last time, more so, but there was the car as if someone was staying. A Chevrolet station wagon with Connecticut plates.

The house was quiet, shades down.

When he looked the other way he saw a man sitting back in one of those lawn chairs in the overgrown garden, his face with its chin pointing into the warm sunlight, a hat on his chest. He thought: It isn't the same man. It wasn't Corbin. There was a leather briefcase against the leg of the chair, a glass balanced on its arm, the man's fingers holding it lightly. He saw the man had opened his eyes enough to look at him. The two weren't more than twenty yards apart. Royal half nodded. The man just stared. He saw it was Corbin but that he was different. He knew him because of the go-to-hell look he had. It was what he remembered about him. That and the porkpie with its camouflage pattern. It confused Royal because he knew he had dropped the hat into the well at the Daley place. The man must have bought himself a new one, that was all. Corbin closed his eyes, turned his face away, chin up for his sunbath: Go to hell.

Four

14

He borrowed Mona's truck and went out the next day. There was no car, nothing. He pulled off near where he and Van had stopped on the night, then walked back to the house. A for-sale sign he hadn't seen was set out of the way behind bushes. It was quiet. If the man had spent the night, you couldn't tell. Maybe he came to get something, went home to Connecticut.

It was suddenly March all over again, gray and cold. The weather was going crazy. It had snowed a little on his way out. Royal walked behind the house. There was a window half open on the second floor.

The place was a mess. Leaves had piled up for the two seasons. Most of the lawn under it would be dead. Where there weren't leaves, weeds had taken over. The man's gardens—different shapes, ovals and horseshoes running down a slope to a stand of trees at the south end of the property—were overgrown, the patterns nearly invisible. A statue of some kind at the fence had vines all over it. There was an orchard beyond the garden, and half the little trees looked dead.

He saw the man's chair where he'd left it, went down, and there was the glass, ants inside it.

Two P.M.

Give it a while. He went back to the truck. He wasn't thinking about anything.

He had Van's 30-06 wrapped in a plastic feed sack on the floor under the passenger seat. He'd made up some joints and put them in one of Van's cigar tins. The pot, good stuff, had been taped in plastic wrap, about an ounce and a half of it, hidden under winter clothes at the back of a drawer in Van's room. He had on Van's old roll-brim rodeo hat, a pair of his boots he'd found.

He lit one of the cigarettes.

By the time he bothered to pay attention it was three-thirty. An hour and a half. He couldn't believe it.

He got out, walked up the road.

It began to snow again.

Each time a car went by, Royal thought it was Corbin.

He thought: Let's go.

He stood looking up at the porch. There was a sheriff's notice there, an orange sign taped to the wall warning trespassers the property was under surveillance. He walked up the steps, the first time since the event.

The floor and walls looked all right. Down near where the back wall reached the floor he saw a puttied-over area about the size of a quarter, which could have been where the second bullet went in, the one Van fired afterward. That was all. He'd imagined there would be a trace on the floor of one of those chalk outlines you see in TV police shows. The sheriff's surveillance sign meant nothing: Jackie or one of the others going by in a county car once a week doing forty, not even looking.

At one side of the porch was the door to the storeroom where he and Van had been surprised. Opposite was the door into the kitchen, a window next to it. At the farther end was a third door, made of square glass panes, which led into the living room. He looked in, making blinders of his hands to shut out the light. Most of the furniture was gone. No rugs. He remembered there had been pictures on the walls. Now they were empty as far as he could see. He could make out the TV, a couple of chairs, the fireplace, a piece of the stairs going up. The door was locked. He tried the kitchen door, and it was open.

He thought: Corbin comes back, sees me on his porch. What are you doing?—in that cocky voice. This and that. They would say things to each other. One thing would lead to another.

He thought he should go into the house, wait for him there, see what he'd say to that. Instead he went back to the truck and smoked again. It made him jumpy, and he got out and wandered around the place wondering what to do next. It was getting late. He kept thinking: What will be will be. Maybe Corbin decided to go home and left the door open because he didn't care if Royal or anyone else walked in, carried out whatever was left in the house.

It snowed off and on, hissing down, melting right away. He found a scythe handle hanging from a rafter in the garage and a rusty blade on the workbench. He sharpened the blade as well as he could with a flat file that was rusty too, then began to hack at the wet dead grass and weeds along the road in front of the house. It was a joke, doing what he'd been doing when he was fired, but he liked the work better than anything he'd done since. You could see where you were with it. The man would give him his job again, another chance. When he finished on the road he went into the little yard in front of the barn and began there, getting into the rhythm, stopping to file the blade once in a while.

He felt himself drop into it, losing time.

He thought probably he'd never worked really hard in his life, or only now and then when it was for himself or Lou, for example the time he had set things up after they were married, fixed their rooms up. Any paying job, he'd found ways to make it easy, do it faster, carry more so he was through sooner. It was like the work was his enemy, and he had to find ways to fool it, beat it, like it was a battle where the smarter you were the less you did, and the one who did just about nothing and didn't get canned won.

He thought: Get the place in order for him. The least he could do.

Corbin showed up around five, when it was nearly dark, took the turn into the drive fast so that his car skidded on the wet surface. He got out. He had the hat on.

Royal stayed where he was on the other side of the drive near the little barn, waiting for the man to see him.

Something was wrong with him.

Corbin stood with his legs spread as if for balance, one hand on the roof of the car to support himself, the other on his hip, breathing with his mouth open. He stared down at the driveway.

Royal saw he was drunk, but he also thought he was sick. Even from where he was he could see the paleness, that he was thin.

The man saw Royal across the hood of his car. He didn't seem surprised. Looked at him, looked down again, his hand lightly on his hip, getting his wind back as if he'd been running. Then up again, gazing at Royal from under the narrow brim of the hat.

The man said in a drunk's voice, "Get the fuck out of here."

Then, as if he had taken care of his problem, he turned and walked up the steps, his knees stiff. He had to support himself on the stair rail, half pulling himself up each step. You could hear his breathing. Drunk as a skunk. Royal waited to see if lights would go on in the house, but they did not.

Ten minutes.

He thought: He'll call the police. Then he thought: No.

Fifteen.

He went to the truck, sat in it, unwrapped the 30-06. He had the cartridges in the glove box, and he loaded the rifle, then took it and went back up the hill and onto the porch. The door was standing open, like he wanted him to come in.

Royal went into the kitchen, feeling for the wall switch. With the light on he could see into the living room. The man was sitting in a chair next to the cold fireplace. There was a cat on the back of the sofa, which surprised him for some reason.

The man was sitting there. No dream.

There was a table, a pizza box on it, a couple of empty beer bottles. The house was cold.

Royal went right into the living room, switched on another light, went to the front windows, and pulled the cords so the blinds closed.

He said, "Now you take it easy."

He wasn't worried, but his voice shook.

Everything he said from now on he was going to have to keep saying in his mind forever, so he didn't say much.

He walked around to where the other could see the rifle, and also so he, Royal, could look at Corbin.

The man glanced sharply at Royal once, not like he was drunk, looked at the gun. Then he shut his eyes and let his head drop. His hands were folded calmly in his lap. It was as if he had fallen asleep. His skin was yellow in color, and it hung slack on him. He was thin. You could see the sockets of his eyes, deep lines like cuts in his long cheeks. There was the mole under one eye, which Royal recalled, and the scar like a hook.

Royal asked, "Are you alone here?"

He could tell the house was empty.

"I remember your son. I remember your daughter too. She had horses. You brought her back from a horse show one time, and she cried."

Royal said, "I guess you believe your son was worth ten of someone like me. I can understand that. It's prob'ly true."

He was saying too much.

"You see the situation you put me in. The position."

He started to say more. There was more. But it failed him.

He thought: It's time to take charge, take responsibility. It wasn't blood. You could choose, like Van said, act.

Now his whole body had begun to work, pulses taking off everywhere, different muscles jumping. It made his hands jump, so he didn't think he could do it. Finally he steadied himself the way you do when you have game in your scope: take a deep breath, let half out, hold it.

He shot him at last.

There was a toilet in a little room under the stairs, and he went in there and vomited into it, then pulled down his pants, sat, and emptied himself, sighing. He was all right now. Once it was done it was a fact of life like any other.

He went upstairs, his ears ringing from the shot, went through each of the mostly empty rooms. Nothing of value. There was a room in back, the one with the open window. It had art posters and Mets and Dodgers pennants on the wall, books, games in boxes. It had to be the boy Michael's room. It looked as if the father had been sleeping here, though not in the bed. There was a cot, its sheets and blankets pulled onto the floor, clothes all over the place. He could see money and keys, a comb and whatnot on the dresser. There was a picture of the boy, maybe ten years old, wearing a bathing suit, his face twisted, looking into the sun. Royal realized he'd been carrying the rifle from room to room and put it on the bed that was probably Michael's. All it had was a mattress cover, the usual stains. Royal looked at the yellowish stains and thought the boy had been like anyone else. There was a piece of paper and a pencil on the dresser, and he wrote his name, Royal West, and left it. There was also sixty dollars, which he took.

He went back down without the rifle.

The force of the hollow point had knocked the chair over with the man in it. You couldn't see much, and Royal didn't try. Suffish it he was dead. He went over and, keeping his face turned away, got the wallet out of the man's hip pocket, which was easy the way he lay, and took off his watch, which was harder because his left arm was folded under him. Blood was beginning to spread, and you could smell the man, his shit. He smelled himself too. He wanted a shower.

He looked in the wallet. More cash. ID. Robert Corbin. A Connecticut address.

He walked out, put away the tools he'd used, looked over his work in the garden, the barnyard. He saw the man's cat sneaking behind the garage, looking worried the way cats do in the open.

He thought that Mrs. Marquette would pick up the news on her scanner, let people know, save him the trouble of telling them. They'd carried him long enough, the people in this town.

He sat in Mona's truck. Pretty soon he would drive somewhere just to be moving. He lit another reefer, which left him one for later. He wouldn't be able to get at the bag of it at Wayne's and Mona's now.

He never knew the daughter's name, the one who had cried, who had brought him the drink of water when he worked there, so he called her Flora after his third-grade teacher who he'd been in love with. They walked around the property. There was just the two of them now. She wanted to know all about his life, so different from hers. He told her frankly and openly, both the sweet and the sour. He told her about Van, everything that had gone down, but he told good anecdotes too, which showed Van in a better light.

They stopped. He kissed her, spoke her name. She wore a white blouse with a round collar that came up high on her smooth sunburned neck. The wool of her sweater under his hand was warm from the sun. There was the smell of clean warm cloth like ironing, the light sweet smell of her skin.